Secretly Kings

Matt Beers

Published by Matt Beers, 2023.

SECRETLY KINGS

First edition. November 9, 2023.

ISBN: 979-8223842859

Written by Matt Beers.

to all the kids who didn't fit in

and who never wanted to

-Acknowledgments-

As with any creative endeavor, this book was not a one-man show. I can take credit for much of it, primarily the plot holes, the curious and unrealistic dialogue, the heavy-handedness in describing Oliver's musical interests, and the parts that drag a little, even though, at their writing, I thought were brilliant.

For the good parts (and especially the really bad parts that are no longer present), I must thank several people...

Brian Foss, who has been a very dear friend since we first met while cutting up a fallen tree in my mother-in-law's backyard. He always knows what I'm trying to say and helps me get there without making me feel like a yammering idiot. And he is very good at making me feel appreciated.

Thank you, Brian, though I'm still in no position to pay you for your editorial contributions.

Lisa Oglesbee, who has been a very dear friend since we first met in high school. She once suggested that I include more girls in my stories. When I took her advice I decided to base one of them on her. Thus was Emma Seaway born. Lisa once questioned whether Emma was "too perfect," and I would like to point out that, if that is indeed the case, it's her own fault.

Betsy Beers, my beloved wife, who tolerates far more of my nonsense and rambling than she signed up for, but sticks around nevertheless.

The fact that this book was ever written is due, in large part, to you laughing at my stupid jokes and not being too hard on me when I get grumpy because my characters won't behave. I love you, dear. Thank you for loving me back.

-August 2023-

a prologue of sorts

The Gladden Antique Store was located on the corner of State and Main Street, an address that would have been enviable in any place other than Gladden, Indiana. The building was well over a hundred years old. It was lined with wooden sidewalks and paneled with ancient cedar shingles which were countless decades past their prime. Out-of-towners found it quaint, but the locals recognized it for what it was: a fire hazard.

Mr. Barrow, the manager of the antique store, sat behind the counter reading a yellowing paperback, some forgotten science-fiction novel prophesying a future of flying cars and robotic servants. Apart from Mr. Barrow, there were only two employees: Tucker and Darby, the Birdly twins. The teenagers were little more than trouble-makers in the eyes of the people of Gladden, but were genuinely appreciated by their employer.

Tucker slipped quietly behind the counter, trying to look unassuming, and sat himself on the stool next to his boss. After a moment, he cleared his throat uncomfortably.

"What's up?" asked Mr. Barrow without looking up from his paperback. "You get that dining set cleaned up?"

"Yeah," said the boy, trying to draw the gaze of the older man. "It wasn't that bad. A little orange oil took care of the worst of it."

"Good," said Mr. Barrow, glancing sideways at the boy and noting the worried look on his face. "What's up?" he asked a second time.

"Darby," said Tucker.

"What about him?"

"He broke up with his girlfriend."

"And?" asked Mr. Barrow.

"He's not handling it well."

"I really don't think I should get involved..."

Tucker wrung his hands together, nervously cracking his knuckles. His blue mohawk, multiple piercings, and tattoos suggested an aggressive, tough-as-nails individual, but he was really just an anxious teenager trying to figure out life. "He's just sitting in the truck listening to that Buzzcocks song over and over..."

"The shop truck?" asked Mr. Barrow.

"Yeah," said Tucker.

"Terrific" said the older man, setting his paperback aside. "And you left him alone?"

"I came and got you," said Tucker, his panic starting to show through. "I didn't know what else to do..." but Mr. Barrow was already gone.

The truck was parked in its usual place in the wide lot behind the antique store. The engine was idling gently, but every few seconds it gave out a threatening roar, reviving unpleasant memories and making Mr. Barrow's shoulders tighten. Darby had shut himself inside and cranked both the A/C and the radio.

Approaching the truck at an angle, Mr. Barrow stayed out of sight as much as possible. It wouldn't do to spook Darby. He was an impulsive boy. He might bolt and there was no telling what kind of damage he might do under the influence of heartbreak and late-1970s punk rock.

Mr. Barrow managed to make it to the passenger door without incident, opening it and climbing inside. One look at Darby's pathetic, tear-stained face was enough to tell him that this was the boy's first heartbreak, but it almost certainly wouldn't be his last. Pain like that can be addictive and Darby's first taste had him locked up tight.

Darby reached over and turned the radio down with a sniff. "Hey, boss."

"Hey, Darby."

"Sorry about the noise." He took a deep, shaky breath and swallowed hard.

"The Buzzcocks are no good for a breakup," said Mr. Barrow gently. "If you really want to feel it, try the Cure."

"The Cure was her favorite band," said Darby with a whimper. His bottom lip bega to quiver.

"She got the kids in the divorce, huh?" said Mr. Barrow, shaking his head. "Did she leave you anything? Who didn't she like? Who couldn't you listen to when you were together?"

"She hated the Ramones..." said Darby.

"Holy..." said Mr. Barrow, running a hand across his bald head. "And you waited for *her* to leave? Darby! You dodged a bullet, kid. *Mondo Bizarro*. One of the Ramones' most underrated albums. 'Poison Heart'...'Strength to Endure'...A lot of good stuff on that album. Give it a listen when you feel up to it."

With another sniff, Darby nodded. "Okay..."

"But in the meantime," said Mr. Barrow, "you're wasting gas running the truck out here with the A/C cranked."

Darby killed the engine and they both climbed out of the truck and walked back toward the building. Just as they reached the back door, Darby reached out and touched Mr. Barrow's arm.

"Mr. Barrow?" he said. "Is it always gonna feel like this?"

The old man sighed. "I've lost a lot of people, Darby. All of them, actually. And the losses don't all feel the same, but right now...the hurt...this is the predictable part. This is manageable." He opened the door and paused, not looking at Darby. "The one thing I know for certain is that the people we lose...they're never quite as gone as you'd like them to be."

Mr. Barrow walked inside, leaving Darby to collect himself.

PART ONE- The Tragedies

"Ladybird, ladybird fly away home,
Your house is on fire and your children are gone,
All except one, and her name is Ann,
And she hid under the baking pan."

-Traditional English Nursery Rhyme

-ONE-

the blame

I set my brother on fire when I was six years old, but he survived. Three years later, I ran over him with a car, which seemed to do the trick.

I don't know what happened to us. I remember that we used to be happy, the whole family. There is photographic evidence to back this up. Christmases, vacations, a dog...I know I didn't imagine it.

But something happened.

You can see it in the photo albums that were left behind, the way scientists can identify different geological eras in layers of sediment. Here we see the 1971 layer, several years before I was born. Mother and Father look so young and fresh and afraid. Grandparents gleefully pose beside a grinning, fair-haired child in a high chair with a birthday cake that says, "Happy Birthday, Reagan!"

The layers stack and blend perfectly with one another so that, to the casual observer, they are one continuous layer. Mother and Father look older, wiser, less afraid. A new baby arrives, a girl. Reagan, now three years old, stands beside the frilled bassinet, still grinning. He is such a proud brother. The layers blend.

Christmas, Easter, summer. A silly tea party, more birthdays, another Christmas. Mother standing next to a new car, another Easter, a fishing trip. Father, now with a mustache, with three laughing children on his back. Reagan looks happy, the sister, Maggie, is laughing, and Oliver, the newcomer who has somehow slipped in without making a ripple in the layers (the sneaky little

9

thing), is seated atop the pile, clearly proud of himself for managing to stick it out with his older siblings. The smile on his pudgy face doesn't seem to reach his eyes, though. He's wondering, even then, what he's doing there, what his role is.

Only a trained eye would notice that there seem to be several layers missing from the family history. Entire years pass without anyone thinking to pick up a camera, feeling no pressing need to document life. Those lost years are dismissed with a shrug. Minor omissions. Anomalies in an otherwise unbroken timeline of happiness.

Let's take a closer look and examine the final layer, the last few album pages recording this once happy family...

It's 1981 and the photos start to take on a more cultivated feel. Smiles sit less naturally on faces. Siblings are more strategically posed.

A birthday party. Reagan is ten. There is cake. There are gifts. Decorations hang from the walls. The celebrant is treated like the little king Mother and Father had always hoped he would become.

Maggie is in every picture, her smile so natural and captivating. It's Reagan's birthday, but she is clearly striving to be the star of the show and it's hard to deny that, between the two of them, she possesses the greater share of personality. Oliver is there, too, somewhere. His messy blond hair is occasionally visible in the background or poking in from the edge of the frame.

The layers become thinner and thinner, the photos fewer and fewer, the memories less and less. Some unnamed thing has interrupted the happiness.

We arrive at the final page of the final photo album. It's Maggie's birthday. The kitchen has been turned pink with decorations. There are so many friends piled around the table, but it's not hard to spot the birthday girl among them. She stands out, her eyes always on the camera, always demanding the spotlight.

Reagan is not in any of these photographs. The little king, it seems, has been overthrown, his place usurped by his younger sister. Oliver, however, makes one, fleeting appearance. There is a picture of a massive pink cake with strawberry decorations. In the bottom corner of the photograph is a chubby, fair-haired child (he looks so much like his older brother) staring open-mouthed at the gigantic confectionary masterpiece.

There are no more photographs. It's as though time stopped on Maggie's seventh birthday.

If you compare that last photograph, little Oliver staring up at the majestic pink cake, with the next chronological photo I have of myself taken a decade and a half later, you would never know they were the same person. Too much happened in the intervening years. Too many scars, both literal and figurative. If I could have told Baby Oliver that, in six years time, he would be an only child and in hiding with his slightly deranged mother, he would still be thinking about that big, pink cake.

I think we might have gotten through it, whatever it was that was tearing our family apart, had we known that, from time to time, every family goes through...whatever it was. Unfortunately, in our little town of Gladden, Indiana, people didn't talk about that kind of thing. Home problems stayed at home. It was considered rude to bring those sorts of things out into the open, so everyone was left thinking they had unique, insurmountable problems.

For years, I thought that Gladden was part of the problem. I used to look back on those people as stuffy, pious, self-righteous do-gooders who never did our family any good. While there were plenty of those types of people living in Gladden, there were also plenty of gentle, caring, kind-hearted people who went out of their way to help my family, and they were so genuine about their motives that I never knew they were there, helping, serving, caring.

That's the terrible irony about truly good people: They don't make a show of their kindness, so the rest of us never get the chance to follow their example.

The blame for the tragedies that befell our family doesn't belong to the people of Gladden, as much as I might like to think it does. And it wasn't my parents or even Reagan. The blame isn't the exclusive property of any single person (though I might argue that I have a far larger claim than most). We all contributed to the downfall of the Barrow family, either by punching holes or by not mending them.

Whoever owns the blame, this is what happened to me. I don't know what to do with it all. Maybe you will.

-TWO-
surely
-(summer, 1984)-

My parents, Rex and Delores Barrow, would never admit that they each had a favorite child, not to their children, not to each other. It was pretty obvious, though...to me anyway. Dad's favorite was Reagan, his little slugger, his photocopy. The heir to the Barrow throne. Mom's favorite was Maggie. Strong-willed, independent, Machiavellian in her calculated manipulation of any and all situations. She would have been the first female president had she lived.

And then there was Oliver.

I was no one's favorite, except, eventually, by default. I was not an athlete. I was neither clever nor ambitious. I didn't have friends. Instead, I was afraid and anxious. I liked to find quiet and dark places to hide with a book and a flashlight. People upset me.

One person in particular.

I don't like confrontation. I never have. I'm happy to let problems fester and grow. In my experience, living with an unaddressed issue is almost always less painful than dealing with it. Avoidance has been my preferred approach to conflict for as long as I can remember and is probably the reason I was so fond of finding quiet, out-of-the-way reading places. If Reagan couldn't find me, there was no conflict.

Unfortunately, I wasn't very good at hiding.

We lived in a two-story farmhouse built by my great-grandfather, John Barrow, who, I suspect, knew more about farming than he did about construction. Nothing in the house made sense. There wasn't a single right angle in the place, but he tried his best and the bizarre result of his good-intentions served his descendants for three generations.

John Barrow was a proud farmer, as was his son (my grandfather), Elmer. Elmer's son, Rex (my father), made an attempt at the family business, but farming just wasn't his thing. When Elmer died in 1975 (three years before I was born), Rex promptly sold off all of the farmland and took a job as a long-haul trucker, no doubt inspired by the C. W. McCall song, "Convoy," which was very popular around that time.

It's absurd to me that the wind that steered the course of so many lives might have been generated by a novelty song about truck drivers chatting on their CB radios. Because there's no question that, had he not spent so much of his time on the road, Dad would have noticed that Mom was growing more and more detached from reality and he might have intervened. He might also have noticed that Reagan was growing more and more aggressive and Maggie was growing more and more devious and Oliver was growing more and more solitary. He would have noticed his family slipping sideways into madness and surely he would have done something, called someone, taken us somewhere to get help. Surely he would have. Surely...

Maybe he did see these things and maybe that's why he stayed away. He knew the ship was sinking and he didn't want to be around when it went under.

Dad and I had the same approach to conflict.

I think we were all born wrong, my siblings and I. We could have been great under different circumstances. As it were, we all suffered or else made sure those around us did.

Reagan tried to act tough but he couldn't stand the thought that someone might not take him seriously. It didn't matter if you were a teacher, a preacher, or a kid on the playground, he wouldn't hesitate to put a fist in your eye if he thought you were laughing at him. He would have been right at home as the hero in a Roger Zelazny novel, running stubbornly toward the end of the world.

Everyone thought Maggie was sweet and adorable, but everyone thought the same about Hannibal Lecter before they found out he was eating people. Maggie could charm anyone, could make them think whatever she wanted. She would lie about anything and everything just for fun, and no matter how much you told yourself you wouldn't listen, you couldn't help it. She used sincerity like a scalpel, and the cuts she made went deep.

As for me, I was Winnie the Pooh, Piglet, and Eeyore, all rolled into one. I was stupid and nervous and depressed, but hopeful that someone would come along shortly and sort everything out. I waited and waited and, when Christopher Robin finally showed up, it turned out that he didn't know any more than I did.

We were all tools in the same toolbox, but we served very different purposes. Reagan was a hammer. He was blunt and he hit things. Maggie was a razor blade. You wouldn't even know she'd cut you until you'd already bled to death. I was a staple gun. Under enough pressure, I'd snap and probably hurt someone, even if I only wanted to help.

How did these three humans descend from the same ancestors? Who knows? Who cares? There's no magic formula that makes a human turn out one way or another. Sometimes we come out broken and sometimes we come out perfect. The perfect ones think they're broken and the broken ones think they're perfect. It's a messed up system, but we're too deep into it at this point to change it. Humanity will just have to keep producing confused humans until the end of time.

I did what I could to avoid my siblings, but that wasn't always possible. Reagan was easy to hide from, but Maggie was more clever. She could always find me and coax me out of my hiding places. She could make anyone do anything.

Reagan would often track me down, but he couldn't always get to me. I'd find tiny gaps under the basement stairs or the barn floor and squeeze into spaces where he couldn't reach. He hated that. It made him feel powerless, and that was the worst thing of all for him. Worse, even, than being laughed at.

One summer afternoon he tracked me to a space under the barn floor where I had made a small space for myself. I had to wedge myself through an opening in the floorboards but, once there, I found a fairly comfortable little area. It was about three feet by four feet and I only had a few inches of headroom, but it was quiet and cool and out of the way. Reagan must have seen the beam from my flashlight shining up through the floorboards because he was suddenly above me, stomping around, shaking dust down onto my head.

"OLLIE!" he shouted. "OLLIE-OLLIE-OLLIE!"

I had no trouble ignoring him. It was my only weapon against him and I knew how to use it. However, after several minutes, once it became evident that he wasn't upsetting me, he grew angry. He always grew angry when his tactics proved fruitless.

I was six years old. Reagan was thirteen. He already hated me. He hated everyone. Even...especially...himself.

"Get out here, Ollie!" he demanded.

"No!" I shouted. "I'm reading! Leave me alone!"

"I SAID, GET OUT HERE!" he roared.

"LEAVE ME ALONE!" Even to my own ears, my voice sounded weak and pathetic, but I knew he couldn't get me, not without pulling up the floorboards.

He stopped raging, but I could hear his breathing, heavy and wet. For several seconds, all I could hear was my heart beating in my ears and his high, agitated breathing somewhere above me. Then I heard a shuffling, a scrape, and the creak of something being lifted by a metal handle. He took a few steps and stood directly above me. Soon, there was a trickle of liquid pouring onto the boards and my first thought was that he was peeing on me. That seemed like his idea of a clever joke. Before I could scurry out of the way, however, the liquid ran between the boards and onto the ground next to me, splattering onto my shirt and in my hair. The smell told me right away that it wasn't urine, but gasoline.

We were taught in school that nature has given us two responses to danger. *Fight* and *Flight*. You either respond to danger with danger of your own or you run away like a sniveling little rat (my preferred reaction). They have since added more responses, but this all happened in 1984, so I only had the original two options to work with.

I suppose my initial response that day would fall under the *Fight* category according to the experts. Although, as the *Fight* and *Flight* responses are meant to give the individual a greater chance of survival, and what I did next suggested that I had no interest in survival, perhaps the experts would have put my reaction in a third category: *Foolishness*.

All I remember is smelling the gasoline and thinking, *He's going to burn me up.* There was no fear. My mind went blank and I switched to autopilot. I tucked my book into my shirt to protect it from the gasoline and began to crawl through the puddle of fuel toward the gap in the floorboards. My hands and legs were slick with gasoline and dirt as I hoisted myself up into the fresh air. Reagan didn't notice me pop out of the floor ten feet behind him.

The gasoline fumes made me light-headed and calm. My sinuses felt raw. I swayed on my feet as I watched Regan in the midst of a war-dance.

"IT'S RAINING! IT'S POURING!" he shouted gleefully as he continued dumping fuel all over the barn floor. It spattered onto his legs as his booted feet slid around on the grimy boards.

I could have run. *Flight* was still an option at that point. Had I been in my right mind, I would have, but I had unplugged from reality. I watched the scene play out as though I were watching a television show, *The A-Team*, perhaps, and I was Mad Murdock. Madder than that, even.

Dad kept that particular can of gasoline for starting bonfires at the far end of the property. He always kept it full and he always kept a box of matches handy. I reached up to the little shelf by the door and there they were. "Swan Vestas," the box said. "Strike anywhere."

"IT'S RAINING!" Reagan screamed. His blue jeans were soaked. "IT'S POURING!" I pulled a match from the box and rested the white phosphorous tip against the rough strip on the side of the box.

Had I taken an extra moment to consider the situation, I might have said something pithy like, "The old man is snoring," before striking the match, but I didn't. I hadn't considered any part of this.

I dragged the match along the side of the box like I was pulling the pin on a grenade. The sound made Reagan spin around to face me, his eyes wide with insane rage. Before he could even react, I flicked the match toward him, like in the movies, but nothing happened. What they don't tell you in the movies is that, when you throw lit matches, they go out.

He was on top of me in an instant, slamming me onto my back. He was straddling me, slapping and punching as I writhed in the spreading pool of gasoline, unable to get my arms up to protect myself.

I screamed and Reagan laughed. He was hanging over me, slapping and punching, drooling like a mad dog. My legs flailed and my bare feet drummed on the floor, but it was a useless effort.

My hands slapped around searching for a weapon, but there was only the matchbox. Several of the matches had fallen loose and were scattered on the floor. Swan Vestas. Strike anywhere.

I don't remember picking one up and I don't remember striking it, but there it was, flickering in my hand, moving slowly toward my brother's face. Reagan froze for half a second before grabbing my wrist and pulling my arm straight up as if it were a weed that he meant to rip out at the root. The flame flickered and danced, crawling up the match stick, reflected in his wide, wild eyes.

"What do you plan to do with that?" he gasped hoarsely. He tried to pour disdain into his voice, but I had seen the fear in his eyes. Even in this moment of weakness, I still held the upper hand. What *did* I plan to do with it? I was just as curious as he was.

Apparently, I meant to drop the match, because that's what I did. It fell in slow motion onto my gasoline-soaked shirt and, before Reagan could do more than swear loudly, we were both in flames.

That was probably the worst possible moment for my *Flight* response to kick in, but it sure did. Reagan fell back and I ran screaming from the barn, my shirt blazing around me, my hair catching up top, my shorts catching below.

I tripped and fell to the ground, stop-drop-and-rolling completely by accident. A moment later Mom was there smothering the flames with a bath towel that had been drying on the line.

Once she was sure I was extinguished, she was gone. I freed my head from the towel and looked up in time to see Reagan stumbling out of the barn, his legs completely engulfed in flames. Mom raced toward him with the garden hose, spraying him and slapping at the flames. It was a long time before they went out.

No one ever asked what happened.

I still have the scars from that day, though they've faded significantly. An ugly red welt runs up the left side of my face and my torso looks like I have a perpetual, albeit patchy, sunburn. There's a rectangle of perfect skin in the middle of my chest where the book had been pressed against me. Had I been reading a bigger book I would have been better protected.

Reagan came through the fire worse than I did. His blue jeans didn't want to stop burning. He had second- and third-degree burns over much of his legs, groin, and torso and had to spend more than a month in the hospital.

And still no one asked what happened.

Dad assumed it had been an accident. He kept a couple of old tractors in the barn and Reagan liked to work on them from time to time. Any number of things could have gone wrong.

Mom knew better. She never said so, but I think she understood the situation about as well as she could have without having any specific details. I think she knew, even then, that Reagan was dangerous, though she never mentioned it at the time.

She must have suspected that I was dangerous, too, but she never mentioned that, either.

-THREE-
home again, home again
-(November, 1987, and June, 1993)-

People used to ask me why I didn't try to escape. Why I didn't run back home. The easy answer is that I didn't know I had been kidnapped.

This was a few years after the fire. Mom found me in my bedroom sitting amongst a pile of toy cars. I wasn't playing with them, they were just scattered around me as I stared blankly at the wall. It had been a pretty rough day.

"Get in the car," she said, and I did. Had she been out to the corn crib? Had she seen what I'd done?

I had always imagined a kidnapping would look different and would be far more traumatic. The trauma was on its way, but I found the initial experience freeing and transformative. Like I said, it had been a pretty rough day. Being kidnapped was definitely the high point.

We drove through the night and stopped somewhere in Michigan. I didn't see Dad again for six years.

Skip ahead to June of 1993. I was fifteen years-old and hadn't seen Dad since November of 1987. During that time I almost never thought of him. That sounds cruel, but it's the truth. Even when we lived together, I rarely saw him. I had only ever been vaguely aware of him at the best of times.

A lot had happened since we'd last seen each other. I'm sure he had loads of questions and I probably could have answered most of them, if not all, but he never asked. I also had questions, but asking them would have meant dealing with a lot of guilt that I'd successfully buried under six years of avoidance. "Let sleeping dogs lie," as the saying goes. As far as I know, there are no sayings about dogs that are dead and buried.

Our reunion was not what I had expected. Dad picked me up at the Greyhound station in Fort Wayne. He didn't recognize me at first. I was wearing blue jeans and a plain, gray t-shirt. My hair was just as shaggy as ever, hiding half of my face, making me look like a juvenile delinquent.

"Hey, boy," Dad said, when he finally recognized me. "Nice hair."

"Hey, Dad," I said awkwardly, trying to match his casual tone. "Nice hat." He was wearing a comically large black Stetson almost as wide as his shoulders. He looked like he was prepared to do magic tricks at a rodeo.

"You like it?" he said, pointing at it. "It's my 'go-to-hell' hat. If you don't like it, you can go to hell." And then he laughed. It was a wheezy, desperate sound. He clearly felt as awkward about the situation as I did.

When Mom and I disappeared, he threw himself into his work. He spent all of his time driving a truck back and forth across the country, interacting exclusively with other sad and lonely people who were doing the exact same thing, but in the opposite direction. I believe that long-haul truck drivers are the largest group of lonely people in the entire world. For a lot of them, that's the appeal.

The forty-five minute drive home was as uncomfortable as you might imagine. Dad kept opening his mouth to talk, but merely cleared his throat. Or he would fiddle with the radio, dancing back and forth between two different country music stations and talk radio. He must have smoked at least half a dozen cigarettes while we drove.

Neither of us knew what to say. Was one of us supposed to apologize? Should we talk about Mom? Reagan? The Ramones? We'd never had much in common, but the kidnapping really widened the gap.

That's one of the many drawbacks of being kidnapped. It tends to interfere with relationships.

The house was a mess. I could tell he had done his best to clean it up before I arrived, but he had been rushed. When word reached him that I had been found, he was in Tennessee with a truckload of romaine lettuce. After he unloaded the lettuce, he was supposed to pick up a load of stereos and take them to Georgia, but the dispatcher told him to drop the trailer and get home, ASAP. Someone else would finish his run. By the time he got back to Gladden, he had two days to get the house in order. He spent most of that time drinking.

The whole place smelled like a very old ashtray. The walls, once farmhouse white, were now nicotine yellow. I doubted if he even realized it. Every surface was either gritty or tacky. When I opened the refrigerator I saw that it was mostly empty except for a lot of expired condiments and plenty of beer.

"You like beer?" he asked when he saw me looking. I thought he was kidding, but he didn't look like he was kidding.

"Uh, no," I said. "I don't think so. I've never tried it."

"Huh," he said, sounding genuinely surprised. I suppose my hair gave him the wrong idea.

My bedroom was pretty much exactly how I had left it, except someone had cleaned up my toy cars and put them away. Dust coated every surface. It smelled less like cigarettes here, but it was still pretty bad.

The closet and the dresser were filled with too-small clothes and the bookshelf was crammed with too-young books. The *Black Hole* bed sheets, the lamp shaped like a wooden soldier, the art-class suncatcher made of crepe paper...It all seemed familiar, but it all belonged to someone else, someone who left this room six years ago and never came back. Even in this tiny world I had created for myself once upon a time, I felt out of place.

Dad watched me from the doorway.

"I suppose we'll need to do some shopping," he said, gesturing toward the closet. "I doubt any of these clothes would still fit you." He laughed but it sounded sad, as if the lost years had slapped him across the mouth.

"I've got clothes for now," I said, pointing to my duffel bag on the bed. "The counselor at the hospital said they would send the rest of my stuff later."

"She the one I talked to on the phone?" he asked.

"Yeah," I said.

"Didn't sound like she knew what she was talking about."

I didn't know how to respond, so I just stood there.

It was a very uncomfortable situation. Even when I was younger and saw him regularly, I didn't know how to deal with Dad. I had learned to expect frequent, unexplained outbursts, but now he was being far too calm. This was not the same man I had known when I was nine. Granted, I was also not the same boy. I kept reminding myself that the situation must have been equally strange for both of us.

I walked to the window and pulled back the curtain. The corn crib was just across the dirt yard. The red doors were as bright and bold as I remembered, though they had been chained shut for some reason. I wondered what it looked like in there.

I would have sworn that the red doors shuddered as I stared.

"You hungry?" Dad asked, making me jump. "Let's go down to the Alpine. I'll buy you a burger."

The Alpine was one of three restaurants in Gladden. The other two were Dairy Treat and Crosscut Junction. They each catered to a different crowd. If you were a teenager and wanted a quick burger and a milkshake, you went to Dairy Treat. If you were in town visiting for the day and wanted overpriced chicken salad and a quaint atmosphere, Crosscut Junction. If you were a middle-aged local and wanted to rub elbows with other middle-aged locals (and didn't give two beans about the government's hoity-toity health standards), the Alpine. Dad was a regular at the Alpine.

We arrived just in time to beat the dinner rush. There was a sign on the wall inside the front door that said, "Smoking Section" with an arrow pointing vaguely toward the dining area. Below that it said, "Non-smoking Section" with an arrow pointing back toward the parking lot.

The whole place smelled like our house. It was dark and smokey and reminded me of a Bob Seger song, but without the charm. You could almost see the hepatitis crawling on every surface.

Dad led me to a table near the back of the dining room, right beside the emergency exit. This was his table. If he came and it was occupied, he waited outside until it was free. He couldn't sit with his back to the room and he absolutely needed to be near an exit. VietNam had done a real number on him.

He lit up a cigarette as soon as we sat down without asking if it bothered me. No matter where I turned or how I leaned, the smoke found me. He must have noticed my discomfort because he made a disgruntled face. "I'll try not to smoke in the house if it bothers you."

"Thanks," I said.

"The burgers are okay," he said, handing me a menu, "but you might want to avoid the fish."

I ordered a chicken sandwich and fries. Dad ordered a country-fried steak with extra gravy and a baked potato. He poured so much melted butter on that baked potato that it looked like soup before he was done. He smoked the entire time we ate. Everything tasted like cigarettes, even the water.

"Guess I'll need to go grocery shopping," he said as we drove home. "You probably don't want to eat at the Alpine for every meal." He laughed, but I wasn't sure what the joke was.

Over the next few days, I studied my father closely, wondering what had happened to him. He used to be such an intimidating man, larger than life, strong and brave and terrifying. Now he just seemed sad, like a birthday balloon with enough helium to keep it hovering above the ground, but only just. He sagged and grunted and told dumb jokes and laughed loudly until he coughed himself dizzy. People knew him, but in the way small town folks know all of their lifelong neighbors. No one seemed overly fond of him. He reminded me of the last, aging clown in a dying circus. All out of jokes. All out of tricks. All out of friends.

I had to remind myself what had been taken from him. All things considered, he was doing about as well as one could expect.

-FOUR-
after the fire
-(October, 1984)-

At the time, the barn fire was the worst thing that ever happened to our family. Gladden was a farming community. A barn fire was nearly as tragic as losing a child. People brought meals and helped clear away the rubble. They prayed for us at church. The Sunday school children made cards.

That sympathy didn't keep me from getting teased about my burned face once school started, though. Barns and burns mean nothing to children. They saw a weakness and were eager to exploit it. Not that they needed the burns as an excuse to tease me as our prior interactions would testify.

"Hey! Elephant Man!" they would yell. This all happened in 1984. *The Elephant Man*, a film about a horribly disfigured individual, had come out several years prior and this was the most relevant insult my classmates could conjure up.

The following summer, *The Goonies* was a hugely popular hit and kids would see me on the playground and shout, "HEYY, YOUU GUYYS!" My classmates watched far too many movies.

Maggie was almost exactly between Reagan and I in age. By the time I came along, they already hated each other.

There were several stories about the two of them that were considered family legends, like the time Maggie broke a valuable lamp and was so sincere with her accusation that Reagan, who wasn't even home at the time, was punished for it. Or the time Reagan was caught furiously forcing a Lincoln Log down Maggie's throat. You know, typical sibling stuff.

When I came along, it gave them a new reason to fight. Reagan assumed that, as we were both boys, he and I would be best friends and team up against our sister. Maggie assumed the same, but she was smarter, more manipulative, and knew how to steer me away from such petty alliances.

One of my earliest memories was of Maggie leading me upstairs to play in her room and Reagan being so outraged by this betrayal that he shoved me backward down the stairs. I must have been about three years old.

Was it Maggie's intention that Reagan push me down the stairs? Was she using his jealousy to drive a wedge between us, to turn me against him? That's some pretty advanced guile for a seven year-old, but I wouldn't put it past her. I can't imagine what she would have been like had she reached puberty. Regardless, she didn't deserve to be murdered.

Neither did Reagan, for that matter.

After the barn fire, I was more afraid of him than ever. My physical scars were superficial. Even my hair grew back. Physically, I was reasonably unaffected by the fire. I had gotten off easy. I hadn't even gotten in any trouble. This must have burned Reagan almost as badly as the actual flames.

He couldn't take it out on me, though, not then, anyway. Any outright attack against me so soon after the fire would look very much like payback, and that would have led to questions about the fire and, once the story came out in full, who would have shouldered the greater portion of the blame? Even Reagan knew enough to leave this one alone.

Instead of taking revenge, he chose to stay angry.

I don't remember the exact date, but it was sometime in October of 1984. Mom complained about the cooler weather because it meant we had to keep the windows closed and the house was still rich with the cloying, acrid odor of the barn fire.

Reagan was still wearing bandages on parts of his legs and groin. The thought of the degree of damage the fire did to him makes my teeth hurt. The doctors weren't able to salvage much...soft tissue. This, despite the decreased production of testosterone that came as a result, no doubt contributed directly to an increase in aggression.

Four generations of Barrows had lived in that house, which meant there was four generations worth of hoarded junk filling the attic and the cellar. Stacks of crates and boxes reached the ceilings, creating narrow paths that snaked through the decades of accumulation. I had made several little nests amongst the trunks and broken chairs, perfect little hiding places where my books and I could commune undisturbed.

Maggie also made a habit of playing in the attic. Our great-aunt Jewel had left behind a massive dollhouse and Maggie had set it up next to the big attic window that peered out over the yard. "That's where the light is best," she said. It was also directly above Reagan's room. He would hear every step and every bump. Perhaps that's why Maggie decided to play jacks next to the dollhouse.

Jacks, in case you aren't familiar, is a very old-fashioned game in which players bounce a ball and try to scoop up sharp, metal pieces (the titular "jacks") before the ball falls back to the ground. The jacks look like something left behind in a World War I battlefield or dropped out of the trunk of a spy's car to deter enemies who might be following. They are jagged and dangerous and someone looked at them and said, "We should give these to children."

The trick is to bounce the ball very hard to obtain greater hangtime and, therefore, greater opportunity to grab jacks. In the mad rush to grab as many of these sharp baubles as possible, one is almost certain to suffer a fair amount of pain, but I don't think Maggie worried too much about that part. It was the bouncing that she was focused on that day.

However, it is very difficult to play jacks without encountering pain, as Maggie soon discovered.

She was usually so smart about her mischief. She could kick a hornets' nest and convince the hornets to sting someone else. Avoiding consequence was her specialty. Somehow on that autumn day she slipped up.

Mom was downstairs. I was in my room. Reagan had just had his bandages changed, which was always a humiliating and painful ordeal. That was when Maggie started bouncing the ball. Even I could hear it in my room at the other end of the house, so I can only imagine how loud it was in Reagan's room.

After a few bounces, he shouted, "Knock it off!"

The ball stopped for about half a minute before starting up again. I heard Reagan's bed springs creak as he got up. "I SAID, KNOCK IT OFF!"

The ball stopped again, for longer this time. Reagan's bed springs creaked as he laid back down. Downstairs, I heard the kitchen door creak open and slam shut. Mom had gone outside for something.

I had been laying on my floor with my toy cars spread out around me, but now I was kneeling, the hair on the back of my neck prickling. There was electricity in the air. I wanted to shout a warning, but I didn't know who to warn. Something bad was about to happen.

Then Maggie started hammering on the floor, presumably with her fists. There was nothing subtle about it. There was no way to deny that she was intentionally trying to upset her brother.

Did Maggie know that Mom had gone outside? Did she expect someone to come to her aid when Reagan finally snapped?

The drumming continued as I peeked around my door frame, looking down the hall. Reagan's door burst open and he flew up the attic stairs two at a time. That must have hurt, with his burns and bandages. The pain, no doubt, made his rage that much more dangerous.

The next thing I heard was a muffled scream. The drumming continued, but it had a much more panicked, frantic feel. It stopped abruptly and, a second later, Maggie tumbled down the attic stairs, coming to rest upside down, her head twisted awkwardly beneath her folded body. From where I stood, shaking and gasping, I could see blood running from her mouth, pooling around her. She was wearing a turquoise turtleneck and magenta corduroy overalls. The blood soaked into her turtleneck, making it almost the same shade as her overalls.

Reagan stomped down the attic stairs, stepped over Maggie's twitching body, and slammed his bedroom door behind him. I couldn't move. I stood there whimpering as I stared at Maggie. The flow of blood gradually slowed. Her face was white as marble and her blonde hair was matted with blood.

I was crying and I had to struggle to draw enough breath to speak. "Get up, Maggie," I whispered. "Get up."

She didn't get up. But she did wink at me.

-FIVE-
someone else's villain
-(June, 1993)-

I had been back home in Gladden, living with Dad, for about a week and a half when he announced that he was going back to work. I was kind of surprised he was willing to leave me there by myself. I kept forgetting that it was my house, too. At no point during that ten days had I felt like anything but an unexpected and confusing guest.

"I'll be gone three days at most," he said. "A few stops in Kentucky and I'll bring a load back north." He left me with fifty dollars for food and a fridge full of beer.

July was rapidly approaching. Families were planning picnics and anticipating massive displays of fireworks. There weren't any official holiday festivities in Gladden, but the residents planted tiny American flags up and down every street. If you wanted to see fireworks, you'd have to drive into Fort Wayne and battle the crowds.

Our house was located on Armstrong Road, just outside of Gladden, well within walking distance of town, surrounded by fields that had once been owned by my ancestors. We still owned about an acre and a half of barren, useless real estate with one house and three ancient outbuildings. There weren't even any trees.

In the winter, wind whipped across the fields and between the poorly-fitted wall-boards. In the spring, the rain found holes in the roof. In the summer, the sun baked and bleached everything. In the fall, harvesting machines worked non-stop on all sides of us, choking the air with dust and noise. Then the icy winter winds would come and we'd do it all over again.

I liked the winters best because it was easier to warm up than to cool off. Everyone has their own brand of misery that they've learned to live with. Mine is the cold.

The actual town of Gladden was very small, only about a half square mile. To visitors, it was quaint, and people often compared it to Andy Griffith's idyllic Mayberry. An ancient windmill stood outside the antique store, looking down on the intersection of State and Main, Gladden's primary streets. There were wooden sidewalks and benches made from rough-hewn logs. You could buy spring-loaded fox traps, electric cattle prods, and hand-cranked ice cream machines at the Gladden Hardware. The Gladden General Store sold Amish-made candles and soaps and old-fashioned candies that you had to scoop out of barrels and weigh on a scale. If you were just driving through, the place looked like a postcard.

For many of its residents, however, Gladden was not the Saturday afternoon country paradise it seemed. There were cliques and groups throughout the town, just like everywhere else, and each clique and group had their own concerns and pet peeves and causes that they championed while vilifying the other cliques and groups for not addressing the same concerns and pet peeves and causes as fervently as they did.

The Gladden Missionary Ladies' Group, for example, thought it was shameful that the Gladden Mennonite Women's Auxiliary didn't host a Veteran's Day dinner, and the Gladden Mennonite Women's Auxiliary thought it was blatantly disrespectful that the Gladden Missionary Women's Group didn't host a Memorial Day dinner, and both groups disapproved of the scandalous Valentine's Day Banquet for Seniors put on each February by the Gladden

Rotary Club. None of the three groups even acknowledged the existence of the Gladden Bridge and Euchre Society, which allowed its members to drink alcohol during meetings.

There were two parks in Gladden, The Old Park and The New Park, and every mother in town had a firm opinion of the type of person who allowed their child to play in one or the other.

The Old Park moms believed that the old ways were best. They had played in the Old Park when they were young and their children would do the same. Besides, the New Park was far too close to the mobile home court, and everyone knew what kind of folks lived there.

The New Park moms believed that the Old Park was too full of rusty metal and offensive graffiti. That was where the teenagers hung out after dark to smoke cigarettes and say swears and kiss girls. The boys all wore their hair too long and the girls all wore their skirts too short.

Both Old Park and New Park moms believed anyone who allowed their children to play in the other park deserved whatever kind of delinquent they raised as a result.

The folks who bought their beer from Jim's Sunoco gas station instead of Eichel's grocery store were cheap boozehounds and the folks who bought their beer at Eichel's instead of at the Cedar Creek Carry-Out were communists and the folks who bought their beer at the Cedar Creek Carry-Out instead of from Jim's Sunoco were conspiracy theorists and compulsive gamblers as it was well known that Harold Bonneville ran a weekly poker game in the back room. My father, eager to avoid any unsavory social labels, bought beer from all three.

Everyone in town was someone else's villain.

-SIX-
definitely not a dog
-(July, 1993)-

Mid-way through the second week in July, a moving truck pulled up the long driveway and a man came to the door. Dad was gone again, working. He had come home for two days and then left me with another fifty dollars for groceries.

"Delivery for 'Barrow,'" said the man at the door, checking the manifest. "Says it's 'personal effects' out of Traverse City." He looked at me and I realized he expected me to tell him where to put it. I couldn't imagine why they had sent an entire 48-foot trailer to transport my meager belongings, most of which I didn't want any more, but I followed him out to the trailer. A second man had unlocked the back doors and was securing them to the sides of the trailer when we walked up.

They had brought everything, all of my personal belongings, our secondhand couch, the kitchen table where Mom had...Even Mom's tiny Chevy Vega was there, secured with canvas straps. I felt a pang of sympathy. It looked so small and fragile in that trailer, almost like seeing a frightened family pet in a cage.

The movers pulled two long, metal ramps from under the trailer and rolled the Vega gently out onto the driveway. It was strange to see Mom's car in Gladden again after all this time. It probably thought the same about me.

I had no idea what to do with the rest of the stuff, so I told them to load it all into the house. We never used the dining room, so I shoved the long table against one wall so they could pile everything in there. While I did that, they pulled the truck up between the house and the corn crib so they could carry everything in through the back door.

When the truck was about half empty one of the movers flagged me down. "Whatcha got chained up in that building back there?" he asked, wiping sweat off his face with one grimy sleeve. With his other hand he pointed toward the corn crib.

"What do you mean?" For some reason, I felt a cold chill working into my gut.

"Is it a dog?" he asked. "Something keeps clawing and sniffing at that door."

I shrugged and he shrugged and we left it at that.

It took the movers about an hour to unload everything from the truck. When they were done, one of them handed me some paperwork to sign.

"So, what's the story?" one of the men asked as I jotted my name on the line marked "recipient." "Someone moving in? One of your folks get married or something?"

I'm sure the poor guy meant no harm and probably would have preferred it if I had made up some happy lie, but I was caught off-guard and told the truth without thinking.

"Uh, no," I said. "My mom kidnapped me when I was nine and then, a month ago, she tried to poison me with sleeping pills. Now I'm back home with my dad."

He blinked at me and said, "Huh."

"Yeah," I said as I handed back the paperwork. "That's kinda how I feel about it, too."

-SEVEN-
mommy's little monster
-(autumn, 1987)-

Before I explain about Mom and the sleeping pills, I should explain why she kidnapped me in the first place. Maybe you can guess.

Maggie's death was considered an accident. She had slipped on the attic stairs, tragically breaking her neck on the way down. I don't know if anyone actually believed that story, but the alternative, that she was murdered, was too disturbing to consider.

It made sense that, with Maggie gone, Reagan would have calmed down. They were mortal enemies and he had struck the final blow. The victory was his, but so was the guilt, and I think that weighed on him far more than he could ever have imagined.

Unfortunately, Maggie was the balancing weight on the other side of the scale. Without her, Reagan had no opposition. He was left to run wild with no one questioning his actions.

He was fourteen now, and in that awkward stage where boys are expected to become men. We treat it like some sort of magical thing that happens overnight.

"You don't have time to play with toys anymore, you have to be a man."

Men don't cry, they don't apologize, they don't waste time trying to understand different ideas or cultures or beliefs. Men fight. Men drink. Men concern themselves primarily with their own convenience.

At least that's what they did in Gladden. So it was with Reagan.

He became something of a menace around Gladden and nearby Leopold, where we went to school. There were constant complaints from the school, from local businesses, and from neighbors. Reagan vandalized and stole, he started fights and sold cigarettes to junior high kids who were too young to steal them from the gas station. He spent less and less time at home, which worried Mom, but elicited no complaints from me.

Dad worked more and more, coming home, at most, one night a week. I got the feeling that Mom felt about Dad's absence the same way I felt about Reagan's: No complaints.

In spite of everything, Mom tried to give me a normal life. I went to school. I ate well. We went to church.

But Mom was never the same after Maggie died. None of us were, of course, but something happened to Mom, inside her head. Some important switches got flipped and her settings got all messed up. Her gears started to turn just slightly out of time with one another, like a clock that loses one or two seconds every week. It's not as reliable anymore, but it will be a while before anyone notices.

I don't know if Dad really understood what was going on, but he came closer to fixing it than anyone else, even if it was purely by accident. I think his primary focus was to give Reagan some kind of outlet in the hopes that he'd stop causing so much trouble. It was a good idea, but it wasn't enough to save the family.

Dad hadn't been home in three weeks when he walked through the kitchen door, dropped his duffle bag in the middle of the kitchen table where I was sitting and said, "Where's your brother?"

I shrugged. "I haven't seen him." I was struggling my way through my math homework. Dad stared at me with his eyebrows raised expectantly. "Well?" he asked.

I shrugged again.

"Is that how you greet your father?" he asked.

"Oh," I said. "Hi, Dad." I got up and gave him a hug. He smelled awful. Three weeks on the road didn't offer many opportunities for bathing.

Dad went to the bottom of the stairs. "Ray!" he shouted.

"What?" Reagan called back.

"Get your ass down here, boy!" Dad shouted. He always swore a lot after long trips. He was a good-natured guy, but he was not rich in social graces.

Reagan stomped down the stairs. "What?" he asked again, making his way to the fridge. As he passed behind me, he smacked me on the back of the head. He always did that. I hated it.

"I found you a car," Dad said.

"You got me a car?!" Reagan asked, pulling his head suddenly out of the fridge.

"I'm not buying it for you," Dad said. "Steve, the night dispatcher, has a '69 Cutlass he's looking to get rid of. He's asking $150, but we can probably talk him down."

Reagan was practically drooling. "You said it's a '69? Two-door or four-door?"

"Four. '69 was the first year they started using the split grille on those Cutlasses."

"Does it run?" Reagan asked.

"How the hell should I know?" Dad shrugged. "It better run, for $150. If it don't, we'll get it for half that and fix it up ourselves. Probably just needs a battery. Clean out the carburetor a bit. Should be good to go."

The Cutlass was a massive thing, longer even than Dad's Ford pickup. It was wide and smooth and the color of very old mustard, the kind that's so expensive you never throw it out, no matter how unlikely you are to eat it. The hard top had almost completely flaked away exposing the rusted metal roof underneath.

Apart from the barn, there were two outbuildings on the property: the granary and the corn crib. I'm not an expert on farming practices, but I'm pretty sure granaries were used to store grain and corn cribs were used to store corn. As we had neither grain nor corn, we used our outbuildings for storing other stuff, mainly old broken things that Dad couldn't bring himself to throw out. Dad and Reagan made room in the corn crib for the Cutlass.

In the past, the corn crib had been used mainly as Dad's workshop whenever he had a project he wanted to work on for six weeks before giving up on it, so it was the perfect place for Reagan to tinker with his car. It had a workbench and plenty of things for him to break when he was in a bad mood. And it kept him out of trouble.

The two months that Reagan spent working on the Cutlass are among the best memories I have of my brother. He was focused and positive and, most importantly, he wasn't interested in me. I could actually sit in my room and read without being afraid that Reagan would burst in and slap me for no reason or steal my book and start ripping out pages. It was almost nice.

There were days, however, when the old Reagan seemed to return. Those days were marked by slammed doors and streams of profanity coming from the corn crib. At first he left the big, red doors standing wide open so we could all see him in there working hard under the hood of the Cutlass, but as problems mounted, he started closing the doors. He was ashamed that it was taking so long to get the car running.

When he finally did, I thought that would be the end of it. Reagan would back out of the corn crib, take off down the long, dirt driveway, turn out onto Armstrong Road, and we'd never see him again. That was not the case, however, because getting the engine running was just one of many hurdles Reagan had to clear before the car was road-ready.

That didn't stop him from revving it every day, especially when he was angry. Sometimes he'd go out to the corn crib, start the engine, and just sit in it. We'd hear that huge engine chugging away, guzzling about a gallon of gasoline every minute, and then he'd stand on the accelerator and the engine would roar. Mom and I would both jump and if you listened closely, you could hear Reagan screaming along with the engine. They were one, man and machine. If Reagan could repair the machine, maybe the man would be repaired, too.

We could tell when things were going well because he would talk lovingly about the car. "That's a 350 Rocket under there," he'd say. "5.7 liter, 350 cubic-inch, V-8 engine...Pure American muscle."

More often than not, though, he complained about some new problem he'd discovered. "The heater core burned out last night," he said one morning with dark rings under his eyes. It made him look just like Dad. "You ever smell burning coolant?" I had not.

"The vents fell out while I was fighting with the old heater core," he announced a few days later. "The damn brackets were held in with just two little screws, can you believe that?"

"The radio keeps shorting out," he said once the vents were back in place. "Dad wants me to keep the 8-track player, but I think I'm gonna buy a new tape deck."

I don't know who he was talking to because neither Mom nor I ever responded to these comments. He just went on as though there was nothing else in the world we could possibly care about.

"Ray!" Dad had come home from a long trip, went straight out to the corn crib to see how the Cutlass was coming along, and had apparently not liked what he found. "Why the hell does the corn crib smell like gasoline?!"

"The fuel line is all dry rot!" Reagan complained. "It keeps leaking!"

"Well, fix it!" Dad shouted, as if this idea had not occurred to Reagan. "I don't need gas soaking into the floorboards! You remember what happened to the barn!"

"I've been looking for the leak," said Reagan, frustrated. "Every time I fix one spot, another leak pops up farther down the line!"

"Dammit, boy! You gotta replace the whole line!" Dad said, poking Reagan in the forehead with a stubby finger. "Stop fooling around and get it done!"

As much as I enjoyed seeing Reagan get berated, even I felt that this was a harsh accusation. Reagan had not been fooling around. He had dumped every spare minute and every extra dime he had into that car. The guys down at the Gladden Napa knew him by name, he was in there so often.

Mom walked in, summoned by raised voices. "Hey," she said, calmly. "What's all this?" Dad stiffened and drew in a harsh breath as though he were in trouble.

"He's got gas spilling all over the corn crib floor," he said in a strained voice. "We're gonna end up having another fire if he's not careful."

"He'll be careful," Mom said sweetly. "He's been working hard. Now all three of you go wash up for dinner." Reagan was sullen and brooding the rest of the night and for several days after.

I didn't realize it at the time, but the Cutlass was Reagan's chance to show Dad that he could be responsible, that he could do something to make Dad proud of him. What Reagan didn't realize was that Dad didn't know that he was supposed to be proud of us.

I don't think Dad ever considered the possibility that his opinion mattered all that much to his sons. No one had ever told him that we needed his approval, so we never got it. I made peace with it and moved on. Reagan couldn't.

The sympathy I felt for Reagan didn't last long. Four or five days later, I was eating breakfast when he walked into the kitchen. I immediately tensed up. I knew what he would do. He would walk past me to get to the refrigerator and, as he passed, he would flick my ear or smack the back of my head. That was his thing. He would find me at peace and remind me that my peace only existed because he allowed it. He would shatter that peace whenever he chose, simply because he could. I was not free to have even a moment of nothingness. He controlled everything.

As he approached, I froze with my spoon midway to my mouth, hovering in anticipation of the smack. Milk dribbled down into the bowl while my cereal grew soggier by the second. He passed behind me and did nothing. He walked to the refrigerator, opened it, and took out the milk.

I was furious. Even when he did nothing, he was still in control. He had me so worked up, so tense, so ready for his aggravating behavior...and then he didn't even have the decency to meet my very low expectations. I stood up, dropped my half-full bowl in the sink, and stormed out of the kitchen.

That was when I truly understood that I would never be free of my brother. I wasn't worried about him killing me like he had Maggie. I was worried that he and I would both live long lives and I would have to deal with him for the next seventy years. We would be old men and he would still be antagonizing me, stealing my medication, kicking my cane out from under me.

The events that occurred later that evening might have taken a different path had they occurred on a different day when I was in a different mood. As it was, I was still pretty irritated with my brother.

"Irritated" may not be the right word, but how can I say that I was feeling an enraged sense of loathing for him, all because he *didn't* smack me in the head?

Reagan had replaced the faulty fuel line, but he needed to make sure it wasn't still leaking at the ends where it was attached to the tank and the fuel pump. Someone had to press on the accelerator to flood the line with fuel while Reagan checked the line from underneath. Dad was out on the road and Mom was busy, so it was up to me to help out.

"Just sit here and press on the gas pedal," he said, pushing me toward the driver's seat. The car was running but I had no idea which one was the gas pedal and I said so.

"Oh, my God!" he shouted, jabbing a finger at the pedal on the right. "That one, retard!" He dropped to the ground and wriggled under the car.

"I'm nine, Ray," I said, as defiantly as I could, though my voice trembled. I'm not sure why I suddenly thought it was a good time to stick up for myself.

"What?!" he said, poking his head out and sneering up at me.

"I'm nine," I repeated, trying to keep my voice level. "I don't know anything about cars. If you want my help..." but before I could finish, Reagan was on his feet, grabbing a fistful of hair at the back of my head and yanking me up onto my tiptoes. I gasped and squirmed.

"If you don't want to fall down the stairs like Maggie, you'll shut your stupid mouth and get in the damn car and do what I tell you!" He shoved me into the driver's seat headfirst and when I turned to face him, he slapped me.

"Now pay attention!" He jabbed a finger at the pedals. "Gas! Brake!" He jabbed a finger into my chest. "Idiot!" Then he slapped me again. "Now wait until I tell you, and step on the gas. You remember which one that is?"

My mouth quivered in spite of myself and I nodded.

"SHOW ME!" he screamed. I pointed to the pedal on the right. He slammed the car door and gave a snort of disgust before crawling back under the car.

I seethed. It wasn't that he had slapped me or called me names, but that he had all but admitted to killing Maggie. He had never been so bold before. And I was next. It was just a matter of time. I'd known as much for three years.

Hot tears spilled onto my cheeks. I hated him so much. He broke everything within his reach. He radiated ruin. Nothing good could thrive while he was around.

"Hit it!" he called from under the car. I had to stretch to reach the pedal and when I did, my toe slipped off.

"I SAID HIT IT, DUMBASS!"

I scooted forward and placed my foot against the pedal and pressed it down. The engine roared and the car twisted beneath me. It wanted to be away from here as much as I did. Maybe we could go together. Neither of us deserved to be abused by Reagan.

"STOP!" he called.

I lifted my foot and wiped away my tears. As I waited, I looked over the knobs and dials and gauges. I'd watched Mom and Dad drive, Mom in her tiny Chevy Vega, Dad in his clunky Ford pickup. It didn't seem very complicated. Everything was labeled.

"HIT IT!" I hit it. The car lurched beneath me again, a dog straining at its leash. "STOP!" I stopped.

I pictured Reagan driving this beast down the road, sneering and shouting at everyone, swerving at passing cars and pedestrians. It seemed unfair for innocent people to have to deal with this monster.

"HIT IT!" I happened to glance into the driver's side wing mirror just then. It was positioned at such an angle that I was looking up at my own bedroom window. Someone was standing there, peering through the curtains, someone wearing a turquoise turtleneck and magenta corduroy overalls. Maggie was watching us.

"I SWEAR TO GOD, OLIVER! I WILL COME UP THERE AND..." but I hit the accelerator hard and Reagan's threats were drowned out by the roar of the engine. He did not like that.

In an instant he was out from beneath the car and had his hands buried in my hair, yanking me from the seat. He threw me face first onto the filthy corn crib floor and dropped a knee into my lower back, right onto my left kidney. I let out a breathless wail and felt his hot breath in my ear.

"When we're done here, I'm going to break your legs and drive you out to Spencerville and you can drag your useless ass back home." He slapped his palm flat against my ear and spit on the side of my face before getting off me. I gasped for breath while I crept back to the car and hoisted myself into the driver's seat, looking up at my bedroom window as I did so. Maggie was gone.

She's gone, I told myself, *and she's never coming back.* I wanted the same for Reagan.

Fight or *Flight*.

Flight had always been my preference. Maybe I could drive the car right out of Gladden and never come back. There had been moments, however, when *Flight* wasn't enough. Sometimes I had no choice but to fight. Did I have a choice that night? Of course, but I was tired of *Flight*. It hadn't gotten me anywhere worth being. But I still had some *Fight* in me.

I had lied to Reagan. I knew a little bit about driving. I knew what all the little letters on the gear shifter meant.

I waited for Reagan to yell, "HIT IT!" When he did, I pulled the gear shifter down to "D" for "drive" and slammed my foot on the gas. The Cutlass leapt forward, slamming into the workbench, which was just hefty enough to hold the car in place. I kept my foot on the gas and the rear tires spun like mad, chewing away, looking for traction. One of those tires was on top of my brother. He might have screamed, but the roar of that 5.7 liter, 350 cubic-inch, V-8 engine drowned him out. The 350 Rocket was louder than everything.

I put the car in park, stepped calmly out of the driver's door, and walked away from the corn crib. I didn't look at Reagan as I passed, but his legs were twitching. One of his boots had come off and I could smell urine and car exhaust. I walked straight up to my bedroom and got out my toy cars.

And that's where Mom found me at the end of what I have already described as a pretty rough day.

"Get in the car," she said, and I did.

-EIGHT-
the library
-(November, 1987)-

I was being kidnapped. Why didn't I try to escape? Again, the short answer is that I didn't know I was being kidnapped. I was with Mom. Considering the day's events, an impromptu, late-night drive to Michigan seemed pretty normal.

Why didn't I try to escape? The long answer is more complicated.

At first I was relieved. I thought I would get in trouble when Dad saw what I had done. Mom had rescued me and I was in no hurry to go back home. Dad would yell and I would get frightened and I would probably cry and then he would yell at me for crying.

I never wanted to go back to Gladden or to my father ever again. No one had to tell me that Reagan was dead. I knew. How could he not be? Dad would be really mad.

As we drove north on the interstate in Mom's 1977 Chevy Vega, I leaned my head against the passenger window and let the lights wash over me at every interchange. I pretended the light was cleansing me of my sins. I grew cleaner with each pass, purer with every mile. The farther we drove, the cleaner I felt.

The radio was on, but it was hard to find a station that stayed in tune for more than thirty minutes or so. It was my job, as we rushed through the night, to find something decent to listen to. It was November, 1987, and the soundtrack was a steady stream of Billy

Idol, Taylor Dayne, and Michael Jackson, though Tiffany was the reigning queen. In those days, you didn't have much choice and took what you could get. Don't like Phil Collins? Too bad.

The hours passed and I snuck little glances at Mom to see if she was mad or sad or worried or upset. Whenever she saw me looking, she forced a smile that told me more than she probably wanted me to know.

She must have known what happened, what I did. Yet, here we were. I should have been in trouble, but instead, I was in charge of the radio. I wasn't too eager to ask questions. I would have run with her as long and as far as she asked me to.

The Vega was a two-door hatchback painted a shade of brown that could have only come from the 1970s. After a few hours, we abandoned the radio and I crawled into the hatch and stared up through the glass at the stars. I remember the roof-lining had a uniform pattern of tiny pinholes. If I let my eyes relax and my mind go slack, the holes on the left side of my vision would drift over, lining up with the holes on the right side of my vision, and I would lose myself in the unknowable depth of a galaxy of pinholes. I would switch back and forth between the two: the twinkling, real stars outside and the manufactured, static galaxy on the inside. They were equally fascinating.

When you're young, you assume that your parents have a plan, whatever the situation. Even when your mom ushers you into the car and drives through the night with no explanation, you assume she knows what she's doing.

We packed nothing, though we'd had time to do so. We even left our toothbrushes behind. Mom could have cleaned out the bank accounts and we could have lived fairly comfortably, just the two of us, but she panicked. All we had was about thirty dollars, most of which went into the gas tank.

The first two nights were pretty rough. We had to sleep in the car. Mom had driven us to northern Michigan in November and we were completely unprepared for the cold.

On our third day on the run, Mom found a flier on a grocery store bulletin board advertising a battered women's shelter. They were kind enough to take us in, give us clothes and food, and not ask too many questions. We spent three weeks there. They helped Mom find a job and an apartment. I would like to say more about our stay at the shelter, but I can't remember much, which is an absolute shame. The way those ladies treated us informed much of my future beliefs: Be kind. Don't judge. Help when you can.

The kindness we received from those chain-smoking, foul-mouthed ladies at the battered women's shelter in Traverse City, Michigan, was perhaps the most impactful, non-traumatic experience of my early years. There was no agenda and there were no expectations. There was just love. These ladies had been through it all...drug addiction, systemic injustice, abuse of every kind...but they were tough as nails and they loved as fiercely as anyone I've ever known. If they could help someone walk through the same fire they'd been through, they were happy to do it. They didn't have much, but they put it all on the table. They held nothing back.

Knowing that there are people out there like that, even tucked away where I can't see them, gives me all kinds of hope for humanity. If there had been more people like that in Gladden, maybe Reagan wouldn't have been so evil and maybe I wouldn't have had to run over him with his own car.

Maybe.

Through the shelter, Mom found work as a night custodian at a
hardware store. After hours, the store needed to be swept and
mopped, and the bathrooms, breakroom, and office needed to be
cleaned. There were floor mats to vacuum and trash cans to empty.
It was a big job and she was a little lady, so I helped and sometimes I
even enjoyed it.

I didn't attend public school. The ladies at the shelter warned
Mom that enrolling me in public school was a good way to get found.
If Dad hired a private investigator to track us down, one of the
first places they might look was school enrollment records. So I was
homeschooled, though Mom's idea of "homeschool" was sending
me to the library while she cleaned other units in our apartment
building.

I loved the library. It was two blocks away from our apartment
and, for the first several months, Mom would walk me to and from,
but once the weather got nicer and she began to feel more
comfortable with our new neighborhood, she let me go on my own.

The employees at the library knew me by sight and, much like
the ladies at the shelter, didn't bother me with a lot of questions.
Sometimes I would approach them for advice on a book or if I had
questions about a certain subject that I was studying (even though
Mom's educational standards weren't very high, I was still expected
to learn occasionally). I quickly found that certain employees were
more dependable than others, based on the topic of my query. For
example, if I wanted some light, non-demanding reading material,
Patty, the old lady with the faded purple cardigan (who was probably
in her early-forties...old...) always had suggestions. If I wanted
something a little more challenging, both in style and theme, Julia,
the pretty lady with the red hair, was happy to help, though her
recommendations were almost always Ray Bradbury novels. Alan,
a heavyset gentleman who wore the exact same short-sleeved dress

shirt every single day coupled with a different poorly-tied necktie, was my source for math questions, and I have since come to suspect that he knew as much about the Pythagrean theorem as I did. Luckily, Pythagoras doesn't come up in conversation very often.

By far, however, my favorite library employee was a guy named Brian. He might have been in his late-twenties or early-fifties. He was lanky and a little goofy and was always reading something interesting. I never had to seek him out. He would find me.

"Hey, man," he would say, sliding into the seat across the table from where I was studying. Our interactions always felt slightly conspiratorial, like an act of espionage.

"You ever read Douglas Adams?" he asked once, sliding a copy of *The Hitchhiker's Guide to the Galaxy* across the table to me. Another time he recommended *Ender's Game,* by Orson Scott Card. He always seemed to know exactly what I would enjoy. And his recommendations weren't limited to books. The library had a wide selection of music as well, mostly on cassette.

"The stuff they play on the radio is okay," he said once, "but if you let them..." he pointed vaguely toward the outside, "...decide what you hear, you're gonna miss a lot of good stuff."

Brian introduced me to bands like The Ramones, The Misfits, Nirvana, The Clash, Bad Religion...If the radio played honey to attract flies, this stuff was pure vinegar. It was, admittedly, not the most appropriate soundtrack for a young child to grow up with, but I loved it.

Have you ever considered the lyrics to "I Think We're Alone Now"? Sweet, teen-queen Tiffany was alluding to sneaky, sweaty romps with her hunky beau. What was wrong with Violent Femmes singing about the same subject matter, albeit in a far more blunt and straightforward manner? They didn't try to hide the truth of their youthful escapades in a pretty package. I have always preferred unabashed straight-talk to subtle half-speak.

I didn't have a cassette-player at home, so I was forced to pursue my elicit punk-rock interests in one of the listening booths at the library. I would spend entire afternoons blasting The Misfits' "Die, Die My Darling" into my ears and then go home and spend the evening with the mournful wail of Joni Mitchell wafting softly from the living room. Brian eventually helped me out with that, too.

"You should start studying Spanish," he said one day, dropping into the seat across from me.

"What?"

"Or French," he said. "It's always a good idea to learn a second language. And start now while you're young. Right now, your brain is still able to form new neural pathways and make all sorts of language associations. If you wait until you're my age, your brain will be so messed up with drugs and booze that nothing new will get in. You should go to the Help Desk and see if Patty can set you up." He stood to go.

"But I don't want to learn another language," I said. "I don't even really like using English."

"Dude," Brian said, leaning over the table, "trust me. Go to the Help Desk and tell Patty that you're thinking of learning a new language. It'll be worth it. You can thank me later."

My curiosity got the better of me and I went over to see Patty. She smiled as she watched me approach.

"Hello! Looking for some more Roald Dahl?" she chirped.

"Not at the moment," I said, smiling. "I was wondering, if I wanted to start studying a new language, like Spanish or French, do you have anything that might help?"

"We absolutely do!" Patty clapped her hands together excitedly and pushed the drooping sleeves of her cardigan up past her elbows. I grimaced internally, wondering what Brian had gotten me into.

"We have dozens of workbooks and different types of material like that," she said, "but what we've found works the best are audio tapes. It's called 'language immersion.' The tapes run you through a course. It starts out real easy, numbers and colors and things like that, and then you move on to different nouns, like 'car' and 'chair' and 'shoe.' And eventually you start to pick it up and before you know it, you're fluent!"

"Oh," I said, once Patty paused for a breath. "Well, I don't actually have a cassette player of my own, so..." I turned to go, but Patty stopped me.

"You can check one out!" she said. "The language program has about two dozen cassette players and headsets that go with the tapes so you're free to study at home!"

Out of the corner of my eye I could see Brian doing a series of celebratory hip-thrusts in one of the aisles, just out of Patty's line of sight. "That sounds great," I said, trying to keep a straight face. "Thank you so much."

What concerned Mom the most was Dad finding us. She would have sold the car, as it was such an easily-identifiable model (not many Chevy Vegas were still on the road in the late 1980s), but that, like enrolling me in public school, was a big no-no. Automobile title transfers are public record, easily tracked by a private investigator. So, the Vega sat in the apartment lot, tucked between a dumpster and a weedy copse of trees.

Mom was also worried that someone would recognize me. This was back in the milk-carton-kid era and Mom was convinced we would one day see my overexposed class photo plastered on the side of a half-gallon at the grocery store. The burn mark on the left side of my face made me far too recognizable.

"We're going to let your hair grow out," she said during dinner one evening. This was right after we moved into the apartment. I hadn't yet gotten interested in the counterculture of punk rock and my opinion of boys with long hair was that they smoked cigarettes and said swears and weren't very nice. I didn't want to be associated with those types.

I killed my brother, but I was worried about what people would think of me if I had long hair. That was Gladden down to the roots.

"Well, maybe you could just grow the front part," she said, pushing my hair over to one side of my forehead and squinting at me. "You could let your bangs grow long. I saw some boys on TV. Skateboarders from California. That's how they wore it."

"We'll see," I said. "Maybe." That was how I handled unwanted conversations back then. It's also how I handle them now.

I really didn't want to grow my hair out, but what could I do about it? If Mom didn't cut my hair, who would? I certainly couldn't do it myself. There was a pair of scissors in a kitchen drawer when we moved in, but they were lefties.

Had I been using the library's cassette player for its intended purpose, I would have been fluent in three new languages for as much time as I spent using it over the next several years. I spent all of my time either at the library, cleaning the hardware store with Mom, or in my room listening to music and reading.

Mom sent away for a homeschool test packet and, in spite of my lack of interest in learning anything, I did fairly well. My math scores were atrocious, but my reading and language comprehension were off the charts. Mom was pleasantly surprised and congratulated herself on supplying me with the proper tools for success.

I would agree that, under the circumstances, she really did well. In my experience, the most well-rounded kids are those whose parents step back and are less imposing, less controlling. Mom made sure I had access to what I needed and then let me try. She was too busy scraping together an income to worry about whether or not I understood calculus, which, for the record, I never have. I'm not even sure what it is. I think it has something to do with math.

Time passed and our weird, solitary life started to feel normal. I liked my limited routine and I liked not having classmates making me feel bad about myself all the time. I especially liked not having to hide from my brother.

At Mom's behest, I let my hair grow. It wasn't so bad. No one treated me any differently. I wasn't accused of crimes and no one offered me drugs. I was just a pale little kid with shaggy hair, which did precisely what it was meant to do, incidentally. It grew down over the left side of my face and hid the red burn marks that made me so identifiable.

I don't know who we thought would turn us in. We had no friends. We saw no one. The hardware store was closed whenever we cleaned. The library staff took my presence for granted and none of the other patrons made eye-contact. Our neighbors came and went so often that we never bothered introducing ourselves. That's the beauty of a six-month leasing agreement.

For six years I lived like that: cleaning the hardware store at night, hanging out in the library during the day, hiding in my room in between. I continued using the cassette player from the library, but by some miracle of shoddy paperwork, no one ever asked me to return it. Brian's doing, I assume. I continued to read voraciously, though I never got any better at math.

Eventually, I began to wonder how much longer it could go on. I wasn't getting bored with life, exactly, but I knew something had to change. Things always do.

On June 9, 1993, it did change, because two days earlier I opened my big, dumb mouth and ruined a perfectly good thing.

-NINE-
unreliable, but dangerous
-(June, 1993)-

One day, I overheard a woman at the library talking to her children and she mentioned that Father's Day was coming up, and I thought, *Hey! A father! I have one of those!* and for some reason I couldn't just leave it at that.

"Father's Day is coming up," I said as Mom and I were just starting to eat dinner later that evening. Mom stiffened as if she had been slapped, her salad fork frozen in midair. After a moment, she forced herself to take a bite.

"Mm-hm," she said, chewing carefully as she stared blankly into the space between us.

"Well," I shrugged, trying to disguise the shiver brought on by the sudden chill, "I thought maybe we could send him a card...or call him..."

Mom stopped chewing and gave me a look that I had never seen from her before. Her nostrils flared and her pupils were wide open, taking in every scrap of information she could gather. I had a crazy notion, just for a moment, that she might try to stab me with her fork.

The moment passed. It couldn't have been more than a few seconds, but I was suddenly sweating. My hair was plastered to my head and my t-shirt clung to my chest.

Mom swallowed her bite of salad and smiled sadly, the same smile she had given me the night we had driven away from Gladden, the night Reagan had died. "I don't think that's a great idea, Ollie," she said. Her voice was so calm, so level. Had I imagined that wild look? I must have.

"You're probably right," I said. My voice was hoarse and shaky. "I need to go to the bathroom," I said, hurrying out of the room.

Mom kept eating. "Don't forget to wash your hands."

I leaned over the bathroom sink and splashed water onto my face, feeling the shape of my eye sockets, my nose, my lips. I looked into the mirror (a thing I usually avoided doing) but my hair, shaggier than usual, hid my features, just like it was supposed to. I wondered idly if I was good-looking and would have been surprised to learn that this is a pretty common question. Everyone wonders.

I also wondered about Mom and what had just happened. Surely that wasn't normal, that sudden, unsettling shift. When I was young, we had an old dog, Conan, and he would go rigid and wary whenever he sensed...or thought he sensed...danger. Eventually, he started to growl and bare his teeth when anyone came near him. Dad said he was unwell and too dangerous and had to be put down. I remember thinking, "He thought we were dangerous, and we killed him. Maybe he was on to something."

I saw that same look in Mom's eyes that I used to see in Conan's eyes. She sensed danger. Was she unwell or was she right?

I dried my face and hands, took a few steadying breaths and returned to the table where everything was magically back to normal. The chill in the air was gone and Mom no longer had that caged look in her eyes.

"Are you alright?" she asked, genuinely concerned. "You look pale."

I nodded and smiled. "I'm fine. Just a little tired, I guess."

"Well, it's been dry all week," she said, "so mopping shouldn't take too long. We'll be done before you know it." She was talking about the hardware store.

We finished dinner in silence. I didn't know it then, but the gears inside Mom's mind had slipped even further out of place. They still turned, but the machine was about to break. The clock was no longer merely unreliable, but dangerous.

By this point, the hardware job was something we barely considered. We had done it so many times over the years that it was just something our bodies did while our brains were busy elsewhere. I would pick up the trash from the register area and swing by to collect the office trash and drop it off by the back door before we had even gotten properly settled in. Then I would grab the vacuum cleaner and hit the office and all of the floormats (rolling these up and moving them out of the way), gathering more trash as I went.

While I was doing that, Mom cleaned the bathrooms and started going up and down each aisle with the dust mop, making note of aisles that needed extra attention or aisles that could be skipped. In the summer, mopping was easy and we skipped most aisles. In the winter, however, we almost always mopped the entire store, often hitting some aisles twice.

When the vacuuming was done, I would fill two mop buckets, one with soapy water, one with clean, and start mopping the aisles she had already swept. Once she was done with the dust mop, she would find me and we'd finish mopping the rest of the store. We had fine-tuned the process and could get the whole thing done properly in well under two hours, barring any nasty surprises.

We grew close, working like that for six years. I think that's what made the situation that evening so much more disturbing. Over dinner she had transformed, briefly, into something terrifying, something capable of anything. I saw it in her eyes. As I vacuumed the floor mats that night, I couldn't get the image of her wide, wild eyes out of my head.

Those weren't her eyes. I knew her better than that. She was sweet and she was brave and she had always come to my rescue whenever I needed help.

That wasn't actually true, though, was it? She hadn't been there when Reagan got really bad, had she? She hadn't been there to protect me when he doused me with gasoline. She hadn't been there when he threatened to break my legs. She hadn't been there for Maggie.

I turned off the vacuum and started rolling up the floor mats.

Why hadn't she protected me?

Why hadn't she protected Reagan?

"You're stronger than you know," she said. I jumped and dropped the rolled-up mat I was holding. She had walked up behind me, silent as a hunter stalking a deer. "Reagan didn't realize it, but that was his mistake."

We had never discussed Reagan. Never so much as mentioned his name in six years.

"I didn't want to hurt him," I said softly.

"He wanted to hurt you, though," she said conversationally, "and he would have." She left something unsaid and that something hung in the air between us, thickening until it found my mouth and forced its way out.

"Just like Maggie," I said.

Mom almost smiled. "Just like Maggie."

There was a flicker of movement at the end of the dark aisle behind Mom. I caught a flash of turquoise and magenta before losing it in the shadows.

"You're stronger than Maggie," Mom said. "Stronger than Reagan, too."

"I didn't want to hurt him," I repeated. My voice was so small I might have been nine years old again.

"What did you want to do?" Mom asked, that same almost-smile on her face.

"I just wanted him to leave me alone."

"He wouldn't," she said. "Ever. No matter how old you got, no matter how far you moved, Reagan could never have left you alone. As far as he was concerned, you belonged to him. He would never give you a moment of peace. If he couldn't have it, you couldn't, either."

I was crying now. Not the wailing, frightened sobs that Reagan used to rip out of me, but thick, slow tears. They rolled down my cheeks, hot as the sun. Grief, remorse, and anger, all of the things that I had been holding on to for so long, flooded out of me.

Mother was not impressed.

"Oh, what's this?!" she demanded suddenly, gesturing toward me. A minor battle played out on her features and I thought her eyes would go wild and wide again, but after a struggle, calm prevailed and she walked forward and put her hand on my arm and said, "Hey now..." I had seen her do this to my father many times.

Her voice had changed. It was soft and sweet again, which scared me more than anything. Who was the real Mom? Soft and sweet? Or impatient and disgusted?

Dad had known. Dad had been afraid and had stayed away. Mom and Reagan were *Fight*. Dad and Oliver were *Flight*. I'm not sure what Maggie was.

Mom walked away from me, disappearing down a dark side aisle, humming quietly to herself. I wiped my eyes, finished vacuuming, and started mopping. Mom caught up with me when she was done with the dust mop. We finished cleaning the store, chatting idly like nothing had happened.

As we were walking home, Mom said, "You know what? I think I'm going to make lasagna. I haven't made lasagna since we moved here."

"I love lasagna," I said.

"How about Wednesday?" she asked. "I need time to remember the recipe and then go to the store."

"Wednesday's great," I said.

There had been nothing at all in her tone that suggested she was going to try to poison me. Honestly, though, her lasagna was so good, I might not have cared even if I'd known.

-TEN-
struggling through the front door
-(June, 1993)-

Mom was nowhere to be found on Tuesday. Sometimes that happened if she got temp work or if the building super needed an empty unit in the building cleaned right away. He paid double for last-minute cleanings, so Mom never passed up the opportunity. Sometimes I helped, if the unit in question was really bad.

I had spent the morning at the library, but went home around noon. Mom still wasn't around and, when the time came to clean the hardware, there was still no sign of her. I double-checked the kitchen counter to see if she'd left a note that I'd missed, then looked in her bedroom. Her purse was gone. I checked the parking lot and the Vega was gone, too. It hadn't moved in at least three years and I was pretty sure it was sitting on at least one flat tire. Its absence felt uncomfortably conspicuous.

Short of calling the police, there was nothing I could do, so I sat on the couch and tried to watch TV. I got through one trailer for a new dinosaur movie and the first 30 seconds or so of a news story about the ground-breaking ceremony for the new Rock and Roll Hall of Fame in Cleveland before I turned off the TV and went to my room. I popped a tape into the cassette player, a new album by a band I'd never heard of, one of Brian's recommendations, of course.

Earlier that morning I was sitting at my usual table at the library when Brian dropped into the seat across from me. He didn't say anything, he just casually slid a cassette across the table. It didn't have the usual library labels plastered all over it. This one was from his private collection.

"'Rancid,'" I read, flipping it over to read the track listing.

"They're new," he said conspiratorially. "It's a couple of the guys from Operation Ivy and a new drummer. All punk, no ska, very raw."

"On a scale from 'Offspring' to 'Misfits'..." I prompted.

Brian considered for a moment before saying, "'Bad Religion'. They're good."

"Thanks!" I said. "I'll give it a listen."

"Just make sure you bring it back in a couple of days," he said as he stood up. "I haven't worn it out yet." He wandered off into the stacks. I still have that cassette.

A few years ago I tried to track Brian down. I wanted to thank him for his kindness and his influence and I wanted to return his cassette and explain why I hadn't done so sooner. I contacted the library and inquired about some of their former employees. To my pleasant surprise, I was connected with Patty, she of the faded purple cardigan, who was still dutifully manning the Help Desk and recommending Roald Dahl to lonely children.

She did not remember me, but she did tell me, sorrowfully, that Brian had passed away a number of years prior. He had an undiagnosed heart-condition and died shortly after an intense pickleball session at the YMCA.

I had a hard time believing that we were talking about the same person. I just couldn't picture Brian lacing up his $25 Walmart running shoes, donning a headband, and putting in a fatal amount of effort for a game of pickleball, but then I realized that there was a good chance that, when he died, Brian had been in his sixties.

As I waited for Mom to show up, I listened to Rancid. "Adina", "Hyena", "Detroit", "Rats in the Hallway"...Track after track, they were incredible. Brian had undersold them.

Sometimes a thing comes along and completely blindsides you. You find yourself leaning on it and wondering what you did without it. That's what punk rock was for me, and, with that first encounter, Rancid jumped to the top of the ranks. I felt about as close to myself as I ever had before. Sure, they sang about homelessness and addiction and class wars, but it wasn't the experiences that I connected with. It was the hopelessness.

They sang about a lot of the bad things in life, but they didn't try to make excuses and they didn't try to pass the blame for their mistakes. I liked that a lot. I appreciated the accountability. It helped me give a name to the shame I had been carrying for six years. I killed my brother and now we were here. Being here was better than being home, but still, being here wasn't easy for Mom or for me and that was my fault. The music, somehow, helped me own it.

I can't really explain it, but something unlocked inside me. If Maggie's death had caused Mom's gears to shift and bump her mind out of whack, punk rock had the opposite effect on me. It rattled my gears into their proper places. It didn't change the facts, it just changed the way I looked at them and helped me process things. It was, quite literally, therapy. Say what you will about those mohawk-wearing junkies with safety pins through their noses, but they helped me heal when no one else did.

Side A had just ended and I was in the process of flipping the tape when Mom came home. I found her struggling through the front door with her arms full of groceries.

I moved to take them from her but she said, "No, no, Ollie. Go down and get the rest out of the car and then lock it up." She nodded toward the keys which were still dangling from the doorknob.

I took the keys and hurried down to the parking lot. I grabbed the last bag of groceries out of the back and walked around to lock the doors. The car was made in 1977 and was far from a luxury model, so the doors had to be locked manually, both of them individually. I went to the driver's side and locked it, then walked around to the passenger side. When I opened the door, a receipt fluttered out. I pinned it to the ground with my toe, locked and shut the car door, and scooped up the receipt, stuffing it into my pocket without a glance before hurrying upstairs with the last of the groceries.

That receipt saved my life.

Summers at the library were not as peaceful as the rest of the year. Parents, suddenly faced with the prospect of having to deal with their own children, sent their delightful little biological burdens to the library for a bit of free babysitting. Patty loved it, but the rest of the staff hated it as much as I did. Fortunately for me, I didn't have to be there.

That's why I spent the morning of June 9, 1993, in my bedroom reading rather than at the library. I had checked out a stack of Vonnegut novels the day before (Brian added *Breakfast of Champions* to the stack as I was checking out and said, "It's not sci-fi, but it's good,") and I was halfway through *The Sirens of Titan* before I staggered out to use the bathroom. Mom was in the kitchen, browning ground hamburger on the stove for the lasagna.

"Hey," I said, opening the fridge and taking out the milk.

"Late start?" she asked. No judgment, just observation.

"Been reading." I poured a glass and drank half of it off in one go. Then I refilled the glass and put the milk away. "We didn't clean the hardware last night." We hadn't even discussed it.

"Nope," she said. "I called Chuck and took a couple of nights off."

"Why?" I asked, sipping at my milk.

"Thought it would be nice to take a break," she said. "Maybe we could drive down to Silver Lake, see the dunes."

"Will the car make it that far?" I asked.

"Don't see why not," she said as she stirred the beef. "I drove it all around town yesterday. Seemed healthy as ever."

"What do people do at the dunes?" This small talk was very normal for Mom and I. She made suggestions, I asked questions, and we would eventually decide to stay home, maybe rent a VCR and a couple of movies.

Mom's mood-shift from two days prior seemed so much less important that morning. I was sure I'd imagined it. I was good at imagining things. I had imagined Maggie in the window on the night Reagan died. I had imagined her again, two nights ago in the hardware. I had definitely imagined those things.

Maggie was gone. She had to be. If she wasn't, then maybe neither was Reagan, and that would be bad.

Mom was fine and Maggie and Reagan were gone. My brain was just totally a mess. I was seeing things that weren't there and would one day need medication and shock therapy and a group home like in *One Flew Over the Cuckoo's Nest,* but not right now because I had my books and my punk rock tapes, and that was enough.

"Oliver!" Mom was calling me. I'd been drifting.

"What?"

"I said, 'Are you going to sit there in your pajamas all day?'" She laughed. "Kinda spaced out, huh? Too many of those sci-fi books."

"Totally rotting my brain," I agreed before finishing my milk and putting the glass in the sink.

I went into my bedroom and read for a while longer before I finally got dressed. I grabbed my jeans from the day before and dragged them on. I'm a firm believer that blue jeans don't even start to get comfortable until somewhere around the second week of continuous wear. I've never seen anything that looked less inviting than freshly-laundered denim.

I was pulling on a fresh t-shirt (these are more comfortable when they're clean) when I noticed the receipt from the night before poking out of my pocket. I examined it and saw that it was from a pharmacy down the street. The pharmacist had scribbled a note at the bottom of the receipt: "I know you feel your situation is more severe than most, but I assure you, the prescribed dosage is plenty! If you have further questions, don't hesitate to call!" The pharmacist had written a phone number below this. The business number at the top of the receipt was also circled.

The order on the receipt was for *zolpidem*. I had no idea what that was, but couldn't imagine what Mom's condition could be. She didn't even get headaches, let alone anything so severe that the pharmacist's concern seemed warranted. What was going on?

"Where are you going?" Mom asked as I knelt by the front door tying my shoes.

"Library," I said. "I'll be back in an hour or so. Just gotta look something up."

"Dinner will be ready around five," she called out as I left the apartment.

I had never had to look up drugs before and I didn't know which employee to ask, but I found Brian loitering in general fiction. He seemed like a safe bet. At least he wouldn't ask any awkward questions.

With no preamble, I blurted out, "I need a book about drugs."

"Aldous Huxley," he said immediately. "*The Doors of Perception*...Jim Morrison was a big fan..."

"Nope," I said, waving him down. "Prescription drugs. Like, an encyclopedia of medicine."

Brian gave me a look of utter disdain and sighed. "God, you're boring..."

The 1993 Consumer Guide to Prescription Drugs was, personally, a disappointment. I don't know what I had expected, perhaps a massive leather tome covered in cobwebs and protected by ancient magic, but the reality was a brand-new paperback, weighing about a pound. There were brightly-colored pills on the cover. It listed prescription drugs and what they treated, what they looked like, what their side-effects were, etc. I couldn't have asked for more, but I was still a bit let down.

It was like hoping for Gandalf and getting Ronald McDonald instead.

Zolpidem is a drug used to treat insomnia and anxiety, neither of which sounded like anything my mother experienced, not with the regularity that would necessitate prescription medication. Could this have something to do with her strange behavior two nights ago? Was she suffering from anxiety? Had she not been sleeping? I kicked myself for not paying closer attention.

(NOTE: Based on my current understanding of the disease, my mother was almost certainly suffering from anxiety. At the time, I had only the vaguest, most elementary awareness of what it was, what it looked like, and how it manifests in different people. The pain that might have been avoided...)

The book had a lot of other information about overdoses and that sort of thing, but it seemed very unimportant at the time, so I didn't give it as much consideration as I could have. By the way, ignoring information when I intentionally asked for it is a personal habit that has never NOT been a problem eventually.

By the time I got home, the lasagna was in the oven and Mom was taking a shower. I looked around for the bottle of pills labeled *"zolpidem"* but couldn't find it. I looked in the trash and there it was, tucked under a bunch of greasy paper towels. I pulled it out, wondering why she would have thrown it away. I first noticed that the bottle was empty, then I realized that it wasn't even from the same pharmacy that the receipt had come from. I pulled the receipt from my pocket and double-checked. Two different pharmacies, two different phone numbers. I searched deeper in the trash and found a second pill bottle, and then a third. All three had come from different pharmacies and they were all empty. My stomach tightened and the sweat on my back and forehead suddenly felt like it had turned to ice.

What was going on?

The quantity listed on each bottle was 500mg. I rolled my memory back in an attempt to recall what I had read about the quantity of *zolpidem* per dose and compared that to what I had read about the quantity required for a fatal overdose. I remembered reading that a person would need 15mg for every kilogram of body weight in order to overdose. Or had it been 150mg? First, I would need to figure out how much Mom weighed, convert it to kilograms, multiply that by 15...or 150...then divide that by however much *zolpidem* was in each pill. I told myself that this must be why math is so important and wondered if I was inadvertently attempting calculus.

By this point I had forgotten what it was I was trying to figure out.

I dropped the empty pill bottles back in the trash and started frantically looking around the kitchen. Mom had already washed all of the prep dishes and left them in the drying rack. The salad was in a covered bowl in the fridge. There was garlic bread laid out on a pan on top of the stove which I assumed would go into the oven at a specific time so that it and the lasagna were ready to eat simultaneously.

(OFF-TOPIC NOTE: One thing I have always admired is the ability to demonstrate flawless time management in the kitchen. You might think it's just basic math, but there's way more to it. One also has to have unflinching confidence in one's calculations. If you're off by just a few minutes either way, your garlic bread...and possibly the entire evening...is ruined. It requires tremendous focus and preparation. If a person wants to intimidate me, all they need to do is casually prepare a holiday feast without any hiccups or casualties. I will not object to any future claims to alpha status. If there's ever an apocalyptic event, I'm showing up at their door. They're the new president.)

There was no sign of what my mother had done with the pills. I cracked open the oven just enough to activate the light and see the lasagna bubbling away, but I wasn't likely to spot anything out-of-the-ordinary in that mess. The waiting garlic bread was equally unlikely to reveal any secrets.

I returned to the refrigerator. The only thing that seemed suspicious was a bottle of wine on the top shelf. I had only seen my mother drink wine once, the night we moved into the apartment, in celebration of our new life. I closed the refrigerator door and leaned against it, scanning the kitchen. I was just about to dig through the trash again when Mom walked out of the bathroom with her hair wrapped up in a towel.

"Hey, Ollie!" she said cheerily. "Smells good, doesn't it?"

"Uh, yeah," I said, trying to look casual as my heart thudded wildly in my chest.

Mom checked the timer on the stove and grabbed an oven mitt. It was time for the garlic bread to go in.

"How was the library?" she asked. When she saw my face, she did a double-take. "Are you alright?"

I swallowed hard and let my head roll slightly to one side.

This, I've found, is a very useful gesture if you want to convince someone that you're feeling unwell. Ferris Bueller advised licking your palms, but I have to disagree with that technique unless you actually want to get sick. The slight head roll gives the impression of dizziness without you actually having to lie about it. Don't stumble or roll your eyes around or try to steady yourself against a countertop. That's too much. Big red flags, there.

Simply let your head drift off-center and bring it back home. Then act normal. After a moment or two, go into the next room and sit down in the nearest unoccupied seat. If anyone asks if you need anything, ask for a glass of water. And don't make eye-contact. You're on the cusp of being sick, you're only vaguely aware of other people in the room until one of them brings you a glass of water, as requested.

Do not drink the water. It's a prop. As soon as the glass is in your hand, set it down on a table and then pause as if the act of setting the glass down has triggered a gag reflex. Excuse yourself. Say you might lie down for a bit. Once you have left the room, you have between five and fifteen minutes before someone checks on you. When they do, be asleep and be fully clothed. Make no attempt to comfort yourself with pajamas or a blanket. Allow your caretaker to infer from your actions that your body went immediately into shut-down mode.

If you have followed these instructions properly, you can now expect to be excused from school or church or whatever family function you are hoping to avoid. Unless your mother has made a lasagna laced with enough sleeping pills to kill a rhinoceros. In that case, you're going to have to be a little more clever.

"I don't think I'm feeling very well," I said feebly.

"Well, suck it up, toots!" Mom said cheerfully as she slid the garlic bread into the oven. "Dinner should be ready in fifteen minutes. Go get yourself cleaned up." She pulled the towel off her head and tossed it to me as I walked toward the bathroom. I hung the towel on the back of the door and stared blankly at the still-foggy mirror. I was nothing but a vague blur, which was a comforting thought.

She was definitely going to poison me. There was nothing I could do about it. Did I even want to stop her?

Yes.

Why?

I don't know.

You have nothing to live for. You have this apartment. You have the hardware. You have the library. You have the sidewalks that connect the three. Your whole world lies within that triangle.

I have friends.

You don't have friends.

The people at the library are my friends.

They get paid to be nice to you. You're a customer to them.

I could make friends.

Really? How? Where?

...

You wanna go across town to the mall? Maybe chat up the pretty girls in the food court?

...

They'll take one look at your face and run screaming in the other direction.

...

You're too afraid to come out from behind your hair. How are you gonna make friends?

"Don't listen to him," a small voice said from behind the shower curtain. I screamed and jumped sideways, smacking my face against the bathroom door.

"Part of him is still in your head," said that small, soft voice. "Part of him always will be."

I slowly slid down to the floor, my legs shaking like mad. I reached clumsily around the cabinet to grab the toilet plunger, falling back against the bathroom door. I clutched the plunger to my chest like a crucifix.

Someone was standing in the tub. I couldn't see them, but I could see the soft reflection of magenta and turquoise against the still-wet, off-white wall. A lock of blonde hair appeared just past the edge of the curtain followed by a large, blue eye. It was rimmed red with dried blood.

I screamed again, a high-pitched shriek that only dogs could hear, and threw the plunger at the shower curtain, but it passed through the plastic drape and clattered in the bottom of the empty tub. There was no one there.

It took several minutes for my breathing to regulate and for my legs to stop shaking enough for me to stand. I filled the sink with water and dunked my face, splashing water up over the back of my neck. I let the water out of the sink and dried my face. When I looked up at the cloudy mirror, I saw that someone had written in tall, dripping letters, "he's still angry."

-ELEVEN-
we all fall down
-(June, 1993)-

When I returned to the kitchen, I was still trembling and I have no doubt that I looked even worse than before, but Mom didn't mention it. The table had been set with two plates of lasagna, a basket of garlic bread, and a drink for each of us: milk for me, wine for Mom.

The thing I had just imagined in the bathroom had nearly distracted me from the more immediate and very real problem that was sitting at the table and staring innocently as if there wasn't a felonious amount of prescription sleeping pills hidden in my dinner.

"What's the occasion?" I asked, indicating the glass of wine. "I don't know." Mom smiled coyly. "I thought it might be nice to pretend that we're rich. A few days off work, a trip to Silver Lake, a glass of wine..."

"I'm not sure Silver Lake is the destination of choice for the world's upper class." I had never been to Silver Lake, but I didn't think there were too many millionaires itching to spend the day scrambling to the top of a sand dune.

"Then we'll pretend we're middle-class," she said. "Still a step up. Now, sit. Eat."

I sat down and eyed my lasagna suspiciously. Mom hadn't started in on hers yet, but was taking a tentative sip of wine. She wrinkled her nose, but gave me a smile.

I picked up my fork and examined the lasagna, looking for anything suspicious. I don't know what I expected to see. Big, white pills poking out from between layers of pasta? I honestly considered trying to switch plates with her, like Vizzini in *The Princess Bride*, but then I remembered how well that had worked out for him. Mom noticed my hesitation.

"Everything alright?" she asked. She cut into her lasagna, forking a piece into her mouth as if to say, *Do you think I poisoned it or something?*

I just smiled at her and took a small bite. That first taste confirmed my suspicions. It was bitter to the point of inedibility. Mom was eagerly devouring hers, eyeing me the whole time. I took another miniscule bite and washed it down with a large gulp of milk.

"Oh! Garlic bread!" she said, offering me the basket. *I'll just fill up on bread*, I thought, stuffing half a piece into my mouth. The garlic bread couldn't chase the bitterness of the lasagna from my mouth.

Mom took a large bite of garlic bread herself and drank off the rest of her wine. The bottle stood beside her on the table and she wasted no time refilling her glass. There was a sudden, manic urgency about her actions. I put my fork down and leaned back in my chair, feeling poison and anxiety churning away in my mostly empty stomach.

"Mom," I said. "We need to talk."

"Mm-hm," she said, chasing down more lasagna with another mouthful of wine. "After dinner."

"Mom," I insisted. "I know what you're doing. I know about the sleeping pills."

This didn't seem to phase her. Her eyes locked on me, but she didn't stop eating.

"You're trying to poison me," I said. "I don't know why, but I think it's because I mentioned Dad. You're afraid I want to go back to Gladden. I think you're afraid I'm not happy and that I'm going to ruin all of this."

Mom leaned back in her chair and stared at me. Her eyes had grown wide and wild again and I felt that frosty chill creep across the table and into my bones.

"You think I'm afraid of losing you to your father?" she asked, sneering. "He doesn't want you. He never wanted any of us. Go ahead and go back to him, but don't expect a warm welcome."

My heart fluttered. At first I thought it was anxiety, but then my head started to swim. I looked at my lasagna. I had only taken two small bites. Surely that couldn't have been enough to affect me so quickly. Then I looked at the garlic bread and my milk. I had thought it was only the lasagna that had been laced with sleeping pills, but I was wrong. Mom raised her eyebrows. She looked almost amused as she took another large gulp of wine.

I ran my hand over my face. How much had I gotten?

Mom could see that I was starting to feel the effects of the *zolpidem*. She laughed bitterly. "Just let it happen, sweetie..."

I looked across the table at her. She was a mess. Wine was running down her chin. In my addled state, it looked like blood.

"So, no Silver Lake?" I said sarcastically. My speech, I noticed, was slightly slurred.

"No Silver Lake," she said, draining her wine glass. She really had to focus as she filled the glass a third time. "And no Gladden, either."

"I never wanted to go back there," I said, my eyes were heavy and the room was beginning to tilt. "Maggie died there. And Ray. That's where I killed Ray."

Mom's head tilted to one side, but her eyes were as clear and as wide and as wild as ever. "You didn't kill Reagan," she said.

"I ran over him with the car," I said.

"He did that to himself," she said, wine and sauce spraying from her lips. "I saw the way he treated you. I saw the kind of abuse you had to put up with every day. He crawled under that car while you were behind the wheel. Only a fool would have been surprised by what happened next."

"It was my fault," I said. My lips felt like rubber and my speech was getting slower, but I forced myself to go on. "He was cruel, but he didn't deserve what I did to him."

"I hated him," she said, her own speech sounding sharp and sure. "I heard you two out there and when you went up to your room, I went out and found him. He was screaming and crying and begging for help, but I hated him. I hated him almost as much as I hated your father. So I left him there and I took you away."

I was slumped in my chair, watching her watch me. I pictured her standing beside the car, looking down at the mess that I had left behind, the mess of Reagan, and tried to imagine her doing nothing. How could my mother, so kind and sweet and wonderful, leave her firstborn to writhe in agony, to suffer a slow death?

"He took my Maggie," she said. Her face had gone slack and her eyes were pale. "He took my baby..."

We sat in silence, watching each other die. I could have let the *zolpidem* take me and wash me away. I felt so heavy and warm. It would have been a peaceful death, but I wasn't ready. I don't know what it was that I hoped to get from the world, but I wasn't ready to die just yet. And maybe I could save Mom, too.

With clumsy hands, I grabbed the salt shaker and my half-glass of lukewarm milk. I got up and fell against the sink, pouring out the milk and refilling the glass with water. I unscrewed the cap off of the salt shaker and dumped the contents into the glass, drinking it all off in one go. The bitter tang of sodium chloride climbed the back of my throat into my sinuses and, though I wretched, I held myself together.

I opened the refrigerator and grabbed the half-full milk jug and began drinking it as fast as I could while my body would still obey commands. My churning stomach accepted the milk willingly at first, but there came a point when it became too much. I could feel the milk sloshing uncomfortably in my middle. My body would soon reject the salty, creamy concoction. I didn't want it to be one of those kinda-sorta upchucking fits. I needed to become a geyser. I had to get it all out as quickly and as violently as possible. I was so close...

In the pantry was a can of tuna that had been among the groceries gifted to us by the kind ladies of the battered women's shelter all those years ago. Neither my mother nor I liked tuna, but Mom refused to throw it out because she didn't want to be wasteful, even though it had expired ages ago. It had become something of a joke between us. We called it our "emergency rations." This seemed like the perfect emergency.

I grabbed the can, pulled the tab on the top and peeled back the lid. I held it to my face and breathed deep through my nose, actually smearing the putrid, congealed grease across my upper lip. I made it to the sink just in time.

I vomited so forcefully that I burst a blood vessel in my eye and pulled a muscle in my neck. I heaved and lurched so violently that I smacked my forehead against the back edge of the sink and my knees buckled beneath me, sending me to the kitchen floor. As my vision blurred and my surroundings grew dim, I had two thoughts. The first was, "I'm going to choke to death on my own vomit, just like Jimi Hendrix."

The second was, "I'm sorry, Mom. I"m sorry I couldn't save you. But you wouldn't have wanted that, would you?"

I woke several hours later, the taste of sick in my mouth, the scent of it in my nose. I sat up, holding my head and groaning, trying to remember how I had ended up on the kitchen floor. I had not choked to death. I was not Jimi Hendrix.

My head was spinning and all I wanted was to close my eyes, but something was prodding the back of my mind like an insistent finger. It all returned in a rush of smells and sounds and I nearly vomited again. I squinted against the unnaturally bright lights of the apartment and saw Mom slumped sideways in her chair. I tried to stand, but my legs wouldn't cooperate, so I crawled to her. Dried wine and pasta sauce were smeared across her chin. I clumsily grabbed her wrist to check for a pulse, but as soon as I touched her skin, I knew she was gone.

The sun had come up before I was able to stop crying and pull myself together enough to call 911. I had to pull the phone down from the counter because my legs just couldn't be bothered to work. When the paramedics arrived, they had to get the super to unlock the door because I couldn't do it.

As they moved me out of the apartment, I looked back at Mom and wondered if I'd made a mistake. It might have been better if I'd just played along.

PART TWO- The Comedies

"Solomon Grundy,
Born on a Monday,
Christened on Tuesday,
Married on Wednesday,
Took ill on Thursday,
Grew worse on Friday,
Died on Saturday,
Buried on Sunday,
That was the end,
Of Solomon Grundy."

-Traditional English nursery rhyme

-TWELVE-
a brief news cycle
-(summer, 1993)-

Most of the three days following my mother's death were spent talking to a counselor from my hospital bed where I was forced to stay for the purpose of observation. I had been poisoned, after all. The police had a lot of questions for me, but the counselor answered most of them for me. I wasn't in any kind of trouble, she assured me, but the police looked like they weren't convinced. They seemed to think that I had something to do with the poisoning.

The pharmacy receipt saved me yet again. The police called the number and spoke with the pharmacist who was very distraught when he heard what had happened. He said he suspected something wasn't right when he filled the prescription.

When news surfaced that a missing child had been found, reporters called my hospital room and even showed up at the door, but the counselor and the police dealt with them. The fact that the kidnapper was the child's mother and had died of an intentional overdose just made the reporters more ravenous. No one cared that it might have been traumatic for me. One photographer was arrested for trying to climb the outside of the hospital to snap a picture of me through my window.

No one ever asked me about Reagan.

When the time came for me to leave the hospital, I was ushered through a back door alongside a cart of soiled linens. Apparently, there were still several photographers out front waiting for me. I've since read some of the articles written about me, but the story didn't hold the public's interest for very long.

I was allowed to return to the apartment to pack up a duffle bag of personal items; clothes, music, a toothbrush, etc. Everything else, I was told, was to be packed up and sent to my father's house in Gladden.

They had called Dad and asked him if he wanted to come pick me up. I tried to imagine what an indescribably uncomfortable experience that would be; an awkward reunion followed by a very long car ride. He must have thought the same, because he declined the opportunity to collect me himself and I was put on a Greyhound bus headed for Fort Wayne, the nearest city to Gladden with a bus terminal.

I had no chaperone on the bus ride home, but no one harassed me. I think my shaggy hair scared them away. I had packed several library books along with my extra clothes and spent the trip reading. Those books are probably listed in some file as "stolen." I still have them. I can't imagine the late fees I must have accrued.

The bus arrived in Fort Wayne and I was reunited with Dad. He pointed at his go-to-hell hat and said, "If you don't like it, you can go to hell."

Welcome home.

My routine that summer was pretty simple. I woke up, showered, cleaned the bathroom, ate breakfast, and cleaned the kitchen, all while listening to music. Since Dad was back out on the road, I didn't need to use my headphones. I just turned up the volume and let it fly.

I often opened all of the downstairs windows and, using several strategically positioned oscillating desk fans, I managed to fabricate a cooling breeze that whirled through the various rooms like a lazy cyclone. I then went through the house looking for things to clean or adjust or arrange. When Dad was home, there were often beer cans and dirty dishes in the living room from the night before. Sometimes he was still on the couch when I came through to clean. I cleaned around him the best I could.

When I was convinced that I had done all I could to improve my immediate surroundings, I grabbed a book and sat in the big bay window in the dining room. With the windows open, there was always a breeze, either coming in or going out and I was usually good for a few hours. Sometimes, just to shake things up, I did a jigsaw puzzle. Under the circumstances, it was as pleasant a way to spend the summer as I can imagine.

Once all of the stuff arrived from our apartment in Traverse City, I spent my time sorting through the boxes. Right away I found a box of cleaning supplies, which I immediately put to good use. All Dad had in the house were half-a-dozen ancient scouring pads and some dish soap, and that really only goes so far. Now that I had things like glass cleaner and a toilet brush and a mop, I could actually do some work.

I started in the bathrooms and worked my way through to the kitchen. My stolen library cassette player sat on the counter spouting divisive, communist rhetoric at me while I cleaned.

Next, I filled a bucket with soapy water and, with a stiff-bristled brush, I attacked every surface. I even scrubbed the yellow nicotine stains off the walls. When I was done, the house smelled amazing. Pine. Lemon. Spring Rain. It smelled like every chemically-manufactured scent that I associated with cleanliness.

Apart from having a clean home, it was such a relief to have all of my books and my tapes back, all of those familiar things I turned to for comfort. Children have their security blankets, adults have their arts. Upstairs in my bedroom, I packed away most of my childhood books, except for *The Chronicles of Narnia*, and replaced them with my meager collection of battered, second-hand paperbacks: Adams, Bradbury, Card, L'Engle, Le Guin, Vonnegut, Zelazny...My friends were finally home.

I went through every box. Mom's personal items brought an unwelcome surge of grief. I found the yellow Elton John concert t-shirt she was wearing the night we left Gladden. I found her green canvas tennis shoes.

She wanted green tennis shoes and she couldn't find any, so she bought white ones and dyed them in the bathtub. We thought the tub would never be white again.

Every time I pulled one of Mom's things out of a box, I spent half an hour crying over it, so I had to stop. I took those boxes down to the basement and hid them.

I now had fresh sheets, a new bedside lamp, and a painting of a London street that Mom had liked enough to pay $3 for at a thrift store, but had never hung up for some reason. It had been sitting in the back of her closet for two years. I only remembered it when I saw the movers carry it out of the truck. I hung it up in my bedroom, opposite my bed. It felt almost like a talisman, protecting me from the spirits dwelling nearby.

I spent a full day arranging and rearranging my books. That's always been a process of great satisfaction for me. I started alphabetically by title and then by color and size (not recommended for long-term storage). Finally, I settled on alphabetically by author, which is the only sorting method that any self-respecting book owner should use.

All the time I was cleaning and organizing, I kept sneaking glances out at the corn crib. The chain on the red door swayed constantly. I told myself that it was the breeze. There really was nothing unusual about a chain swaying in the breeze. What the movers had heard was probably a groundhog that had burrowed up into the corn crib. That was nothing out of the ordinary on an old farm.

I had nearly persuaded myself that there was, in fact, some wild animal living in the corn crib and not something sinister and vengeful. I could have gone on believing that for a very long time had gravity and fate not intervened.

One of the great tragedies of electronic equipment produced in the 1980s is that, while the technological components were usually very sound, the physical components in which they were housed were often less so. It was rare to find any electronic appliance of advanced years that didn't require, to some extent, the assistance of duct tape to keep everything in place.

One fateful evening in the middle of August, I was walking up the stairs to my bedroom, carrying the stolen library cassette player by the handle (which had never, in all my years of using it, given any indication of failure), when the whole thing abruptly fell with a crash, cartwheeling wildly down the stairs. The handle remained in my grasp, but the important parts, those that made the music happen, broke free and bounced from step to step, the components, fragile and varied, scattering across the floor.

My reaction was not that of a mature individual. There were incredulous gasps, angry tears, and I very nearly said a swear. Music, specifically MY music, was important to me in a way that I have, hopefully, made very clear, and now my only means of accessing that music was gone.

I've heard stories of addicts going through withdrawal...the cold sweats, the tremors, the paranoia...and it all sounds very familiar, because that's how I felt during the days that followed. The only radio in the house was a massive console stereo that sat in the living room. It had a turntable and an eight-track player, but I didn't even know if it worked. Mom's turntable had been delivered with all of the old apartment stuff, but there was no tape deck and I had stashed it in the basement with the rest of her belongings. The stolen library cassette player was all I had, unless I wanted to listen to Kenny Rogers, Loretta Lynn, or Joni Mitchell.

I know it sounds like I was being dramatic. Even in 1993, that ugly old tape player was a piece of laughably outdated technology, but it meant the world to me. It was a gateway to a place I couldn't access on my own. And in that place, I found myself. The music had helped me process loss after loss, trauma after trauma.

The loss of my music left me with no way to process my grief.

Now, when I say that there was no other cassette player in the house, I mean, there was no other cassette player in the house that I felt safe using. There was one other cassette player, and it was reasonably nearby. Just down the hall, in fact.

It was in Reagan's room. And it looked to be my only option.

I initially told myself that there was no way on Earth, no way above or below it, either, that I would consider using Reagan's radio. Three desperate days later, however, I felt very different.

I stood at the top of the stairs, just outside of my bedroom, and looked at the three doors at the far end of the hall. To the left, Reagan's room. To the right, Maggie's. In the center, the attic. I had no desire whatsoever to open any of those doors.

In the two months that I'd been back, I hadn't gone poking around in their rooms. It seemed like a violation, especially since I had reason to suspect that they were...still around...in one form or another. I had imagined Maggie in Traverse City. What was stopping me from imagining her here, as well? And the swinging chain on the corn crib? Probably my imagination, too, but why roll the dice?

In the end, my desperation outweighed my fear and my respect for other people's property. I needed that radio and I would have it.

I spent all morning hyping myself up. Normally I would have listened to the Misfits or Rancid, maybe. "Hyena" at full volume would have been like a shot of pure adrenaline.

I would have marched right down to Reagan's room, kicked in the door, and looted the place with no fear or shame. But that didn't happen. I tried humming quietly to myself, but that had the opposite effect I was hoping for. In the end, I decided just to get it over with.

The hallway was upholstered in the same ancient, threadbare carpet as the rest of the second story. The padding underneath was packed flat and offered about as much cushion as a concrete slab. There were several places where both the carpet and the padding had worn through completely and the floorboards were visible.

I tried to ignore the nagging sensation in my middle that suggested I was doing something foolish and unforgivably stupid. With every floorboard creak and labored step down that impossibly long hallway, the nagging sensation intensified, as did my heart rate. My mind raced with dozens of imagined scenarios, none of them pleasant, but there was no turning back. I was nearly there.

I looked down at my feet and realized that I had not moved. I was still standing right outside my bedroom door.

They say the first step is always the hardest. I think they only say that to trick you into taking the first step. I found the first step to be the easiest. Steps two and three were significantly more difficult. Step four was nearly impossible.

Halfway down the hall, I put my hands against the walls on either side of me and braced myself. I thought about when I was very little and I was unable to reach the walls with my outstretched hands. As I grew, I was able to stretch and would climb the walls, "chimneying," as rock-climbers call it. I pretended I was Spider-Man. Mom was always worried I would hurt myself. That seems ironic now.

So much had happened to me since I was small enough to climb the walls like Spider-Man. So much loss. So much anger and fear. Those seemed to be recurring themes in my life. I'd overcome a loss, stand up to a fear, and then be faced with another. No matter how much I grew, I still felt like the same frustrated little kid, unable to reach the walls that held me in.

But you did reach the walls, I told myself, *and you climbed them. You were Spider-Man.* I took a deep breath and shook the hair out of my face. The first four steps had seemed to take forever, but the next four went way too fast and I found myself standing at the end of the hallway before I was ready.

Reagan's door was painted the same grimy, farmhouse white as the walls. The doorknob was an ancient thing, original to the house. No one had bothered to remove it when the door was painted and there were half-century old paint streaks on the door plate. I touched the cool, tarnished brass knob, but didn't open it.

Instead, I turned across the hall, to Maggie's room. Same grimy, farmhouse white, same half-century old paint streaks on the door plate. When I touched the knob, however, it was warm.

My fingertips rested lightly on the brass and I became aware of a soft, smooth sound on the other side of the door. It was a repeating sound: a whispery creak...and a pause; a whispery creak...and a pause. I pictured a rusty pendulum swinging back and forth, lightly brushing the ground with each pass.

I don't know what I expected to find when I opened the door. Maybe I thought I'd find an empty room. That would be proof enough for me that Maggie's ghost in Traverse City had all been in my mind. I certainly didn't expect to have my fears confirmed.

I turned the knob and opened the door and saw an empty, child-sized rocking chair under the window gradually come to a stop. The carpet beneath the rocking chair was worn where the runners had been rubbing for the last nine years. There were also two bare spots the exact size and shape of Maggie's tiny feet. She was nowhere to be seen.

I didn't enter the room, but stood looking in from the hall. As my eyes roamed slowly over the room, unchanged since her death, I felt a pang of loss and an ache for a sister I barely remembered. A white wicker vanity sat across from the door and, in the mirror, I could see my reflection standing in the door frame. The mirror was cluttered with photographs tucked into the antique frame. One photograph was of me as a small child. I recognized it, even in the low light, even from several feet away. In the photograph, I was being madly and gleefully licked to death by a puppy. The photographer, probably Mom, had caught me in a rare moment of carefree, childhood joy. That laughing, chubby toddler was a far cry from the gangly, anxious teenager I saw in the mirror. I was touched that Maggie had kept the photograph.

I was wondering if I had frightened Maggie away (what a thing to do, to frighten a ghost), when I studied the reflection again. Just inside the door frame, six inches from my right hand, was a turquoise-clad shoulder with a magenta shoulder-strap. A lock of blonde hair was just barely visible. My breath left me in an involuntary gust. I had to fight to inhale.

"Hello, Maggie," I whispered shakily.

"Hello, Ollie," she whispered back.

"I didn't mean to bother you," I said.

She did not reply.

"Would you mind closing the door?" I asked, my throat starting to close up, "I don't think I'm up to it."

The door slowly swung shut, seemingly of its own accord. I drew a ragged breath and hurried back down the hall to my own room.

I slept with the lights on that night.

-THIRTEEN-
out of the frying pan
-(summer, 1993)-

I woke early the next morning, intent on getting Reagan's radio while there was plenty of daylight. I'm not sure why I thought daylight would help. He wasn't a vampire.

Nevertheless, I got dressed and, with none of the hesitation from the night before, I marched down the hall to Reagan's room. I could hear the whispery creak of Maggie's rocking chair from behind her closed door.

"Maggie?" I called through the door. I didn't feel like whispering. I needed to be bold, not timid. Whispering was timid. But being bold seemed wrong, too, and my stomach clenched into a tight ball. "I'm going into Ray's room. If you know of any reason why I shouldn't, now would be the time to tell me."

Maggie made no response. Her rocking chair didn't even stop.

But someone thought it was a bad idea. From outside came the roar of a 5.7 liter, 350 cubic-inch, V-8 engine. The Cutlass, still locked in the corn crib, gunned to life and screamed. It screamed just like it had the night Reagan died. It startled me and I jumped back from Maggie's door. The sound was like a heart attack. It was such an intense, angry noise that I pictured the dial on every gauge buried deeply in the red. How long could a machine, how long could a heart, take that kind of abuse before the stress became too much and it gave out?

After half a minute, the roar died down. My heart was racing, my breathing was ragged, and my ears were ringing.

"Does he do that often?" I asked once my breathing eased up a little.

"Sometimes," she said mournfully.

I placed one hand against the door.

"That's all he can do," I said. "He can yell...he can make scary sounds, but he can't hurt us anymore."

I could actually hear the silence coming from Maggie's room. Even her chair was silent. It suggested that she did not completely agree with me.

I went into Reagan's room anyway.

It was a mess, but no more so than the bedroom of any average sixteen year-old boy. There was a Black Sabbath poster pinned to one wall and abandoned clothes on the floor. His bed, surprisingly, had been neatly made. Well, neat-ish. Car magazines lay on his nightstand and I had a feeling I knew what I would find if I looked under his mattress. The dust-rich air smelled stale and moldy and forgotten.

Reagan's stereo normally sat on top of his bookshelf. It was what we used to call a boom box, or a ghetto blaster. The thing must have weighed fifteen pounds once you loaded it up with batteries...but it wasn't there. The electrical cord was plugged in, but it wasn't attached to anything. I took the cord and rolled it up before checking in the closet and under the bed. The radio was not there. I stepped back out into the hall, pulling the door shut behind me.

If the radio wasn't in his room, there was only one other place it might be: the corn crib. He liked to listen to music while he worked on the Cutlass. I returned to my room and lay face down on my bed, trying to convince myself that I really didn't need a cassette player that badly. It was just music, after all.

If you tell a man that he can't eat, that there is no food to be had anywhere, he can survive for quite a long time before hunger starts to drive him mad.

But, if you tell a man that he can't eat, though there is plenty of food and it's accessible, it just isn't for him, he'll start to go mad pretty much immediately.

Had Reagan's radio not been sitting right there, forty feet away, I might have been content to go on with life without my music. I would have found ways to occupy my mind. There were plenty of hobbies to try. Wood carving, for example. I might have learned to knit.

But the radio was so close I could practically hear it singing to me.

I waited until noon. I thought it might give me some kind of mystical, supernatural advantage should Reagan, like Maggie, be lurking about. Putting faith in sunlight is such an adorably human flaw.

I grabbed a flashlight from under the kitchen sink and marched out the back door. Though there was not an ounce of confidence in my body at that moment, I thought that, if I hurried, I might be able to trick myself into being brave.

The air was sticky and wet and thick with tiny, hungry bugs. I was sweating through my t-shirt and my hair lay plastered over the left half of my face. The closer I drew to the corn crib, the more my old burn scars itched. I wondered if Reagan, wherever he was, was itching, too.

Though there was no breeze, the rusty chain on the red door started to sway, its trailing end banging rhythmically against the weathered planks. I paused halfway across the yard. There was plenty of sunlight beating down on me, but I turned on the flashlight anyway. Nothing happened. The flashlight was dead. I nearly said a swear.

The chain continued to sway in the non-existent breeze, banging faster and faster against the door. Then the door itself started to rattle and shake, straining against the chain holding the sliding panels closed.

I gripped the flashlight and gritted my teeth. I suppose I should have prayed, but it didn't occur to me. There was a shrill, silent tension in the air, increasing every second, making my eyes water and my skin ache. I braced myself for whatever was about to happen. The tension rose, building to a painful crescendo before abruptly stopping. The crickets continued to chirp and the flies continued to buzz, but the chain on the door stopped swaying.

It felt like a trick, but I pressed on across the yard. *I killed him once*, I told myself. *If necessary, I can do it again.* I didn't believe a word of it. If anything, he was even more formidable now that he was dead. Like Obi Wan Kenobi.

The corn crib was divided into three stalls. The center stall, where Reagan and Dad had parked the Cutlass, was the largest. The stalls to the left and right were little more than storage areas, narrower than my bedroom, but quite a bit longer. I approached the narrow door on the left-hand stall, lifting the bolt and pulling the door open. The ancient hinges shrieked in protest and I stepped back quickly, just in case there really was some wild animal living inside. Leave it to Reagan to have adopted a large and angry rodent. When nothing attacked me, I leaned tentatively through the door.

The air smelled musty, much like the air inside Reagan's bedroom. I scanned the floor and the opposite wall, everywhere light fell, but could find nothing that would qualify as an excuse for not proceeding, so I reached around the corner and ran my hand along the wall. There had been an overhead light in here when I was younger, controlled by an old-fashioned switch (it was a twisting knob instead of the more modern toggle), but the bulb must have burned out because when I twisted the knob, nothing happened. Again, I nearly said a swear.

They say that you're not actually afraid of being alone in the dark, but that you're afraid of NOT being alone in the dark. This is true.

I inched forward into the darkness, feeling along the ground with one outstretched foot. Bright sunlight stabbed through the holes in the ceiling, but the contrast was so dazzling that it hurt more than it helped. Roughly halfway along the inside wall was a low doorway leading into the center section of the corn crib. My plan was to rush through the door to the workbench, grab the radio and rush back out before...something happened. I just needed to be quick.

I held the useless flashlight tightly in one sweaty fist as I shuffled across the floor looking for the doorway. Once in the shadows, my eyes adjusted and it was easier to see. I spotted the low doorway, but someone, clearly Dad, had nailed plywood over it.

Why had he done that? Probably for the same reason he'd chained the sliding door shut.

I pulled at the plywood, working my fingers around the edge and wiggling it loose, little by little. The nails creaked loudly as they gave up the fight. It took a few minutes, but the plywood finally came loose suddenly and I almost tumbled backward. The flashlight slipped out of my slick grasp and, when it hit the ground, it flickered feebly for a split second before going dark again.

Struggling to see in the inconsistent darkness, I felt around for the flashlight, and when I finally put my hand on it I was not exactly pleased to discover that someone else was already holding it. Cold, dry, thin fingers were wrapped around the base. I screamed and fell back, scurrying across the stall. The flashlight flickered on again, the beam falling upon a bloodless face with wide, wild eyes and a dry tongue protruding from between cracked lips and greasy teeth. Reagan grinned evilly at me and I scrambled for the door screaming. I flung myself out into the sunlight and landed face down in the dirt. I scampered forward unflatteringly on all fours and I didn't stop until I was about fifteen feet away. I turned to look at the corn crib, breathing hard and whimpering.

Laughter has never sounded less joyful than it did coming from the dry, dead throat of my brother. I couldn't see him, but I could see the flashlight beam flickering on and off.

"Ollie-ollie-ollie," he said, gleeful and gravelly. "Ollie-ollie-ollie..."

This wasn't fair. He couldn't do this to me, not anymore. Even dead, he was still destroying my peace. I had won this fight six years ago. I shouldn't still be fighting it. I began to get angry.

I was on my feet before I knew what I was doing. I rushed toward the thin wooden door, slamming it shut and dropping the bolt in place. From the other side of the door, I heard sniffing and scratching and that dry, dead chuckle.

"Ollie-ollie-ollie..." he said. "Ollie-ollie-ollie..."

I ran across the yard to the granary, one of only two buildings on the property that wasn't haunted. I slid the door open and looked around. I didn't know exactly what I wanted, but I'd know it when I found it.

The granary was a stout, square building with stalls along one side, presumably for storing grain. It was where we kept our bikes and lawn furniture in the winter. There was also a riding mower (almost the entire yard was dirt, so I don't know why we needed a mower), various car parts, an ungodly amount of old newspapers, and the types of odds and ends that one only finds on an old farm: bent and rusty sickles, bed springs, lanterns, bags of seed, feed, mulch, and manure, old hoses, old ladders, old ropes, and at least a dozen five-gallon buckets overflowing with crushed aluminum cans.

A collection of broken rakes and shovels and other long-handled implements stuck out of an old galvanized steel garbage can. I searched through them quickly and found exactly what I wanted: an ax. It was dull and rusty and weighed a ton, but I hoisted it onto my bony shoulder and lugged it back to the corn crib.

I stopped along the back wall and listened.

"Ollie-ollie-ollie," he whispered softly through the boards.

"I've heard that one, Ray," I said brashly. "Try something else."

Something struck the wall, sending a cloud of dust into the air. I marked off roughly where I thought the center stall began and tried to picture in my mind where the workbench was. There was a place where the boards bowed out slightly and I realized that this was where the Cutlass had run up against the workbench. I was lucky the car hadn't pushed right through the wall. Who knows where I would have ended up.

"I need to borrow your radio, Ray!" I called, wedging the ax blade between two boards and prying them apart. "I'll take good care of it, I promise!"

The gap between the boards widened and when I pulled the ax away, four pale, blood-stained fingers pushed through. There was grease under the chipped and split fingernails. I struck at them with the ax, but Reagan was too quick, pulling his hand back before the ax fell. I wondered casually what would happen if I actually hit him with the ax. How much damage could I really expect to do?

I went back to prying the boards apart, trying to get a glimpse inside. I just needed a hole big enough to grab the radio and pull it through.

On my third attempt, I found it. The radio was just on the other side of the wall. If I could remove one board, I'd have it. I levered the ax in and began working the board loose.

Reagan saw what I was doing, saw that I was going to succeed, and he couldn't have that. The Cutlass roared to life. The engine screamed, the lights flashed, the horn blared...but I kept working. It didn't take long to pull the board back far enough to reach my hand through and grab the radio, but as I did, Reagan's bony, bloodless arm shot out and grabbed me by the hair. I struggled, but there was nothing I could do as he pulled my face up to the hole I had made.

We were face to face now. I could smell death and rot as he chuckled. "Ollie," he sighed. "Welcome home." He ran a finger along my cheek and I could feel it burn. He snapped his teeth at me like a piranha and every time he opened his mouth, I could see that there were far too many teeth inside. He saw the fear in my face and started laughing in earnest, a strained, hysterical, manic laughter that made my head feel like it was about to split open.

Just when I was sure I couldn't take another second of his breath and his insane laughter, someone grabbed me from behind and yanked me back. I found myself falling backward into the weeds, Reagan's laughter still ringing in my ears.

"What the hell do you think you're doing?" Dad was staring down at me as I lay gasping. He was grimacing and rubbing his chest. "I didn't chain that door up for nothing, boy!"

All I could do was look up at him and catch my breath. I could feel a thin trickle of blood running down my cheek where Reagan had scratched my face.

In answer, I held up the radio which I had managed to hold onto. "Mine broke," I gasped.

Dad stared at me incredulously. "You're out of your damn mind, boy." He picked up the ax and used it to hammer the loose board back in place. "Stay out of there," he said, pointing at the corn crib. "You got it? There's nothing in there for you, so just stay the hell out."

"Got it," I said, standing up and cradling the radio. "Thanks."

As we walked back to the house, Dad said, "You know, I woulda bought you a new radio."

That certainly would have been a simpler solution.

-FOURTEEN-
into the fire
-(August, 1993)-

Dad's work schedule was unpredictable, so I never knew when to expect him home. Jobs came and he went. When the job was done, sometimes other jobs came, sometimes they didn't. Him showing up to pull me, quite literally, out of the jaws of death could not have been a bigger or more welcome surprise.

"I used to tell people you were the smart one," he said, draining his third beer. "Now I gotta think of something else to tell 'em."

"I know it was dumb," I said. I was sitting at the kitchen table with a damp cloth and a bunch of cotton swabs, cleaning cobwebs and dust out of the radio's many crevices. "I just wanted to listen to some music."

"We have a radio in the living room," he said, tossing the empty beer can into the kitchen sink. He started to leave the kitchen.

"Dad?" I said. "How long...?" I let the question hang unfinished, unsure of how to frame it so it didn't sound insane.

He stopped, but didn't look at me. "'How long,' what?" he asked. He sounded exhausted.

"How long has it been going on?" I asked. "In the corn crib?"

Dad was silent for a long time. "I don't know what you're talking about," he said, still not facing me. "Just stay out of there."

I didn't see him for the rest of the day.

I spent most of the day cleaning the radio. The batteries, after six years of exposure to the elements, had burst and there was a significant amount of corrosion that needed to be dealt with. I even took out several screws and opened the exterior case so I could clean away the cobwebs and dirt that had accumulated inside. Reagan should have thanked me. I took better care of that radio than he ever did.

It was an admirable piece of equipment. It had two cassette decks which presented me with the hitherto undreamt-of opportunity to make my own mixtapes.

If you never had the pleasure of living in the cassette tape era of the music industry, you cannot grasp the frustration of purchasing an album and finding that there were only three good songs on it, four if it was an uncommonly good album. And they never grouped the good songs together in the tracklist, either. You had to either sit through a bunch of bad songs or fast forward to the good ones. Listening to music could be a very stressful and time-consuming experience. Once we had the technology to make our own mixtapes, we were free. We could put all of our favorites on one cassette and go live our lives. It was magical.

The following morning, I stole a few blank cassettes from Reagan's room, risking another vehicular outburst from the corn crib, and set to work making mixtapes. I was sitting on my bedroom floor with all of my punk rock tapes stacked neatly around me, writing a detailed list of songs on a notepad (my mild, undiagnosed OCD wouldn't allow me to fully embraced the punk ideals of anarchy, chaos, and disorder), when Dad walked in.

"Let's go," he said. "Get in the truck." I flashed back to six years earlier, me sitting in the exact same place, surrounded by my beloved toy cars following a stressful experience involving Reagan in the corn crib. Mom told me to, "get in the car," and I did, no questions asked. For six years I lived like that, no questions asked, and it almost killed me. I narrowly avoided death by lasagna.

"Where are we going?" I asked, getting to my feet and stepping carefully over the stacks of cassettes.

"We gotta get you registered for school," he said, like it was the most normal thing in the world.

I had completely forgotten about school. I found myself thinking, not for the last time, that it might have been less trouble if I had just eaten the lasagna.

The high school that served Gladden was two miles away in Leopold, the next town over. Dad had called and talked to someone who told him that I needed to come in and fill out a few forms.

"Did you bring a copy of his transcript?" asked one of the secretaries. The nameplate on her desk said, "Carolyn Auburn." She kept trying to smile, but it just wouldn't take.

"A transcript?" asked Dad. "What the hell's that?"

Mrs. Auburn took a deep breath, blinked once slowly, and said, as politely as she could manage, "The records from his previous school."

Dad jerked back and looked dumbfounded. "Previous school? He ain't been to school since the fourth grade!"

Mrs. Auburn's eyebrows rose sharply, though the rest of her face remained stony. Thankfully, another secretary hurried over to Mrs. Auburn's desk and leaned down, whispering something in her ear. Mrs. Auburn looked at me and her eyebrows gradually lowered. The other secretary held out her hand and Dad shook it.

"Hi, I'm Jo Kline," she said with effortless cordiality. "Would it be safe to say that Oliver was homeschooled?"

Dad looked at me and I shrugged. "I read a lot," I said, "and I took some tests to make sure I was on track."

Mrs. Kline nodded and said, "That's terrific. We don't need a transcript, but you will need to take some placement tests."

Mrs. Auburn sighed, got up from her desk with a huff, and walked away, mumbling something about, "...dealing with all of these jackasses..." She came back a moment later, still mumbling, with a packet of forms from which she pulled several pages, handing them to Dad.

"Fill these out," she said. "I'll start preparing the placement tests."

We were directed to a table in the teacher's lounge and together we got everything filled in. There was a section on one form labeled, "Reason for missing documentation and/or enrollment records." Dad stared at it for a long time.

"I don't even know where to start..." he said. He sounded so lost. It was the first time I really appreciated what he had been through. Mom and I had each other. Dad had no one.

But he hadn't exactly been alone, had he? No wonder he spent so much time on the road.

I took the pen from him and wrote, "Longer than expected absence due to family tragedy."

Dad read it and snorted. "That's pretty good," he said. We finished filling out the forms and returned them to Mrs. Auburn, who looked them over. Once she was satisfied, she handed me a stack of papers.

"The placement tests," she said dryly. "Take your time and take it seriously."

I returned to the table in the teacher's lounge and got to work. The first test was math and my heart sank. I was sure they would put me back in fourth grade to pick up where I had left off.

In the end, it wasn't as bad as I thought. My math scores were pretty dismal, but my reading and language scores were high enough that there were no objections to me rejoining my former classmates. By the time Dad and I walked out of the building, I was enrolled as a sophomore at Leopold Jr./Sr. High School.

Dad surprised me by taking me into town to do some proper back-to-school shopping. "Into town" is what folks in Gladden said when they were going into Fort Wayne. I got some new blue jeans, some new t-shirts (nothing fancy, thank-you-very-much, just plain colors, mostly black), and a brand-new Walkman. The thought of listening to my tapes whenever and wherever was a luxury I had not allowed myself to consider.

I still had my old *Incredible Hulk* backpack from the fourth grade, but I didn't think I was ready to expose myself as an eccentric just yet. Instead, Dad took me to an army surplus store.

"Those backpacks they sell at Sears and JCPenney are overpriced garbage," he said. "They'll wear out before the end of the year. The stuff here will last you a lot longer. And some of the better ones will stop a knife."

"How likely is it that I'll get stabbed?" I asked.

"I don't know," Dad shrugged. "Leopold has changed a lot since I went there."

I picked out a heavy canvas backpack that the guy at the register called an Australian rucksack. It seemed unnecessary at the time, but Dad was right. I still have and use that bag to this day, thirty years later, though I have not tested its effectiveness against knife attacks.

-FIFTEEN-
Simmy and Seaway
-(August, 1993)-

When I boarded the bus on the first day of school, the plump, bearded bus driver nodded genially as I climbed the steps. I made my way down the aisle to take a seat near the middle. There were half a dozen other kids on the bus, all of them reduced to a pair of eyes peering over the seats, watching me with varying degrees of curiosity. I was aware of how it worked in Gladden. Even though people knew who I was and knew parts of my story, they would wonder about the parts they didn't know. I decided to let them wonder. I put on my headphones, pressed play, and let Minor Threat carry me to school.

The bus dropped us off behind the school gymnasium and I followed the crowd of students inside. All around me were teenagers in a wide range of height and appearance. It was impossible to tell how old anyone was. They might have been seniors or they might have been junior high students. Puberty had made us all vague and indecipherable.

Friends greeted each other and laughed and chatted animatedly. Groups assembled in the halls, huddled around lockers or drinking fountains, comparing class schedules. The crowd swirled around me like shallow tidal water, neither sweeping me along nor hindering my progress. It took no notice of me. I felt anonymous, almost as though I belonged there.

I thought, *I'm one of them.*

It was the first and last time I had that thought.

The loudspeakers overhead crackled to life, emitting a stream of announcements, though I seemed to be the only one paying attention. I thought I recognized the voice of one of the secretaries who had helped me with my enrollment.

One of the announcements instructed new students to come to the front office. I had a general understanding of where the front office was from my earlier visit with Dad, but finding my way through the churning mass of teenagers wasn't easy. Things look different when they're empty. Rooms, shoeboxes, journals, schools...They have so much promise and hope until we start filling them up. Schrodinger's Potential.

I must have looked lost, wandering through the halls, because a teacher stopped me. "Can I help you?" he asked, taking in my long hair with no attempt to disguise his disapproval.

"I'm looking for the front office," I said.

He stared at me skeptically for a long moment before finally pointing down the hall in the direction I had been going. "It's that way."

I thanked him and continued, feeling foolish for some reason.

That teacher's name, I would later learn, was Mr. Kelly. He taught eighth-grade health and PE and had no time or patience for any students who did not participate in the athletic department. He was not well-liked by either the staff or the students.

At the end of the hall, I looked back and Mr. Kelly was watching me suspiciously over the heads of the other students, hands on his hips, a deep wrinkle creasing his brow.

The office was busy. Students were lined up to talk to different secretaries and I could hear Mrs. Auburn's voice over everyone else.

"This should have been turned in over the summer," she was saying heatedly. Mrs. Kline hurried to assist before the situation boiled over.

"Excuse me!" I heard someone calling. "Excuse me!" I looked to my left and saw a smiling woman waving at me from one of the side offices. I stepped out of line and approached her.

"Are you Oliver Barrow?" she asked excitedly.

"Yes, I am," I said.

"AH!" she shouted, clapping her hands together and making me jump. "I'm Miss Simms, one of the guidance counselors. Give me just one second..." She hurried over to Mrs. Auburn's desk, grabbed an intercom microphone, pressed the button, and said in a low, steady voice, "Emma Seaway to the front office. Emma Seaway...front office, please."

She scurried back to me, still wearing her humongous grin. She was wringing her hands together excitedly. "I've been waiting all morning," she said. "We've all heard about you. Your whole story was on the news."

"The news?" I said, nonplussed. This was the first I'd heard about it. I looked around at the other students in the office. Most of them were pretending not to listen in on our conversation. I could still hear Mrs. Auburn yelling across the office.

"What your family has been through," she said, shaking her head sadly. "First the accident with your sister, and then the...the accident with your brother..."

I stared at her, still baffled. Now the other students weren't even trying to hide the fact that they were listening in. Leopold Jr./Sr. High School was not a large building. There were, give or take, eight hundred students. Everyone knew everyone, or at least knew a rumor about everyone. It turns out, I was something of a celebrity. Any new information the students could pick up was currency, like cigarettes in prison.

"...and then you disappeared for all those years. And now here you are!"

"...here I am..." I murmured through numb lips. How much did people know, exactly? What had the news said? Was it my imagination, or had Miss Simms hesitated when she mentioned the...the accident with my brother? I looked back at the other students who were once again pretending to mind their own business.

"My little girl is going to be showing you to your classes. She's been looking forward to this," said Miss Simms, clearly very proud. "Don't tell her I told you that. She'd probably think it was embarrassing."

Just then, the door to the hallway opened and a tiny girl entered. Her mouse-brown hair was very long and frizzy. She wore huge, purple-framed glasses and a giant, rust-colored cardigan that looked like it was trying to swallow her. She was small enough to have passed for an elementary school student. Her skin was so pale that she was almost translucent.

"Hey, Simmy," she said, casually waving to Miss Simms. Then she gave me an appraising look up and down. "This the kid?"

"Be nice," warned Miss Simms as she handed the girl a folder with my name on it. "This is Oliver. I shuffled some things around and put you in the same fourth period class, so you don't need to worry about tracking him down for lunch."

"Excellent work, Miss Simms," said the girl in a fake British accent as she flipped open the folder and looked over my schedule. Then she looked up at me and held out her hand. "I'm Emma Seaway, currently the most important person in your life."

Miss Simms rolled her eyes and murmured something that sounded like, "...oh, good lord..."

Emma threw Miss Simms some kind of look, a little amused, a little annoyed, but rich with affection. She grabbed me by the arm and marched me out into the hallway, knocking people out of her way with the confidence of a person three times her size.

"Your first period is Algebra," she said, not checking to make sure I was following her. I had to scramble to do so. "Mr. Cross is okay, but his class is upstairs, so we have to hurry. Don't be afraid to ask questions if you don't understand something, but don't yawn or put your head down. He likes to throw chalkboard erasers at sleepy kids. I'll come get you at the end of class and take you to your locker. There really isn't time now. The bell's about to ring."

Emma barely paused for breath as she weaved in and out of the crowd. I almost lost her several times, but I kept catching glimpses of her rust-colored cardigan between bodies. She led the way up a flight of stairs and down a second-floor hallway before stopping in front of a classroom.

"Any questions?" she asked, turning abruptly to face me.

"Yeah," I said, a little breathlessly. "Did Miss Simms say she was your mom?"

Emma's face darkened, as if she was bracing for something. "Simmy's my foster mother. Does it bother you that she's black? Or that I have a foster mother?"

I thought about it for a second. "No, it doesn't bother me," I said. "I don't have a mom at all. Should it bother me?"

Emma shrugged and relaxed a little. "Bothers some people."

"People around here get bothered by everything," I said.

"But not you," she said, giving me a sideways look.

"Oh, they get bothered by me plenty," I said. "I think it's probably the hair."

Emma responded by turning and walking away. "I'll be back to get you before the bell rings for second period."

"Thanks, Mom!" I called. I wasn't sure if that was how teenagers talked to each other, but it's how they talked in John Hughes movies. Emma gave me an amused glance over her shoulder before she disappeared down the stairs, so I guess I was doing okay. The bell rang and I walked into my class, feeling strangely optimistic.

It did not last long.

When Emma came to collect me from Algebra, I was feeling suffocated, not just by the content, but also by the sterility of the experience. It felt so rigid and hopeless, nothing like school as I remembered it from my younger days. Where were all of the decorations? Walls covered in rainbows and smiling cartoon characters holding up numbers and symbols? I was a long way from Mrs. Foster's fourth grade classroom.

The teacher, Mr. Cross, was okay, just like Emma had described him. He made a few jokes and seemed reasonably friendly, but it still felt too regimented. We were seated in tight rows, all facing the same direction. No one but Mr. Cross spoke. The message was clear, "There is one way. Do not deviate. Deviation upsets the balance and balance is imperative to the system."

I was probably being a little dramatic, but I kept picturing the scene in *A Wrinkle In Time* where all of the children are conditioned to bounce a ball in unison and, when one child bounces out of sync with the others, he's punished.

This type of education was a thing that was done to you rather than a thing in which you participated. It was a procedure, not a partnership. I much preferred studying on my own in the library, like I had done for the past six years. This method of learning didn't work for me and left me absolutely exhausted.

And it was only first period.

"That bad, huh?" Emma asked as we walked out of the classroom. Because she was showing me around to my classes, she had permission to take me out a minute early. A whole minute! And she had permission! More regimentation.

"Don't worry. You have Social Studies next. Easy stuff." As she led me down the hall, the bell rang and I could hear the bustle of movement from the surrounding classrooms as students jumped up from their desks.

"Is it always like this?" I asked, dodging a student who burst blindly from a classroom on my right.

"Like what?"

"I don't know," I shrugged. "Relentless, I guess?"

She didn't answer right away, but ran down the stairs. I almost fell trying to keep up. She stopped at the bottom and turned to face me and I nearly ran over her, which, considering her diminutive stature, could have been disastrous.

"Yes," she sighed. "It's always like this. And, in the end, it might be worse for you than for most."

She turned to merge with the flowing crowd. As I followed her, darting clumsily through the swaying bodies, I noticed that I was drawing a lot of looks.

"Worse for me because I'm new?" I asked.

"Oh, no. Quite the opposite," she said over her shoulder. "A lot of people remember you from before."

I had never really had any friends and I had never done anything remotely memorable, so how on earth did anyone remember me? Oh, right. The news.

They don't remember you, I told myself. *They remember the kidnapping. And they remember Maggie and Ray.*

"There are loads of rumors going around," Emma was saying, "about what you were like in elementary school, about where you've been all this time. It's not just the students, either."

I looked around at the anonymous faces surrounding us. I wondered how many of them I had known once upon a time. "So what are they saying?" We had stopped in front of a bank of lockers.

Emma ignored my question and spun the combination dial around.
The numbers were a blur as she flicked the dial back and forth. She
yanked up on the handle and the locker snapped open.

"This is you," she said, stepping back to reveal an empty metal
closet with a bare shelf and a couple of empty hooks. All that hope
and promise, just for me. "Leave your backpack and whatever books
you don't need in here. The teachers don't like it if you carry all your
stuff with you from class to class."

"Okay," I said, unslinging my backpack. "How do I open it?"

Emma spent the next few minutes explaining how to open my
locker. She explained, I did it wrong. She corrected, I did it wrong
anyway. Eventually I got it but I was pretty sure it was a fluke.

"Forget it for now," she said. "You'll be late to second period."

Social Studies was better than Algebra. The desks were arranged in
small clusters, which I took to mean that we would be doing plenty
of group projects. I didn't know how I felt about relying on other
students for a grade, but I could tell by the others sitting in my desk
group that they shared my trepidation. Judging by the way they all
nodded to each other, they were already acquainted, but they weren't
talking, and none of them would make eye-contact with me. All of
the other groups were chatting and there was a generally friendly
mood...except for our group. I assumed I was the problem. I always
do.

"Hi," I said, trying to sound cheerful and confident in spite of
having limited experience with either trait. "I'm Oliver."

The other three kids in the group just stared at me. I wondered
what rumors they had heard about me and was tempted to ask.
Even with my sorely underdeveloped social skills, I knew that was
probably a bad idea.

Third period was Study Hall. Everyone sat in rows, like in Algebra, but it felt like it was more for the sake of storage rather than for readiness. Sitting in rows in Algebra felt like we were live rounds in the magazine of some huge machine gun, primed and ready for battle, but in Study Hall we were just trying to stay out of the way, which had become sort of my happy place. Staying out of the way was one of the few things I could do with any amount of confidence. I liked Study Hall.

Fourth period was Journalism. We were responsible for writing, editing, and arranging the school newspaper. I wasn't too sure how well I would manage in that class, but it became something I looked forward to every day. It offered many interesting opportunities. Teachers and administrators had no problem letting journalism students roam the halls as long as it was for some article they were writing. They never even asked to see a hall pass.

Emma was in that class, as well. We were a long way from being friends, but she was at least friendly. At first I thought she was being especially nice by sitting next to me instead of with her other friends, but I eventually learned that she didn't have any other friends, not in that class, anyway.

Halfway through fourth period was lunch.

"I haven't seen Fern all day," Emma said as we walked to lunch. "I have no idea what lunch mod he has."

"Fern is a boy?" I asked.

"It's short for 'Fernando,'" she explained. "Fernando Hanson...A bunch of kids started calling him 'Fern' in the seventh grade, you know, to tease him, but he started using it and they didn't know what to do."

I admired the 'disarm' method of dealing with bullies. It was much better, in my opinion, than my methods of arson and vehicular manslaughter. It's less messy and you get to laugh as your bullies struggle to figure out how the situation got away from them.

"Why were they picking on him?" I asked. I know bullies don't need a motive, but I wanted to keep the conversation going.

"Pick a reason," she said. "He's Vietnamese, he's adopted, he's gay... But mostly, they pick on him because Fern's not one of them. He doesn't want to be one of them. The idea that someone might not idolize them is very threatening for some people."

I hadn't met Fern yet, but I already liked him. "Being Vietnamese in this community?" I said. I thought about my VietNam vet father and how some of the less tolerant comments he'd made proudly in public were met with no challenge. "That's a pretty bold choice."

Emma nudged me out of the flow of students to stand against a wall of lockers. We watched the other students pass by on their way to and from lunch.

"These kids are all normal. They live average, typical lives." She said this like it was an accusation, like being a normal kid was some kind of disease that they had chosen. "They only know what they're taught. They can't read between the lines. They need everything laid out for them in clearly defined terms. They can't decide anything for themselves. They only know a song is good because it gets played on the radio constantly. They can only laugh at a joke if someone else laughs first."

She sounded like Brian from the library. He was always pushing me toward counterculture, non-conformity, self-discovery. He wanted me to ask questions, always.

"Believe what you believe," he told me once, "but know why you believe it."

"They're so afraid of doing the wrong thing," Emma was saying, "that they never do anything different or unexpected."

I had been seeing the other students walking through the halls and sitting in classrooms all day and I had been thinking of them as one single organism. They all bounced the ball in unison. Instead, I tried to think of them as a collection of individuals, each one matching his movements with those of the person next to them lest they be exposed as an imposter. When I thought of them in those terms, it seemed like they were all living a constant nightmare.

"They're afraid," I said. "They're afraid of not bouncing the ball in unison. They're afraid they'll be punished."

Emma gave me a curious look.

"*A Wrinkle in Time*," I said, by way of explanation.

"Yeah. Like the children on Camazotz," she said, nodding. "I guess I never thought of it like that."

Every choice was a risk. Any decision could be the one that ruined their lives. Each and every one of these kids was balancing on a razor-blade tightrope above a flaming pit full of zombie crocodiles. None of them liked it, but no one knew how to get down safely.

"They're all just babies," Emma said, almost compassionately. "Little, idiot babies with no life experience. They go to parties and they have no problem drinking and fooling around with each other because those actions have known, documented consequences. We all know what those things lead to. We all went through the D.A.R.E. program. We all went to MacMillan Health Center and watched the documentary on the human life cycle."

I hadn't done either of these things, but she was on a roll, so I didn't interrupt.

"But none of them has ever tried to do anything meaningful because they don't know what might happen if they actually change the world."

We stood and watched them pass until the crowd slowed to a trickle.

"They've never survived anything," she said, watching the last of them disappear around a corner, "so they don't know they can."

-SIXTEEN-
the lunch table
-(August, 1993)-

People often reminisce about school lunch, either fondly or otherwise. The floppy, rectangular pizza slices. The boiled, gray hot dogs. The cold spaghetti and soggy garlic bread. My first impression of school lunch had little to do with the food. As we entered the cafeteria, what I saw looked like a scene from *The Lord of the Flies*. There were no adults that I could see, just dozens of confused, chaotic children experiencing a rare moment of freedom and having no idea what to do with it.

Emma and I moved through the madness with our trays held in front of us like priests entering a temple bearing sacred offerings, she with far more grace than I. I kept my eyes on my tray with Emma's rust-colored cardigan in my periphery, guiding me through the fray. I was so focused on not spilling my food that I was only vaguely aware of what was going on around me. Chairs screeched across the floor, kids shouted back and forth at each other. A wayward apple rolled across our path and Emma deftly kicked it back in the direction it had come. I didn't look up until we stopped at a nearly empty table against the far wall of the room.

"Oh! You found a stray!" someone called out. I looked up to see a thin Asian boy eyeing me with amusement and interest.

"He followed me home," said Emma in a simpering voice. "Can I keep him?"

"Is he housebroken?" asked the boy, skeptically.

"Nearly," I said. "I've got the 'broken' part down."

"Fern, this is Oliver Barrow," said Emma, examining the food on her tray. She pulled a small notebook from a pocket in her cardigan and started jotting down notes. I learned that she did this for every school lunch. She kept notes on lots of things.

"I know who you are," said Fern. "You should hear all of the crazy things people are saying about you."

"Like what?" I asked, trying to sound only politely interested.

Fern sat up straighter, eager to share the gossip and, maybe, learn more. "They're saying that you killed your sister." He started counting rumors off on his fingers. "You set your brother on fire. Your mother kidnapped you and no one knew where you were for, like, six years. Then your mother died in a failed murder/suicide attempt."

"What?!" I almost shouted. "That's crazy!"

Emma stopped taking notes. Several heads turned toward us.

"I didn't kill my sister!" Then I started spooning flavorless vegetable soup into my mouth while Emma and Fern looked at each other, shocked and confused.

While I enjoyed watching them struggle with the broad array of thoughts and emotions they were experiencing, I was also surprised by how much everyone seemed to know about me. I had never made any effort to hide it, but how were they so right about so many things? They didn't know how Reagan had died, though. I still had that secret.

Fern burst out laughing and I was yanked back to reality.

"So, what's the deal?" he asked. "Are any of the rumors true?"

"Let him eat, Fern," said Emma. She was back to taking notes. Fern looked like he wanted to keep prying, but he changed the subject.

"I can't believe I got stuck with Perch for Chemistry," he said, rolling his eyes. "I had her for Earth Science last year and she *hated* me."

"You almost set her desk on fire," said Emma, not looking up from her notebook.

Fern gave me a mischievous grin. "It was mostly an accident."

Emma looked up and said sternly, "You put a lit bunsen burner in one of the drawers!"

Fern's grin faded under Emma's disapproving gaze. "I said 'mostly,'" he mumbled.

"If you're going to cause trouble," she said, pointing a finger at him, "at least do it for a good reason and not just because you're bored."

"I wasn't bored," argued Fern. "I did it because I hate Mrs. Perch."

"Not good enough," said Emma, finally sampling the food on her tray. "Personal reasons don't count. You got suspended for two weeks and the world was in no way better for it."

I ate while they talked. Listening to them banter back and forth was like watching a sitcom, but starting halfway through the third season. I forgot for a moment that I was in school.

A group of boys walked past and one of them shouted, "Hey, Fern! That your new boyfriend?!" The other boys laughed and the group continued through the cafeteria.

Fern looked at me and raised his eyebrows. "You interested?" he asked. "I'm available."

"I'm all good," I said, not sure if he was joking or not.

"One of these days, Fern," said Emma, picking up her mostly untouched tray of food, "you're going to flirt with the wrong person and he'll either punch you or date you." She started walking away and, though I wasn't done eating, I collected my tray and hurried after her. She was, as she had previously stated, currently the most important person in my life.

We made our way back to our fourth period classroom where the teacher, Miss Levine, asked us to write a paragraph about ourselves so she could assess our writing style and our attention to relevant details. This is what I turned in:

"I've never been the type of person comfortable with making decisions. Whenever I do, things go wrong. I find myself far more comfortable in the passenger seat. I'm a follower, some might say a coward. I'm okay with that."

Boring, but accurate.

-SEVENTEEN-
suspicious sausage
-(late summer, early autumn, 1993)-

That first day of school was pretty overwhelming. There was so much to learn, and not just academically. The social culture was so intricate, had so many folds, and I was so far behind. Emma and Fern didn't seem too worried about fitting in, but they were dynamic and intimidating. Anyone messing with them would end up with a bigger fight than they wanted.

There are certain animals who avoid the notice of predators by blending in with their surroundings. They resemble leaves or sticks and are overlooked. Other animals take the opposite approach, standing out so blatantly due to their vibrant colors that any predator would assume that they must be poisonous.

Some animals choose clever camouflage while others choose a dangerous reputation. Either way, they're all hiding behind something.

Historically, I was a camouflage kid, but now I found myself with a reputation, even though I wasn't entirely sure what that reputation was.

I won't lie and say that anyone was particularly mean to me those first days of school. People mostly kept their distance. The rumors about me kept them at bay, as did my unforgivably shabby appearance. Mom had always kept my hair trimmed to a reasonably unkempt length, just above my shoulders, but Dad was no barber and I hadn't bothered to find one on my own. I hadn't had a haircut in four months. I looked like a caveman.

I ate lunch with Emma and Fern every day and we became friends. I'd never had friends before. It was nice, though I wasn't sure what the rules were. We joked around and laughed and asked each other for help with homework and shared our struggles and victories. We talked about our favorite books and movies and music. I gave Fern one of my mixtapes. They didn't seem too bothered by my long hair or my bad reputation or any of the other things that seemed like such a big deal to so many other people. Turns out, that's what friends are. They like you for you, and they don't care if you have weird hair.

But my hair was starting to become a nuisance and I mentioned it one day during lunch.

"Does it get in the way when you eat?" asked Fern. He rarely ate anything but bread, preferring to build sculptures with his food.

"It's not that," I said through a mouthful of chicken sandwich. "It's just...everywhere. I can't really do anything without moving it out of the way."

"So, it doesn't, like, get in your mouth?"

"I floss with it sometimes," I said. Emma choked on her milk and made a mess all over her cardigan.

"What about when you sleep?" Fern pressed. "Does it get all tangled up?"

"Look at me," I said, gesturing to the mess on top of my head. "What do you think? It's constantly a problem. Why do you think I brought it up?"

"Okay, calm down," said Fern. "I'm just gathering information so we can come up with a solution."

"The solution is to cut it," I said. "I just can't do it myself."

"How's your article coming along?" asked Emma as she dabbed spots of milk off of her cardigan. It was the same cardigan she'd worn on the first day of school. She wore it every day.

"I'm almost done," I said. I had been assigned an article about school lunches, whether they were increasing or decreasing in quality based on student opinion. All of my research had come from the notes Emma took every day. "I just need to interview a couple of students."

"Well, my lunch was just as delightful as ever," said Fern. He had eaten the bun off his sandwich, but everything else on his tray had been piled into something resembling a volcano. "However, last Thursday's promising 'breakfast-for-lunch' was brought to a screeching halt by what I can only describe as a very suspicious sausage."

"What about you?" I asked Emma.

"It was fine, I guess," she said, double-checking to make sure she had cleaned up all of her milk. "I cannot confirm the sausage rumors, however."

I pulled a crumpled sheet of paper out of my pocket, jotted down what each of them had said, and handed the paper to Emma. "And that's the article," I said.

Emma looked exasperated. "No, Oliver! That is not good enough!"

"You haven't even read it," I protested.

"Yeah, Emma!" Fern said, pretending to be stern. "You should...read..." He lost interest halfway through supporting me.

Emma stuffed my article into her pocket and then grabbed her tray off the table. "Come on," she said. "We've got time to rewrite it before the end of class. I'm skipping sixth period to work on page layout, so I can type it up for you. Miss Levine will skin you alive if you hand it in late."

I honestly wouldn't have made it through those first weeks of school without Emma. She was hyper-organized and she actually cared about how well Fern and I did in school. She seemed very intent on helping us realize that we had potential.

Fern joined us in the Journalism room for the rest of the lunch period while Emma rewrote my article. I briefly pretended like I was interested in helping, but she was clearly not interested in my help, so Fern and I made a paper football and tried to flick each other in the face with it.

"That's about all I can do," she said, handing me a fresh sheet of paper onto which she had transcribed my story. When I say "my story" what I mean is that some of the original words were there...several "the"s and a "with" or two...but it was not remotely recognizable as the story we had started with.

"This is actually good," I said, reading it. "I mean, I thought it was a joke when Levine assigned it, but this is...You made it interesting."

Emma held up her hand as though she were offering a papal blessing. "Now, go and do likewise."

I felt guilty for not making more of an effort on the article. Words were actually something I was comfortable with and I hadn't even tried. I was acting like Fern, which wasn't the worst thing in the world, but Emma already had a Fern. She deserved wider diversity among her friends. I endeavored to do better in the future.

"Hey, listen," I said to Emma as I tucked the freshly edited story in my notebook. "Would you mind cutting my hair for me?"

"I'm not remotely interested in cutting your hair," she said, dismissing my suggestion with a wave of her hand. "I'd make a huge mess of it. Find someone who isn't afraid of making you look like an idiot."

I sighed and looked to my left where Fern was grinning and nodding and bouncing excitedly on the balls of his feet.

I almost said a swear.

I was not a hooligan. I didn't steal or vandalize. I was polite and clean. I respected different cultures and beliefs. I lived a peaceful life and supported the rights of others to live equally peaceful lives, whatever that looked like for them. I was a terrific kid that any parent would be proud to claim. In spite of that, people had always been uneasy about my long hair.

Fortunately, my long hair wouldn't be a problem much longer.

We decided to do it at school, for some reason. The three of us skipped lunch and found an unoccupied boys' restroom in the freshman hall. Emma stood at the door as a lookout, and I straddled a toilet backward with Fern standing over me.

"Take it easy," I told Fern. "Just cut off enough to make it manageable. I'm not looking for a whole personality change."

"Calm down, man," said Fern. "I know what I'm doing."

"Do you?" I snapped waspishly. "Do you know what you're doing, Fern?! Because I'm pretty sure you've never done this in your life, and I'm the one who has to live with the consequences if you mess this up, so don't tell me to calm down!"

"God, you're tense," he said. "You should have paid extra for the massage. We could do a whole spa treatment."

"Fern!" hissed Emma from the doorway. "Speed it up!"

"NO!" I yelped. "Don't speed it up! Take your time!"

"WOULD YOU TWO KNOCK IT OFF?!" Fern shouted. "You're making me nervous!" He sounded more giddy than nervous.

I clamped my lips together and squeezed my eyes shut. Fern turned on the electric clippers and the hum made me break out in a cold sweat. I tried to remind myself of a time when this had seemed like a good idea, but I couldn't quite summon that particular memory.

It went alright for a while. Fern was doing fine, trimming here and there, doing his best to make sure it didn't look like a budget haircut done in a highschool bathroom.

"How much longer?" called Emma. We'd been at it for about ten minutes and, miraculously, no one had come in, but we were pushing our luck and we all knew it.

"I'm almost done," Fern said. "I just can't seem to get this part on the side to look right. The other side is fine, but...Ohhh...I see the problem..." He was silent for much too long.

"What?" I said urgently. "What's the problem? Fern? WHAT'S THE PROBLEM?!"

"I just...cut it too short in this one spot..." He was trying not to laugh.

I jumped up from the toilet and went around to the mirror above the sink. "FERN!" I shouted.

"No, no, it's fine," he said, still laughing. "If we put up the side, you'll look like the guys from Flock of Seagulls."

I looked ridiculous. The hair on the left still hid my scars, but the entire right side was patchy and bristling.

"We need to hurry!" said Emma. "The lunch bell rings in three minutes!"

"Screw it," I said, snatching the clippers out of Fern's hand and pulling off the guard. I took a deep breath and tried to pretend I was doing this to someone else. It was the only way to salvage the mess Fern had made.

There are three really terrific things about mohawks:

1. They're hard to mess up, even for an unqualified hair-stylist,
2. they make people angry for no reason,

3. they give the wearer an abrupt and unexpected sense of defiant confidence.

I worked as quickly as I dared, knowing I only had one chance to get it right. The lunch bell rang, but I kept working. We heard people filling the hall.

"Go use a different one," I heard Emma say to someone on the other side of the door. Grumbling voices trailed off into the distance.

When it was done, I stepped back and took a good look in the mirror and my heart almost stopped. With the long hair out of my face, I looked just like Reagan, albeit with a long, ugly burn mark running down the left side of my face. I was nearly the same age he had been when he died. We had the same blue eyes, the same dour expression...It was uncanny. I didn't like it.

"Don't go falling in love, Romeo," said Fern, dragging me away from the mirror. "We gotta go!" There was hair all over the sink and floor, but we had no time to clean it up.

The three of us filed out of the bathroom and joined the flow of students. I couldn't get over the shock of seeing Reagan looking back at me in the mirror. In spite of my best efforts, he was still disrupting my peace.

As we walked down the hall, I became abruptly aware that Fern was staring at me. I looked over at him and his mouth was hanging slightly open.

"What?" I asked,

"Your scar..." he said. "It looks..."

I had momentarily forgotten about my scar. My hand went reflexively to the place where the skin was raised ever so slightly. I traced a finger from my scalp down to my jaw.

"Yeah, I guess it's pretty bad," I said. "That's why I grew my hair out in the first place."

"No," said Fern earnestly. "It looks awesome."

-EIGHTEEN-
Oscar
-(autumn, 1993)-

Our principal, Dr. Jeffries, did not like his job. That was obvious to everyone who had ever set foot in his office. Or had ever spoken with him. Or had ever heard of him. It was his defining trait.

Since the beginning of school, I'd had several conversations with Dr. Jeffries, all of them very superficial and very forced. He would find me at my locker or stop by our lunch table. In every interaction, he managed to work in the fact that he had studied child psychology and, if I ever needed to talk, his door was open.

I tried to be polite and receptive at first, thinking that he was actually a pretty nice guy, but after he called me "Oscar" for the third time, I realized that he wasn't actually interested in me, he was just making the rounds. I was apparently on a list of troubled youths that he was required to check in with every so often and these little impromptu interviews were the best he could give me.

I decided that I had no interest in helping him feel like he was doing a good job. I didn't mind him being a bad school administrator, but I wasn't going to bend over backward to facilitate his narcissism. Quite the opposite, in fact. Whenever he spoke with me, I adopted a rather combative and unhelpful tone, and the more I dealt with him, the easier and more entertaining it became to antagonize him.

He would approach me at my locker and say things like, "How are we today, Oscar?"

I would respond with something like, "Our condition cannot be summed up with a single adjective, Dr. Jeffries, as we are two different people and, therefore, are experiencing two different lives. I can tell you that I am doing well and, judging by your posture and the general unhealthy pallor of your skin, I would say that you're not getting enough sleep, which can have a profound effect on a person's condition. If I was pressed for my opinion, I'd say you're on the verge of a nervous breakdown. But I'm fine."

After a handful of these encounters, Dr. Jeffries stopped approaching me in the halls.

The day following my haircut, I was called into Dr. Jeffries's office. Mrs. Kline ushered me in, though Dr. Jeffries wasn't there yet. While I waited, I looked around his office. On the wall behind his desk was a diploma, proof of his child psychology-based education. Next to that was a large Magic Eye poster, a novelty interactive artform which was extremely popular in the 1990s.

The idea with a Magic Eye poster was to stare at the image, allowing your eyes to shift gradually in and out of focus until they settled on pairs of subtle, identical shapes hidden within a complicated pattern, shapes which were, at first glance, invisible. Once your eyes found these matching shapes, a three-dimensional image appeared. It was a very cool effect and reminded me of the sensation of hidden depth I got staring at the ceiling of Mom's Chevy Vega.

I stared at the poster over Dr. Jeffries's desk for several moments before I could discern what the image was supposed to be. I let my eyes fall out of focus and was able to find the three-dimensional shape easily enough, but it didn't make sense. I just couldn't identify it. Then I realized that I was looking at a sailboat, but Dr. Jeffries had hung the poster upside-down.

He arrived a few minutes later.

"Do you know why I called you in here, Oscar?" he asked, steepling his fingers in what I'm sure he thought was a menacing way.

"Oliver," I said.

"Hm?" he asked, leaning forward as if to hear me better.

I leaned forward and said slowly and clearly, "MY NAME...IS OLIVER." He smiled as if to say, "Just as impertinent as I had expected."

"Someone left a large quantity of hair in the boys' restroom in the freshman hall," he said, looking up at my mohawk.

"Those freshmen," I said, shaking my head sadly. "Puberty hits so fast. Body hair starts sprouting and they don't know what to do about it. I think they're embarrassed, Dr. Jefferies. I feel sorry for those kids, to be honest. Maybe they should spend more time talking about that sort of thing in eighth-grade health. You should bring this up with Mr. Kelly."

Dr. Jeffries didn't interrupt. He just sat there looking at me over his steepled fingers. "I know it was you, Mr. Barrow," he said when I had finished.

"Why do you say that?" I asked, scratching at the stubble on the side of my head.

"I am neither amused nor entertained by your attitude," he said in a bored voice.

"Okay," I said, sitting up a little straighter. "Okay. I did leave some hair in the bathroom, but I didn't know that was against the rules."

"Mr. Barrow," said Dr. Jeffries with a heavy sigh, "our custodial staff does not have time to clean up after inconsiderate students."

"They only have time to clean up after considerate students?"

Dr. Jeffries's nostrils flared. "No more messes in the bathrooms, please."

I stood up and opened his office door. "Got it. No more messes in the bathrooms."

"Or anywhere else, for that matter," said Dr. Jeffries. He was a sharp one.

"I'll do my best."

Outside of Dr. Jeffries's office sat two anxious-looking youngsters looking dutifully ashamed. Apparently, they were the reason he was late to meet with me. "You're up," I said.

As I passed through the office lobby, Mrs. Auburn looked like she was trying not to laugh and Mrs. Kline gave me a very encouraging smile. Miss Simms, standing in her doorway across the room, waved me over.

"I like the new look," she said, pointing up at my mohawk. It was tastefully done, as mohawks go. It wasn't so tall that I had to duck through doorways or anything. "Thanks," I said.

"You didn't have to do that here at school," she said. "You could have come to our house. I wouldn't have thrown a fit over the mess."

Miss Simms invited me over for dinner at least once a week and I often accepted. She was a terrific cook and very funny. She, Emma, and I would eat dinner, have hilarious conversations, and then clean up after. It was nice, being part of their family, even briefly.

The conversation sometimes drifted into territory that felt like it was getting personal, but Miss Simms was very good at steering us back out of those waters. As a person with secrets, I appreciated her delicacy. It didn't occur to me that I might not be the only one there with secrets.

"I guess I should have thought of that," I said. I looked across the office at Mrs. Auburn and Mrs. Kline, they were watching me. "What's up with them?" I asked, trying not to make it obvious.

Miss Simms stifled a laugh and pointed to a very old speaker box bolted to the top of her desk. She turned a dial and Dr. Jeffries's voice crackled out of the speaker.

"...isn't the kind of behavior I've come to expect from the eighth-graders at Leopold Jr./Sr. High School," he was saying. "We have standards, gentlemen, and those standards dictate that, while in school, we keep our pants on at all times..."

Mrs. Auburn spit coffee all over her desk, Mrs. Kline was bracing herself against the back of a chair, and Miss Simms was shaking in silent laughter. From across the lobby, I heard Mrs. Auburn mumble, "What a jackass..." They were eavesdropping from a similar intercom box on Mrs. Auburn's desk.

"You listen in when he's having meetings with students?" I asked, gleefully. "Does he know?"

Miss Simms merely handed me a hall pass and said, "You oughta get back to class, Oliver."

School was a pain, especially after I had gotten so used to life with Mom. In Traverse City, I came and went as I pleased, studied whatever interested me, moved at my own pace, and no one harassed me or unjustly accused me (though Mr. Jeffries was right to blame me for the hair in the bathroom). With the exception of my time with Emma and Fern, I hated school.

That being said, I never missed a day. I may have found high school to be regimented and cruel, but it was still a routine. I didn't have to make decisions. My actions were determined by the bell. It rang and I sat. It rang again and I stood. Once you got over the childishness of the demands (both from the students and the teachers), it was simple.

Some kids had it worse than I did. They had to get good grades or they'd hear about it at home. Dad didn't really care what I did as long as he didn't have to get involved. And a lot of my teachers seemed to think I'd been through enough, so I got a lot of grace from them. So, in some ways, school was easy for me.

I'm not saying that being at home was bad, though it wasn't the most pleasant place. I liked being alone, but I was never really alone at home and Maggie and Reagan liked to remind me of that fact.

Sometimes Reagan would rev the Cutlass in the middle of the night, pulling me up from a dead sleep. Sometimes the lights would flicker (though that might have just been due to old wiring). Once, the smoke alarm at the bottom of the stairs started going off for no discernible reason and when I inspected it I found that it had no battery.

"You should really replace those every six months," Maggie said from the top step.

"What happens to you if the house burns down?" I asked her. "Where would you go?"

She shrugged and returned to her room.

Sometimes I found the goblins at school easier to cope with than the ghosts at home. At least the goblins were predictable.

"Hey, Oliver," Fern asked at lunch one day. "Do you have any more copies of that mixtape you gave me?"

"Why?" I asked. "Was something wrong with the other one?"

"I just need another one, is all." He was deconstructing his chicken noodle soup, arranging the noodles by length, and measuring them with a tape measure he had stolen from the Home Ec. room. He called out the lengths and Emma wrote them in her notebook.

"Alright," I said. "Any requests? You want different stuff or just another copy of the last one?"

"Whatever's fine," he said. "Two and seven-sixteenths."

Emma wrote it down.

"Actually," said Fern, "I'll take another copy of the first one and if you want to make another one with all different songs, that would be awesome."

"Yeah, no problem," I said. I loved the process of making a mixtape, especially for someone else. The fact that Fern was enjoying the music so much was very encouraging...at first.

I realized that I had been swindled (a harsh word, perhaps, but definitionally accurate) in Social Studies about a week and a half later. We were seated in our little groups, mine still not talking to me, when the kid across from me started digging through his pockets. He extracted folded notes, a house key, a cassette tape, a pack of gum, etc. The cassette tape immediately caught my eye. On the cover was a skull with a mohawk. The title of the album was *Jewels for Fools*.

"Can I see this?" I asked and the kid, though looking a little trepidatious, nodded. I opened the case and found that the tape was a homemade compilation with a very cool jacket insert. I made a note to start making inserts for my own mixtapes. I looked at the track listing and found, much to my surprise, that not only did I know every song, but I had put them all on my own mixtape and in the very same order.

"'Clash City Rockers,'" I read. "'Blitzkrieg Bop', 'Police Truck'...Where did you get this?"

The kid across from me (I really wish I could remember his name...maybe our animosity wasn't as one-sided as I thought at the time) said, looking defensive, "I got it from my little brother. He's in junior high. He bought it from someone, I don't know who."

I handed the tape back and spent the rest of the class staring into the middle distance. When I finally saw Fern at lunch, I didn't hesitate.

"Hey!" I slammed my tray down on the table, making both Fern and Emma jump. "Have you been selling copies of my tape?"

Fern at least had the decency to look ashamed, but only for a moment. "Yeah." he said. "I've been making copies and selling them to junior high kids for five bucks each. I asked you to make me another one because I accidentally sold my master copy."

"And what about the new tape?" I asked angrily. "With the new songs? You been selling that, too?"

"Oh, yes," he said cheerfully. "*Volume Two* is very popular."

"Volume...two?" asked Emma. At least she hadn't been in on it.

"Yeah!" said Fern. "These junior high kids are eating it up! Their parents won't let them buy that kind of stuff at the mall, so they buy it from me."

"How many copies have you sold?" Emma asked.

"About...twenty-five?" Fern calculated. "Thirty, maybe?"

He pulled one out of his pocket and slid it to Emma who picked it up and looked it over.

"'*Jewels for Fools*,'" she read. "You made this?"

"Oliver made the playlist," he said. "I designed the sleeve and made the copies and put it all together."

"So, this is Olliver's," said Emma.

"Yeah!" I said. "I made this!"

"Oh?" asked Fern, his eyebrows elevated. "You're The Clash? And The Ramones? Which of the Violent Femmes are you, again? You didn't make any of this music, Oliver. You stole it, just like I did."

I tried to think of an argument, but there was none.

"You still should have told him what you were doing," said Emma.

"I couldn't," said Fern, looking embarrassed. "It was a surprise. I'm saving up money to get you guys Christmas presents."

"Fern," I said, "it's the middle of October."

"And at five bucks a pop," said Fern, "it'll take me until Christmas to get what I need."

Emma and I looked at him. He wouldn't meet our gaze. I started to feel guilty now. He had been trying to do something nice.

"I don't buy it," said Emma, breaking the spell. "You've never once bought me a gift in the three years we've been friends."

"Damn," said Fern, grinning. "Busted. Look, I'll split the money with you."

"No," I said, looking at the cassette. The design was really well done. "You did way more work on this than I did. Just don't...don't feel like you need to hide things from us, okay?"

"Okay," he said. "Starting now, I won't keep any more secrets from you."

"What does that mean?" asked Emma. "'Starting now'?"

"You don't want to know," said Fern. "Trust me, the less you know, the better."

"This isn't your pitching machine idea, is it?" I asked, referring back to a conversation we'd had earlier in the week. "Because I thought we agreed that it would be considered 'felonious assault.'"

"No, no," said Fern. "Nothing like that."

Emma looked anxious. "What did you do, Fern?"

"Do you remember that giant roll of plastic wrap I found last year?" he said.

"You didn't find it," said Emma. "You stole it."

"Let's just say it was procured through larcenous means," admitted Fern. "Anyway...I was finally able to put it to good use."

"Please elaborate," said Emma in a monotone.

Fern shook his head. "You're right," he said. "The less you know, the better."

"I didn't say that," she said. "You said that."

"It was very wise advice," said Fern. "I'm going to follow it."

"Just tell me one thing," Emma said. "Does this have anything to do with Mrs. Pitt?"

When I first enrolled at Leopold, one of the things I was actually looking forward to was having access to the school library. I had hoped that it would be something like the public library back in Traverse City, a treasure trove of novels and media, free to the curious explorer, but that, it turned out, was not the case. The school library was run by an angry woman named Mrs. Pitt who could not abide idle students. She abhorred loitering, once calling Fern and I "Dickensian miscreants" as she forcefully ushered us out of the library.

Students weren't allowed to browse the shelves on their own. If you wanted a book, you had to fill out a request card with the title and author as well as your reason for wanting the book. Mrs. Pitt could reject your request for any reason. Even if she didn't reject your request, it often took a week or more to get your book. I had no love for the Leopold Jr./Sr. High School librarian.

It just so happened that Mrs. Pitt lived a few houses down from Fern and his parents. Irritating her was one of his favorite pastimes. He had organized neighborhood kickball games in her backyard, posted fliers at the grocery store advertising free-babysitting and listing her telephone number, and regularly had unwanted pizzas delivered to her house.

So, when Emma asked Fern if his unspoken secret had anything to do with Mrs. Pitt, it wasn't actually a question, but, rather, more of a confirmation.

"You're going to get arrested one of these days," I said.

"Let's hope so," said Fern. "I don't feel safe with these pranksters and hooligans running around my neighborhood. It's about time the police in this town did their jobs."

There are three basic pranks teenagers have relied on since the Dawn of Man: T.P.ing, egging, and doorbelling. If you have never been a teenager, please allow me to explain.

T.P.ing, or "toilet-papering," involves acquiring as many rolls of toilet paper as you can (via means both legitimate and otherwise) and draping said toilet paper amongst tree branches and over shrubbery in the dead of night. This requires a fair bit of coordination and planning and can be done on private property or public property, as the perpetrator sees fit. It is essentially artistic and graceful littering and, if done correctly, takes many hours to clean up.

Egging is the act of throwing eggs at things such as vehicles and buildings. This has the potential to cause a significant amount of damage and is rarely viewed as good-natured fun. It requires almost no coordination or planning and often results in criminal charges.

Doorbelling, the least clever or complicated of the three, is when you ring someone's doorbell and then run away real fast. Giggling may or may not be involved.

These tried-and-true tools of the prank trade have been used by teenagers for decades because they are simple concepts, fairly easy to execute, and the materials, if any are needed, are easy to acquire.

And none of them were good enough for Fern.

When Mrs. Pitt walked out of her house that morning and discovered her car wrapped in a solid quarter-inch of plastic wrap, she didn't have to rack her brains to come up with a probable culprit. Fortunately for Fern, she couldn't prove it was him, but she was especially unpleasant toward him after that.

-NINETEEN-
use other door
-(autumn, 1993)-

Fern's most disruptive prank, though, wasn't even a prank. It was just a thing he did that led to another thing that someone else did which ended up spiraling out of control. But, in true Fern fashion, he took the credit.

And I took the blame.

A few weeks after Fern wrapped Mrs. Pitt's car in plastic, we were walking back from lunch and we passed a classroom door onto which someone had taped a sign that said, simply, "USE OTHER DOOR."

Fern, being Fern, plucked the sign off the door as we walked past. I don't think he even did it consciously. It was compulsory for him to cause trouble. He should have been the one with the mohawk.

He threw the sign into the air and it see-sawed to the floor. Me, being me, picked it up because, in the same way that chaos is compulsory for Fern, cleaning is compulsory for me.

So now I'm holding this USE OTHER DOOR sign with a piece of tape on it and I have no idea what to do with it, so I stick it to Fern's chest. He wore it all the way down the hall until we passed the library at which point he took the sign off his chest and stuck it to the library door. That was it. That was the big prank. We thought no more about it...until later.

The library had two entrances, but the only one anyone ever used was the door off the main hallway, right next to Mrs. Pitt's desk. It was impossible to walk into the library without her knowledge and then she badgered you about what you wanted, why you were there, what you were up to, etc. She was not interested in fostering a love of reading in any of the people with whom she interacted.

The other door was on the opposite side of the library and was not visible from Mrs. Pitt's desk. No one ever used that door because it necessitated walking all the way to the other side of the building.

But then there was the USE OTHER DOOR sign.

It probably wouldn't have caused any trouble on its own, however, Mrs. Fitzpatrick had chosen that day to walk her eleventh grade English class down to the library so they could work on their research papers. Imagine Mrs. Pitt's confusion when the library, which she assumed was empty, began filling with students. People started appearing abruptly from behind shelves. They'd been wandering around, touching books, looking at things, unsupervised for countless, untold minutes. Mrs. Pitt was apoplectic when she discovered the sign on the library door.

Had it just been the sign, it would have stopped there, but Mrs. Pitt's reaction was what got people's attention. She could be heard screaming at Mrs. Fitzpatrick and the students all the way from the main office. Dr. Jeffries was seen sprinting through the halls to intervene before anyone got hurt. I didn't witness any of this, nor did Emma or Fern, but the fact that the gossip reached the three of us, who interacted with almost no one but each other, suggested that it had spread to every corner of the school.

Fern was overjoyed. With almost no effort, he had struck a significant blow against his greatest enemy.

"Imagine what I could do if I tried," he said with a far-off gleam in his eye.

"That's what I've been saying about your grades," said Emma, but Fern brushed her off.

"What do you mean, 'if I tried'?" I asked. "What are you planning?" Fern just grinned evilly and said no more about it.

A few days later, however, we understood. USE OTHER DOOR signs started popping up everywhere. They were on bathroom stalls, classroom doors, lockers. The entire junior high boys' locker room had been wallpapered in them. Mr. Kelly's car had been covered.

"Well, you've certainly been busy," said Emma, sliding a USE OTHER DOOR sign across the lunch table.

"Oh, it wasn't me," Fern said sincerely. "I might have made a few suggestions, but...It wasn't me."

"To whom," I asked slowly, "did you make these suggestions?"

Fern sagely held up an index finger. "A stone on a hill will roll farther than a stone in a valley."

"What the hell does that mean?" asked Emma.

"Junior highers," he said, smiling broadly. "They know a good idea when they hear one, and they don't know when to quit."

They sure didn't know when to quit. Even when an announcement went out through the school directing the perpetrators to stop, it continued. Eventually, a letter was sent home to every family in the school.

A word of advice: If you're trying to find the culprit, never include the phrase, "We don't know who is behind this, but when we find out..." It merely encourages those responsible to be more cautious, but it does nothing to discourage the offending behavior.

So much aggravation over a sign...

It didn't take long for Dr. Jeffries to call me into his office about the signs.

"Mr. Barrow," he said, barely looking at me, "I'm not interested in wasting either your time or my own..."

"I appreciate that, Dr. Jeffries," I said, getting up to leave.

"Sit down," he said and I did. "What can you tell me about those signs?"

I looked at him blankly for a long time. "I don't know what you're talking about."

"See? That's the thing, Oscar...Oliver," he said. "You know exactly what signs. Everyone knows. But you sit there and act far too innocent. The police accuse a man of murder and he responds by acting like he doesn't even know what murder is. That's suspicious."

"I thought this was about the signs," I said, crinkling my brow. "Now someone's been murdered?"

"Oliver..." said Dr. Jeffries rubbing his forehead.

"But it sounds like you caught the guy," I said. "Good work, sir." I held up a hand for a high-five.

"Oliver!" Dr. Jeffries looked mad now. "You sat in this office not six weeks ago and promised me no more messes. Do you remember?"

"Yes," I said seriously. "I remember."

"And here we are with another mess," he said.

I shrugged. "I agree, it's a mess, but I had nothing to do with it."

"Do you honestly expect me to believe that?" Dr. Jeffries was almost shouting. He steadied himself with a deep breath. "I studied child psychology, did you know that?"

I pointed to the framed diploma hanging on the wall above his desk. "Yes, sir, I did."

He forced a chuckle in an attempt to change tactics. He was going to try to be understanding, though I might have told him that it was a little late for that.

He tapped a drab, olive green folder sitting in front of him. "Oliver, I've read your personal file," he said, and that kind of shook me a little, though I couldn't have said why. There wasn't much in my life that wasn't widely known. I doubted my personal file held many exclusive secrets.

"You've been through a significant amount of trauma," he continued. "If not addressed, that kind of thing can build up until it changes you. Fundamentally."

"Did you know your Magic Eye poster is upside down?" I asked.

"It seems to me that you're a good kid at heart," he said. "You mean well, generally, but you've lost two siblings and a parent, and during most of your formative years, you were isolated. You never developed the appropriate social skills to deal with..." he gestured broadly around us.

"So, I'm a good kid," I said, "but you think that might change if I don't...deal with my past?"

Dr. Jeffries looked at me. He may have been bored, he may have hated his job, but he looked at me. He didn't look at my hair or my scar or even at the crumpled USE OTHER DOOR sign laying on the corner of his desk. He looked at ME.

"I think you should consider that what you went through would destroy the average person," he said finally. "The fact that you're doing as well as you are suggests to me that you're well above average. I'd hate for you to slip into a pattern of delinquent behavior just because you made friends with the first group of kids who let you sit at their lunch table."

And he had been doing so well. He almost had me, but then he went after Emma and Fern. Whoops.

"You're right, Dr. Jeffries," I said, feeling the heat rising in my cheeks. "Emma and Fern were the first kids to let me sit at their lunch table. They were the first kids to talk to me, to be nice to me, to make me feel welcomed and loved. In fact, they're the only kids who have treated me like a human being. Ever. They're unique and interesting and smart and funny and if you think they're the problem, you're wrong! The problem is that you have hundreds of frightened, clueless kids wandering through your halls, doing their best to blend in because they don't know who they are and they're terrified of finding out! And you think Emma and Fern are the problem?! You need to open your eyes, Dr. Jeffries! Open your eyes and give that diploma back because you have no idea what you're doing!

"Do you want to know something that isn't in my personal file, Dr. Jeffries? Do you want to know what none of the rumors or reports have touched on? Do you want to know the awful truth about Oliver Barrow?"

My hands were shaking and at some point I had risen to my feet and was now leaning over the desk, staring down at Dr. Jeffries who was leaning way back in his seat, pale as a sheet, eyes wide and twitching.

"My brother Reagan was an absolute monster! He killed my sister who was probably a monster herself! And then I killed Ray, because I'm a monster, too! We're all monsters! My mother knew it! That's why she tried to kill me! My father knows it! That's why he's never home! He's afraid of me! AND SO AM I!"

Dr. Jeffries was leaning back in his chair as far as he could. His eyes were wide like he was looking for some place to run.

"But Emma and Fern aren't afraid of me," I said calmly. "And, when I'm with them, I'm not either. I actually like myself when I'm with them."

I turned away from Dr. Jeffries and opened his office door. A USE OTHER DOOR sign had been taped to it while we were having our meeting.

"You're afraid my trauma will change me?" I was no longer shouting, but my hands were still shaking. "Maybe it already has, Dr. Jeffries. Maybe it changed me for the better. Let's hope it has. I mean, I haven't killed anyone in six years. That's gotta be a good sign, right?"

I walked out into the office lobby and Mrs. Auburn, Mrs. Kline, and Miss Simms were all there, watching me. They all wore identical looks of alarm. I knew they had been listening. As I walked through the lobby, Miss Simms's look of alarm turned to a look of...fierce pride? It certainly seemed like it. She gave me an approving nod as I passed her on my way to the door.

I had never experienced that before, someone being proud of me. It was a strange sensation, but nice. I carried it close for a long time.

-TWENTY-
no snacks
-(still autumn, 1993)-

"We need to talk," I said to Emma and Fern at lunch later that day. "Like, really talk."

"I can't stop the signs, Oliver," said Fern in a panicked voice. "Those junior high kids are out of control." He looked worried, like a mad scientist realizing that his violent creation is no longer under his influence.

"That's not what I mean," I said. "But we can address that later, if you want."

"I think we'd better," he said faintly. "I'm scared..."

"What's going on?" asked Emma, ignoring Fern. "Simmy said you were in Dr. Jeffries's office this morning and that something happened."

Something had, indeed, happened. I had said some things out loud that I hadn't meant to, things I would have preferred to keep secret. Sometimes thoughts aren't real until you say them, and then you realize that they have an unanticipated weight.

The thought that I had said out loud was this: "Emma and Fern aren't afraid of me." I hadn't known how important that was to me until I heard myself say it.

I had to acknowledge, however, that they didn't know the whole truth about me. Would they still like me? Would they be afraid of me if they knew what I had done? And how do you bring that up in conversation? My social skills were limited, primarily, to sharing meals and music. How did one confess to murder without making it sound like a big deal?

"Would you be willing," I asked, looking back and forth between Emma and Fern, "to come to my house after school?"

"I have football practice," said Fern. Emma threw a fork at him.

"We'll be there," she said.

"I've got snacks," I said, knowing I had no such thing.

"Coach'll be mad," said Fern, sighing, "but, yeah. I'll be there."

I spent the next few hours in a daze, wondering how I was going to tell them. And how much I was going to tell them. Did I want them to know everything? If I wasn't going to tell them everything, what was the point of telling them anything?

"I set my brother on fire when I was six years old," I said, "but he survived. Three years later, I ran over him with a car, which...seemed to do the trick."

We were in my kitchen. Emma and Fern were sitting at the table while I walked laps around the room.

I told them about Reagan and how scary he could be. I explained about how Maggie liked to make Reagan mad, just for fun. Then I told them about how I learned to hide from them both and about how neither of them liked that very much.

"They both had their own methods for getting me out of my hiding spots," I said. "Maggie would trick me into coming out, which always worked because I'm not smart, and Ray would try to force me to come out, which never worked because he's not smart, either."

I described the events leading up to the barn fire and about what happened after, about the scars and about getting teased in school. I told them how it had been so much worse for Reagan, physically and emotionally. I told them about Maggie pounding on the attic floor. I told them about seeing her fall down the stairs. When I told them that she winked at me, they exchanged nervous glances and I stopped talking. The plan was backfiring. They liked me just fine when I was just a local legend with a murky past. Why spoil it by oversharing?

"You know what?" I said nervously. "Maybe we should stop. I mean, none of this makes any difference at all. I don't know why I thought I needed to do this."

"No!" Emma said, jumping to her feet. "You've been living with this for six years. You need to talk about it. You won't be free of it until you do. Trust me, I know about this sort of thing. And this is why we came over, isn't it?"

"I was promised snacks," said Fern.

"Okay, listen," I said, leaning heavily on the table. "Up to this point, it's pretty bad, but not, like, crazy, you know? But it's about to get a lot worse...and I understand if you want to leave. I mean, I want to leave."

"No," said Emma, sitting back down. "We don't want to leave. Keep going."

I took a deep breath. "Right..."

I talked about Dad and Reagan coming home with the Cutlass and about how hard Reagan worked on it and how frustrated he was getting. Dad was riding him pretty hard about it, and that just made things worse. That car was Regan's entire identity at that point, and every failure and every criticism felt personal.

Then I got to the night Reagan died. I walked Emma and Fern through the whole event, pausing when I got to the part about seeing Maggie standing in my window. Did I want to admit that I was seeing ghosts?

I had just decided that, no, I was not ready to admit that I was seeing ghosts, when Emma looked past me and smiled sweetly.

"Hi, there," she said. I turned around and there she was, standing in the shadows beside the staircase. Turquoise turtleneck, magenta overalls. "Who's this, Oliver?"

I drew a ragged breath. I was not prepared for this. "This...this is my sister," I said hoarsely. "This is Maggie."

There was a long, vacuous silence before Fern knocked his chair over and ran out of the house. I followed.

"Fern!" I called, the screen door slamming behind me. He was pacing back and forth in the dirt yard, his hands buried in his hair, a pained look on his face.

"WHAT THE HELL, OLIVER?!" he screamed. "ARE YOU SERIOUS?! IT'S IN YOUR HOUSE?! WHAT THE HELL?!" He started to hyperventilate and had to sit down with his head between his knees to keep from passing out.

I walked to him and patted him on the back. "Yeah," I said. "That's Maggie. She's...She's the good one."

Fern looked up at me. "You've got to be kidding," he said. There were tears in his eyes. "There's more?"

"Yeaaahhh..." I said apologetically. "And I lied about the snacks."

"Damn you, Oliver Barrow," he said. "On top of everything else, no snacks."

I helped him to his feet. He wiped his eyes and we went back inside where, I realized, I had left Emma alone with a ghost.

Fern stood behind me just inside the kitchen door, both of us scanning the room as though Maggie would be there making sandwiches. Emma was sitting at the table, wiping away tears of her own with the sleeve of her cardigan.

"She left," Emma said. "After you two went outside, she said, 'We need him and he needs you,' and then she walked into the next room. I followed her, but she was gone."

"What the hell, Oliver?!" Fern said in a harsh whisper, still hiding behind me.

"Who did she mean by 'we'?" asked Emma.

"Well, that's the part I was getting to," I said.

I told them the rest of the story, holding nothing back. Maggie had come out to make sure she wasn't left out of the story. I didn't want Reagan to do the same.

Emma and Fern listened in absolute silence as I described what I did to my brother. I cried through most of it, but I felt a lot better when that part of the story was done. I stopped pacing and sat down across the table from my friends and wiped my eyes.

I told them about being kidnapped, how it didn't feel like being kidnapped. I told them about the ladies at the battered women's shelter in Traverse City and about Brian and Patty at the library. I told them about Mom and the *zolpidem* and the lasagna.

"Lasagna sounds really good right now," said Fern.

"My mom's recipe still has some wrinkles in it," I said, "but once I get those ironed out, I'll be sure to share it with you."

By the time I was done, all the way up to that morning in Dr. Jeffries's office, the sun had gone down and I was exhausted.

"What does your dad think about all of this?" Emma asked. Her eyes were red. She'd been crying the whole time.

"I don't know," I said. "We haven't talked about it. He's not really around much."

"When was the last time you saw him?" she asked. I thought back. He had gotten me enrolled in school back at the end of August, and I knew of at least two other times he had been home, but one of those times I hadn't actually talked to him. I only knew he had been home because the fridge was full of beer again and there was more grocery money on the kitchen table.

"Maybe, a week ago?" I ventured. "Maybe?"

"What did he say about your hair?" she asked.

"I don't think he's seen it like this," I said.

"Oliver!" Emma shouted, slapping the table and making Fern and I jump out of our chairs. "We cut your hair almost six weeks ago! You've been alone here this whole time?"

"He's not exactly alone," murmured Fern.

Emma got up and went to the phone, dialing it and waiting for an answer. "Hey, Simmy! Yeah, I'm just about to head home. Would it be okay if Oliver and Fern came over for dinner? Pizza sounds amazing, thank you so much. No, it's fine, we can walk from here. Love you, too. Bye."

Emma and Miss Simms lived about half a mile away, in Gladden proper. At the back of our property was a lumpy farm trail that opened out right next to the baseball diamonds at the New Park. To reach the lumpy farm trail, however, we had to pass the corn crib. As we did so, the red door rattled and the chain started swinging, banging against the weathered planks and causing Emma and Fern to stop short.

"Just ignore him," I mumbled, leading the way around the building. I made sure to give it a wide berth, though, just in case Reagan had something more sinister than chain rattling in mind.

Once we were in the New Park, it was just a matter of crossing the parking lot, crossing the playground, and then crossing a narrow footbridge that spanned what we locals called "Gladden Creek," but was actually a ditch filled with animal waste and industrial chemicals and disgusting farm run-off.

As we crossed the parking lot, I looked up and the park sign caught my eye. Normally it read, "Gladden Community Park," but someone had altered it. I started laughing and Emma and Fern looked to see what had gotten my attention.

Emma read the sign out loud. "'Gladden Communist Party.'"

"Oh, my God," said Fern, starting to laugh. "That's fantastic..."

I wondered how long it would be before Dr. Jeffries called me into his office for an explanation. It was so good I might have been tempted to accept the blame.

"What do you suppose she meant by, 'We need him, he needs you'?" asked Emma while we ate pizza in her living room.

"They're probably recruiting spirits for their ghost army," said Fern, "and they need Oliver to harvest the souls. We're at the top of the list."

"Mm," I said, skeptically. "I'm not sure you'd be considered prime material for haunting."

"What are you talking about, Barrow?" Fern asked, offended. "I'd be an amazing ghost! There'd be cabinet doors opening and shutting all hours of the night."

"Oh, please," said Emma, waving him down. "You'd just sit on the couch and complain about whatever is on TV."

"She's right, man," I said. "It's not like you're gonna die and THEN develop productive habits."

Fern sighed. "TV does suck, though. Have you noticed?"

"But, seriously," said Emma, steering us back on track. "What do you think she meant?"

"When she came to see me in Traverse City," I said, feeling very weird talking about it, "she wrote on the mirror, 'he's still angry,' and I didn't really give it much thought. I mean, until I told you guys about it, I sort of forgot she had done that. She clearly meant that Ray is still angry, but why would that matter? He was always angry."

"Maybe she was warning you," said Fern. "Maybe she didn't think you should come back here."

"I don't think so," I said. "It didn't feel like a warning or a threat, but more like...like she was asking for help."

"You don't think he's hurting her, do you?" asked Emma. She looked pale.

"If there's a way, he will," I said. "Even when he was in a good mood, he'd hurt people, but ever since I murdered him his mood has only gotten worse."

It was amazing that, in spite of the heavy theme of our discussion, we could sit on Emma's living room floor, eating pizza and laughing. I felt such a lightness in my heart. The guilt and shame of what I had done in my fear and anger all those years ago, it didn't weigh any less, but now my friends were helping me carry it.

I don't remember arriving at any kind of conclusion that evening. We didn't make much effort to translate Maggie's cryptic messages. There wasn't any intent of any kind. We were all just processing, which was something I had needed for a very long time.

We might have figured things out sooner if we could have stayed focused, but my dead siblings were certainly not the only problems we had that semester.

-TWENTY-ONE-
"...a very serious crime..."
-(November, 1993)-

Fern's bootleg cassette business was drawing a fair bit of attention. Between the first and second volumes of *Jewels for Fools*, he had sold nearly sixty cassettes, almost all of them to junior high boys. As previously stated, junior high boys are easily influenced, but not easily dissuaded. They're like boulders at the top of a hill. Once they start rolling, they won't stop until they run out of hill.

Holy crap. I just understood what Fern was talking about at lunch that day...a stone on a hill versus a stone in a valley...

Anyway...

A growing group of parents had become increasingly concerned about the kind of music their children had been listening to and brought their concerns to Dr. Jeffries, who could not have been less interested. Still, he was honor-bound to address the issue. Also, the parents threatened to take the matter to the school board, so Dr. Jeffries was kind of stuck.

Instead of sending a letter out to all of the families, Dr. Jeffries skipped straight ahead and called me into his office.

"Sit down, Mr. Barrow," he said.

"Hang on just one second..." I said, staring at the Magic Eye poster, which soon resolved itself to reveal a sailboat, now right side up. "Hey! You fixed it." I held up my hand for a high five and, again, was denied.

"Why are we here again, Mr. Barrow?" he asked, looking as bored as ever.

"I don't know, Dr. Jeffries," I said, "but considering how these meetings usually go, I'm surprised you keep calling me in here." I heard Mrs. Auburn laugh from the other side of the door.

Dr. Jeffries held up a copy of *Jewels for Fools*. "Did you make this?" he asked.

"I don't...I don't think so," I said, taking the tape. I flipped the case open and read down the track listing. "Huh, that's weird..."

"I beg your pardon?" Dr. Jeffries braced himself for another bold lie.

"I think I DID make this," I said. "I make compilation tapes for my own personal use, and this is definitely the track list from one I made a few months ago, but this isn't the brand of blank tape I use. And I definitely don't have the artistic talent to design a cover like this."

Dr. Jeffries stared at me, caught off-guard by this partial admission. "What...what are you saying?" he asked.

"This is my track list," I said, passing the cassette back to him, "but I didn't make that."

"How do you explain this, then?" he asked.

"I lost that particular compilation a while ago," I said. "Maybe someone found it and made copies."

He watched me closely, clearly looking for holes in my sincerity. "So, you made this tape, but you didn't make this tape?"

"No," I said. "I didn't make THIS tape, but I made another tape, which I lost, which someone else found, which they then used to make this tape."

"That sounds...far-fetched," he said.

"You know what else sounds far-fetched?" I asked. "The fact that Australia is wider than the moon, but it's true."

Dr. Jeffries didn't know what to do with that. He tapped his desk and sighed deeply. After a moment he said, "We'll be looking into this further, Mr. Barrow. Whoever is behind this..." he gave me what I'm sure he thought was an intimidating glare, "will be punished. Selling pirated music is a very serious crime."

"I'm sure the music industry is glad of your support, sir," I said, getting up to leave.

"Mr. Barrow," he said, leaning forward, "I trust this is the last time we'll have a meeting like this."

"Well, that's up to you," I said. "I'm not the one scheduling them."

I opened the door, but instead of leaving, I turned to face Dr. Jeffries.

"Can you tell me something?" I asked. "Why do adults get so upset when kids get excited about anything? Is there some kind of rule prohibiting unsanctioned enthusiasm? What are you people so afraid of?"

Dr. Jeffries looked like he was biting back some kind of knee-jerk retort. He settled for giving me a dismissive wave out the door.

I relayed Dr. Jeffries's warning to Fern at lunch later that day. He didn't seem worried.

"What's he gonna do?" asked Fern. "Call the CIA?"

"Actually," said Emma, writing in her notebook, only half-listening to our conversation, "I think the FBI handles stuff like this. The CIA gathers information. The FBI investigates crimes."

"And Jeffries is neither," said Fern.

"Right," I said, "but he can still cause a whole lot of trouble and the only person he has on his list of suspects is me. So knock it off!"

"What did he say, exactly?" Fern asked.

"He said that 'selling pirated music is a very serious crime,'" I said.

"So, don't sell it," said Emma.

"I'm not gonna back down just because of Dr. Jeffries," said Fern.

"I'm not saying that you should back down," said Emma. "I'm just saying, don't *sell* them."

Fern and I looked at her for a moment and then at each other. "You want me to give them away for free?" Fern asked slowly.

"We can't do that, either," I said. "It's a miracle that no one has turned you in yet, Fern. How hard would it be for one of these kids to say, 'I bought it from an Asian high schooler'? It wouldn't take Jeffries long to figure out which Asian high schooler they were talking about."

"True," said Fern. "I do have that particular demographic locked down pretty tight."

"So if you go around handing out cassette tapes," I said, "they'll have you for sure."

"Then what do we do?" he asked.

"Treasure hunt," said Emma, still mostly focused on her notebook. "Hide them around the school."

A wide grin slowly spread across Fern's face. "We're gonna need a lot more tapes."

I decided to make an entirely new mixtape. Knowing that I was making it for a wider audience really informed my track list. When I say "wider audience," I don't just mean the directionless junior high boys who had so embraced *Jewels for Fools*, but their parents as well. I intentionally chose songs that had some kind of positive message, though probably not the kind of positive message most of the parents around Gladden would appreciate. Still, it was better than just choosing the angriest, loudest songs I could find. Why feed into the negative stereotype when there were so many better options?

Most people think of punk rock as angry and antisocial, but it's really not. At its core, it's music written by kids who have been through a lot and it's aimed at other kids who are going through the same. As a kid who had been through a lot, I found it encouraging. It was a promise that I wasn't alone, that somewhere out there were people like me who would understand. And against all odds, I had found them.

The tape was short, only eight songs, but since we were giving them away, no one could complain. Fern and Emma listened to it.

"It's good," said Fern, his eyes sparkling. "It's so, so good..."

Emma shrugged. "I'm more of a Smashing Pumpkins fan," she said, "but this isn't bad."

"It's so..." said Fern, slowly twirling his hands as he searched for the right word. "I always thought punk was just people screaming about their dads or the police. This makes me want to go out and...vote...or volunteer. It's weird. Weird in a really good way."

"*Jewels for Fools, Volume Three*?" asked Emma.

"No," I said. This compilation wasn't like the others, which were combinations of my favorite songs, songs that got me amped up, and songs that sounded good through headphones with the volume turned all the way up. *Jewels for Fools* was just for fun. This was something else entirely.

These songs made me think of all the people who had made a difference in my life, the ones who weren't doing it because it was their job or because they were earning points in any way, but the ones who did it because it was the right thing to do, because they couldn't NOT help. The good people society overlooked, like the ladies at the battered women's shelter, Brian at the library, Miss Simms...

These songs reminded me to fight for myself because so many amazing people thought I was worth fighting for.

"We'll call it *Secretly Kings*," I said. "Fern, it needs a cover. Do your thing."

We made one hundred copies and numbered them. That was Emma's idea. "Even if people don't like the music," she said, "some of them will want to collect as many as they can. It turns it into a game. More people will want to get involved."

It seemed like she was overthinking it and I argued against it at first but, as it turned out, Emma Seaway was an absolute marketing genius.

While the goal was for people to find copies, Emma, Fern, and I made our own game of hiding the tapes. We hid them on top of cabinets and behind drawn blinds. We focused on easy to reach places where people seldom looked. I managed to slip one into the card catalog in the library while Mrs. Pitt was shouting at Fern for propping his feet up on a table. Fern one-upped me by taping a copy to the underside of Mr. Kelly's chair.

Emma outdid us both by stashing one in the sanitary napkin dispenser in one of the girls' bathrooms. She paid the price for her cleverness, however, by having to explain to Fern what a sanitary napkin was.

Thanksgiving was a week away and people were already pretty excited about the long weekend, but when Fern started telling his regular junior high customers that there was a new tape, a free tape, hidden somewhere in the school, they went a little wild. The search for *Secretly Kings* inspired a level of chaos that I had yet to see at Leopold Jr./Sr. High School.

We decided to start slow, only hiding ten cassettes. We checked on them often and, within a few days, they had all been found. Two days before the holiday break, we hid another ten. All but two had been found when we left school the day before Thanksgiving.

"What are you two doing for Thanksgiving?" Emma asked.

"We're going to my grandma's," said Fern gloomily. "So, that should be fun. She never wanted my parents to adopt me in the first place, which she brings up every chance she gets."

"That sucks, man," I said. Having had plenty of family issues of my own, I could relate.

"It's fine," said Fern, shrugging. "I just pretend I don't speak English. It drives her crazy."

"What about you, Oliver?" Emma asked.

"I think my dad and I are going to do a big traditional Thanksgiving dinner," I said, knowing that we would do no such thing. Dad had been home a week before, but I hadn't seen him. His passing was marked by a few empty beer cans in the sink and an envelope of money on the kitchen table with a note that said, "For food, not hookers."

"That'll be nice," she said.

"What about you?" I asked.

"Simmy and I are going to rent a bunch of old movies and spend the weekend in our pajamas eating junk food," she said.

"Can I come over?" pleaded Fern, hanging on Emma's arm and almost pulling her to the ground.

"No," said Emma, slapping him away. "Girls only."

We parted ways and I spent the holiday reading and listening to music. On Friday morning, the day after Thanksgiving, I stepped out of my bedroom and Maggie was at the end of the hall, watching me from around her door frame.

"We're waiting," she said.

"For what?" I asked. My voice was barely a whisper, but I didn't doubt that she could hear me.

Maggie watched me for a moment longer before sliding back into her room and shutting her door. I waited a few moments before going down to the kitchen for breakfast. No matter how many encounters I had with her, my legs always shook afterward.

As I spooned cereal into my mouth, I wondered what it was Maggie was waiting for. Obviously she was waiting for me to do something, otherwise, why tell me? And if I was supposed to do something, then what? Why couldn't she just come out and tell me?

That had never been Maggie's style. She never asked outright if she could get what she wanted any other way. I guess she thought that asking for help was a form of weakness. Better to manipulate someone into doing what you want instead of appearing weak.

Was this the same thing? Was she trying to manipulate me? Was she afraid of appearing weak? Death must really suck if you still have to deal with that kind of self-doubt.

Once I had cleaned up breakfast I took a notebook out of my backpack and curled up on the couch, making a list of all of the cryptic messages Maggie had brought me.

I still have that list. At the very top, in big letters, it says, "The Maggie List." This is what I wrote:

"The first time I saw Maggie was in Traverse City. In the shadows at the hardware. Pretty sure I thought I was losing my mind at that point and didn't think much of it. Later, she wrote on the bathroom mirror, 'he's still angry.'

"The next time was when I tried to get Ray's radio. I opened her door. She was hiding around the corner. Not even sure this counts, because she didn't come to me.

"When I went back for the radio and the Cutlass revved up and I asked her if Ray does that a lot, all she said was, 'sometimes'. I told her that he couldn't hurt us anymore, but she didn't say anything. She made it really obvious that she wasn't saying anything. Almost like she WAS saying something. Maybe? Maybe not.

"She told Emma, 'We need him and he needs you,' but we don't know what that means.

"Day after Thanksgiving, saw me in the hallway and said, 'We're waiting,' didn't say for what, though."

I put the Maggie List aside and spent the rest of the morning reading.

At some point, either that day or the next, I noticed something new written at the very bottom of the page, something I had not written: "That wasn't the first time you saw her, dumbass."

-TWENTY-TWO-
ghost chores
-(November, 1993)-

The thought that Reagan might have been in the house filled me with all sorts of anxiety. I had believed that he was trapped where he was. What were the rules here? Where could he go? Maggie had made it all the way to Traverse City. What was stopping Reagan from leaving the corn crib?

Apparently nothing, judging by the note he'd left at the bottom of the Maggie List.

And he was right. Traverse City wasn't the first time I saw her. I had seen her the night Reagan had died. She was standing in my bedroom window, watching. I saw her in the wing mirror.

But even before that, the day she died, when I saw her lying at the bottom of the stairs. I thought I had imagined it at the time, but didn't I see her wink at me?

Was she manipulating me, even then? Was it such a part of who she was that, even in death, she couldn't escape the impulse?

If that were the case, what was it she needed so desperately but couldn't outright ask for? I didn't know, but I needed to figure it out before Reagan got much bolder. The idea of him leaving me passive-aggressive notes was unsettling enough. I didn't know what I would do if I woke one morning to find him standing over me.

"Okay," said Fern, looking over the Maggie List, "they want you to do something, but what?" We were, of course, at the lunch table, where all of our important conversations happened.

"Not 'want,'" said Emma, tapping the page. "'Need'. They need him to do something. And he needs us. That's what Maggie said."

"She didn't actually say they needed me to do anything," I said grimly. "She just said they needed me."

"They need you...what? Dead? To complete the collection?" asked Fern. "Or maybe they need your blood to open a portal into the afterlife."

"Please stop talking, Fern," I said, rubbing my eyes.

"I doubt it's anything like that," said Emma. "It sounds more like there's a task that needs to be done, something they can't do."

"Your dead sister is giving you a to-do list," said Fern. "Ghost chores."

"I can't deal with this right now," I said, putting my head down on the table.

"Why not?" asked Fern incredulously. "You got a lot of backlogged requests from other ghosts? Is your ghost inbox too full? The ghost-boss breathing down your neck? You're not exactly breaking your back with school work. What's got you so busy?"

I sighed deeply, still face-down on the table. "This is just...a lot. Emotionally."

"That's why you need us," said Emma.

"They need me," I said, lifting my head off the table, "and I need you."

"We're not going to let you do this alone," said Emma.

"I'm happy to support you from a distance," said Fern. "Feel free to call and leave a message with my secretary."

"But first things first," said Emma. "Let's get rid of the rest of these tapes."

All of the copies of *Secretly Kings* that we had hidden the previous week were gone, but that didn't stop kids from searching for more. They had no idea how many we'd hidden, only that, according to the numbering on each cassette, there were supposedly one hundred copies.

They searched insatiably. Boys were constantly being chased out of girls' restrooms or the teachers' lounge. Two boys crashed through the ceiling into an eighth grade social studies classroom and were suspended.

A sort of club formed around the search. They started documenting which tapes had been found. Every now and then, one of them would find Fern and ask for leads on hidden tapes, but he denied having anything to do with it.

"It's not me, man," he would say whenever they asked. "I don't give anything away for free, but if you want a copy of *Jewels for Fools*, I've still got plenty for sale."

"Tomorrow night we should stay after school," said Emma. "That way we can unload the rest of these tapes without anyone bothering us."

"Emmaaahhh..." whined Fern. "My only goal every day is to get out of here as quickly as possible. Don't take that away from me."

Emma smiled sweetly as she picked up her tray and left the cafeteria. Fern and I looked at each other, both feeling miserable.

"She's just as manipulative as your dead sister," said Fern, "but she's not as nice about it."

It was one thing to roam the halls in the middle of a school day when the classrooms were full of students. It was quite another thing entirely to be roaming after the students had gone. Teachers still puttered about, going to the teacher's lounge to make photocopies or lingering in their classrooms to plan for the next day or just chatting in the hallways with their coworkers.

Emma was a regular fixture in the school after hours because she waited for Miss Simms to finish for the day, so no one really paid us any mind. We had free reign to hide the rest of the tapes. We had already gotten rid of twenty copies, which left us with a whopping eighty to go.

"Don't spend a ton of time on any single hiding place," Emma said. "But don't make them too obvious, either."

Our backpacks were full of cassettes and we rattled suspiciously with every step. Fern had a roll of packing tape and was sticking cassettes under drinking fountains and behind fire extinguishers. Emma slipped silently into classrooms, depositing four or five cassettes at a time, in and out in under two minutes.

Near the band room was a large display case that was standing wide open. Someone had been in the process of rearranging trophies when they were called away. I slipped five cassettes inside the display case where they would be visible, but inaccessible once the case was locked.

Later, we passed one of the custodians as he pushed a dust broom down the hall. He was wearing headphones but I could still plainly hear Violent Femmes' "Kiss Off." Apparently, *Secretly Kings* appealed to a much wider audience than just junior high boys.

We'd been at it for over an hour. Nearly all of the teachers were gone. Some sort of sports practice had just finished and several students were wandering back through the hall in a straggling line. They looked flushed and sweaty, though they had clearly just come from the showers. They all carried the musky scent of body heat and cold humidity.

"How many tapes do we have left?" Emma asked.

I shook my backpack. "I'm out," I said.

"Me too," said Emma, feeling around in her backpack.

"I have three left," said Fern, handing one each to Emma and I, and keeping the third for himself.

"Uh, oh," I said, looking past Emma and Fern. Mr. Kelly was marching angrily down the hallway toward us. I slipped my cassette into my pocket and Emma and Fern, seeing the urgent look on my face, did the same.

The student athletes scattered as Mr. Kelly pushed past them. His eyes were fixed on us.

"What, exactly, do you think you're doing here at this hour?" he demanded.

"Heyyy, Mr. Kellyyy," said Fern flirtatiously. Emma elbowed him.

"We're writing an article for the school paper," she said. "We've already received permission to be here." We'd gotten an awful lot of mileage out of that excuse.

"Oh!" said Mr. Kelly, not believing a word of it. "And what, pray tell, is this supposed article about, may I ask?"

Fern leaned toward Mr. Kelly. "You smell nice," he whispered. Mr. Kelly gave him a sharp look of alarm.

Behind Mr. Kelly, the student athletes were all entering a single classroom, welcomed at the door by Julie Birdly, the President of the Fellowship of Christian Athletes. She wasn't an athlete herself, but she couldn't stand the thought of a student Christian organization being run by anyone but herself. Her father was, after all, an ordained minister.

"We're doing an article on the FCA," I said.

Mr Kelly, looked taken aback. "The FCA?" Fortunately, he didn't notice the similar looks of surprise from Emma and Fern.

"They're having a meeting tonight," I said, pointing up the hall. "They have to wait until practice is over, so the meetings always start a little bit later."

Mr. Kelly, trying not to turn his back on Fern who kept leaning closer, shot a glance up the hall. The last few students were lined up at the door, Julie Birdly smiling her wide, fake smile.

Fern reached out a hand to stroke Mr. Kelly's arm, but Emma slapped it away.

"They're going to start without us if we don't hurry," she said, tugging Fern away and motioning for me to follow.

"Have a terrific evening, Mr. Kelly," I said, walking past him.

I was about fifteen feet past him when he called out to me. "You look just like your brother, you know," he said, disdainfully. "And you have the same bad attitude."

I turned back to him and said, "Have you seen Ray lately, Mr. Kelly? Because I have, and I can tell you, he looks way worse than I do. But as for my attitude..." I shrugged. "Some people bring out the best in me, some people don't."

-TWENTY-THREE-
nice things
-(November 30, 1993)-

Every Tuesday after school, the Fellowship of Christian Athletes met in Mr. Kurtz's classroom. The meetings were led by Julie Birdly while Mr. Kurtz graded papers or napped at his desk. As far as I knew, no one went to FCA meetings because they wanted to, but because someone would think poorly of them if they didn't, or, on rare occasions, because they were pretending to write an article to avoid getting in trouble.

"I'm going to murder you," Fern whispered to me as we entered the room.

"I might help," Emma murmured, "but let's do this first."

About twenty desks had been arranged in a circle. Julie Birdly positioned herself in the center, so she could better lead the meeting.

A brief word about Julie Birdly...

I knew Julie from my fifth period Biology class where she constantly argued with Mr. Reynolds whenever he mentioned anything about the Big Bang theory or evolution or about the Earth being billions of years old. Thanks to Julie, we heard as much about the first chapter of Genesis as we did about science.

Any time there was a political issue or a moral question or, really, any conversation at all within earshot, Julie Birdly chimed in forcefully with her stance on the matter. She was louder than anyone else and often steered the debate toward unrelated topics in which she was more well-versed, so even when her arguments made no sense, she won. She was a Maggie-level manipulator.

And, that night, we had the pleasure of spending forty-five minutes listening to her preach.

Julie opened the meeting with an impromptu prayer, which she read off of a notecard pulled surreptitiously from her pocket. She then passed around sheets of paper with song lyrics and led the group in a couple of hymns. Fern folded his lyric sheet into an origami frog and made it hop across his desk. Julie pretended not to notice. When she collected the sheets and Fern proudly presented his frog, she forced a smile but made no comment.

Two boys stood and passed out Bibles. They had a whole box of them and everyone got one. I flipped through mine and saw that most of it had been underlined.

"Please turn to John 13:34," she said. "We're going to be talking about love today."

The last time I was in church, Reagan was still alive, so I was surprised to discover that I actually remembered where the book of John was. It only took me a moment to find the verse Julie had indicated. Emma was only a moment or two behind me. Fern was thumbing through the old testament, looking for who-knows-what.

Julie asked for a volunteer to read the verse out loud. Everyone awkwardly avoided eye-contact and, when no one came forward, she called on a scrawny kid who looked like he was trying to melt into his chair. I recognized him as Julie's younger brother, Lewis. He whimpered feebly and started to read, but we could barely hear him.

"Louder, Lewis," Julie said.

"'A new commandment I...'" he read, still quietly, but we could hear him well enough to follow along.

"LEWIS! LOUDER!" Julie tugged Lewis to his feet. "Stand up on your chair so we can all hear you."

The poor kid was beet red. He stepped up onto his chair and almost dropped his Bible, so Julie sighed heavily and held it up for him. He was completely humiliated and I was growing angry on his behalf. It was the kind of thing Reagan would have done.

While I'm sure Julie Birdly had some lovely traits, manipulation and bullying were the ones she chose to present to the world while claiming to be the herald of Christ's love. I really hated her.

"'A new commandment I give you,'" Lewis read.

"You already read that part," Julie snapped. "Get down. I'll do it."

"'A new commandment I give you,'" she said sweetly, "'As I have loved you, so you must love one another.' Now, let's talk about what that means."

The verse was, as I understood it, a very straightforward statement, but Julie's interpretation was...interesting. She suggested that there were certain people who had already moved past a point of lovability and were "in a season of intervention," as she put it. These included, but were not limited to: atheists, alcoholics, homosexuals, and the foul-mouthed. She glanced pointedly at Fern and I when she made this point.

Those were literally the four examples she gave. I heard Fern whisper, almost to himself, "Three out of four. Damn. Not bad." I glanced at him and we tried very hard to not burst out laughing.

"Jesus wants us to love those who are still open to receive His love," Julie said. "The Bible warns us against throwing our pearls to swine. Let us not be wasteful with the gift of love God has given us. We need to share His love with others who can appreciate how pure and wholesome God's word is."

Emma raised her hand. This was apparently not something that happened often in FCA meetings and Julie looked alarmed.

"God's word is pure and wholesome," Emma said. "You want others to see how nice it is so they'll stop drinking alcohol and being gay and murdering and all of those other horrible things that nonbelievers do." There was not a single drop of sarcasm in her voice. Even I believed that she was just asking for clarification.

Julie smiled at her. "Yes," she said. "Once people know how *nice* God's word is, they won't feel the need to sin."

Emma returned Julie's smile and leaned back in her chair.

"I want us, now, to go around the room and share ways that we can show love to others." Julie went from student to student listening to their suggestions, all of which were fine. Most of them were unoriginal, but they were fine. Some of the suggestions Julie actually corrected, as if there was a wrong way to love someone. She skipped over her brother Lewis completely, giving him a look of deep disgust as she did so.

As I watched her walk around the room spreading her false idea of what she called "love," I grew angrier and angrier. These kids actually believed her when she suggested that some people didn't deserve love. She was lying to them and she was using the Bible to do it. I may not have been a big advocate for the Bible at the time, but she was trying to amputate the best parts of it and that infuriated me.

When Julie made her way around to Fern, he was flipping through the old testament. "How about you?" Julie asked, hesitantly. "Can you give us an example of how to love others?"

"Well," Fern said, looking a little lost, "there's a story in the old testament, a really *nice* story about love, but I can't find it."

"Can you tell us what it's about?" asked Julie.

"It's about Lot and his daughters," said Fern, and Julie turned very red. A few other kids in the room snickered. If you're not familiar with the story, don't feel bad. It's not one they usually share with the kids in Sunday school.

Julie turned to me. She didn't even try to disguise her disapproval as she glared at my hair. "You?" she said briskly.

"There's a quote that I think sums up Jesus's views on love very succinctly," I said. "'A purpose of human life, no matter who is controlling it, is to love whoever is around to be loved.'"

Julie thought about this, decided it wasn't strictly offensive, and said, "That's awfully close to the mark," she said. "Who said that?"

"Kurt Vonnegut," I said. "He was a foul-mouthed, alcoholic, atheist and he had a much better grasp on what Jesus meant by 'love others' than you do."

Julie's face turned an even deeper shade of red. She was especially splotchy around the cheeks. She pressed her lips together and looked at Emma to whom she merely nodded.

"I was just thinking about what you said about the Bible being...pure and wholesome," Emma said slowly. "And I'm...I'm confused about a few things."

"Go on," said Julie, hope returning to her tone. Correcting misunderstandings was familiar ground, a place where she could regain control of the meeting.

"Well, you said we wouldn't feel the need to swear once we knew more about the Bible," Emma said, flipping from page to page. "But here I see a lot of not-nice words...'hell'... and 'damn'..."

"Okay," Julie said hastily, "I see what you're..."

"...and 'ass',..."

"THAT'S ENOUGH!" Julie shouted and the whole room fell deeply silent.

Emma locked eyes with her and said dryly, "... and 'whore.'"

Julie ended the meeting shortly after that. Before we left, I dropped my last copy of *Secretly Kings* into Lewis Birdly's backpack.

-TWENTY-FOUR-

a swear

-(December, 1993)-

We had hidden all of the tapes. Our part of the game was done. The only thing left to do was to sit back and watch the search grow more and more chaotic. It had been a lot of work, and it was to no one's benefit, really, but there was something very fulfilling, in a puckish sort of way, about creating this harmless thing that would aggravate Dr. Jeffries and the uptight parents who held him hostage with their moralistic demands.

It was childish, we knew that, but we were children. So often children are told, simultaneously, to grow up and to act their age. Those are pretty confusing instructions. No wonder so many kids feel confused and anxious all the time. No matter what they do, they're wrong.

"Grow up and act your age," is terrible advice for anyone. And if you're already grown up, don't be afraid to backslide a little. I say, be a child always. Be a child of such magnitude that the miserable, stuffed-shirt abominations calling themselves "grown-ups" have no recourse. Their insults can't hurt you and their powerlessness will eat them like a cancer. Research will be done, textbooks will be written, and new fields of psychology will emerge because of your monumental childishness. The system loves to solve problems, so give the system some problems to solve.

"Why can't she just tell you what she needs?" asked Fern at lunch two days after the FCA meeting. While students searched for cassettes all around us, we were once again focused on the Maggie List.

"That's not how girls work," said Emma. "We like to be mysterious."

"And that's why I prefer guys," said Fern. "True, they smell worse, but they're also less complicated. I never have to guess what they want."

"Unfortunately," I said, "none of them want you." Fern threw a half-eaten dinner roll at me.

"Maybe we don't need Maggie to tell us," said Emma, sitting forward in her chair. "If she's anything like you describe, Oliver, she's probably having more fun stringing us along."

"Yeah," I agreed. "That would be something she would do. Even if she desperately needed our help, she would drag it out just to drive us crazy. She can't be too eager to give up what little bit of power she has."

"We just need to make it less fun for her," said Emma. "We need to act like we don't care, like we're not interested."

Fern scoffed loudly. "Are you honestly suggesting that we play hard-to-get?" he asked. "That's not going to work with someone like her. She holds all the cards and she knows it. She's so much better at this than we are. 'What little bit of power...'? That's a joke! She has ALL the power! We can't do anything to ruin her fun."

"No," said Emma, "but Reagan can."

I immediately broke out in a cold sweat. "You don't want to do that," I said in a low voice. "You don't want to get him involved."

Fern reached across the lunch table and picked up the Maggie List, pointing at the bottom line. "I think he already is, Oliver."

That Friday afternoon, Emma and Fern came over to my house after school. We stood huddled in the yard next to the corn crib, no one talking much. It was early December and, though there was no snow yet, everything on the ground felt crunchy and our breath came out in puffs. Emma and Fern were wearing hats and gloves and heavy coats. I had on my regular blue jeans and high tops. My own winter coat had gone missing somewhere between Traverse City and Gladden, so I was wearing a green, military-issue coat I found in the closet by the front door. Judging by the decades-old pack of cigarettes I found in the pocket, it had once belonged to my father. It smelled terrible.

I moved forward and lifted the bolt holding the narrow side-door closed.

"Oliver?" said Fern in a higher-than-normal voice. "I think you were right. I don't know if this was a good idea."

"Too late," I said, opening the door. The hinges were stiff with rust and cold, but they didn't make a sound. We had all brought flashlights, good ones this time, and I raised mine, casting a dull yellow light into the storage area.

"Ray?" I called. My voice sounded strong, much to my surprise. "Ray, we need to talk."

I heard a very low, very raspy chuckle coming from beyond the storage area wall. He was in the center bay with the Cutlass. I moved forward cautiously.

"Oliver!" said Emma in a harsh whisper. "Don't!"

The chuckle stopped abruptly. "Ollie...did you bring a friend?"

"Listen, Ray..." I said, noticing that my voice was starting to shake.

A pair of gleaming eyes appeared in the gap between two of the boards. He was looking past me at Emma and Fern. "Oohhhh...Ollie brought me some friends..." The chuckling resumed.

"Oh, my god..." I heard Fern whimper.

"We have a couple of questions," I tried again, my voice shaking more.

"Bring them closer, Ollie," he said. "I wanna see them better."

"Ignore them, Ray," I said. I was pleading.

"Let me smell them," he said eagerly. "Just a little..."

"Stop it, Ray," I said. I was getting angry.

"I'll start with the little one," he said. "She won't last long. But the other one...I'll take my time..."

Ray started scratching and clawing at the boards that separated us. His fingers, bloody and split, poked through the gaps, yanking on the flimsy planks.

"BRING THEM HERE, OLLIE!" he demanded, straining against the boards. "BRING THEM TO ME!"

"Ray! Stop it!" I begged, but my voice was feeble compared to his. I was six years old again.

"BRING THEM! BRING THEM! BRING THEM!" His voice was ravenous. "I WANT THEM, OLLIE! I WANT THEM!"

I looked behind me and Emma was holding her head in her hands, shaking it back and forth, her mouth opened in a silent scream. Fern tried to hold her, but she broke loose and fell to her knees. I shouldn't have brought them here. I was asking too much.

Why were we like this? Why couldn't we have been a normal family? Even just a little bit normal? Mom and Dad could have just gotten divorced. Ray could have gone with Dad, Maggie could have gone with Mom, and I could have dissolved into nothing. Instead, I was here while my dead brother tormented my only friends in the whole world. I felt utterly helpless and stupid.

I was suddenly angry at the unfairness of it all and something inside of me snapped.

"SHUT UP, RAY!" I shouted. "JUST SHUT YOUR MOUTH FOR ONE SECOND! WE'RE TRYING TO HELP, ASSHOLE!"

There it was. I'd said a swear.

There was an echoing silence across the yard. It only lasted a moment.

"Oh, Ollie. Now you want to help me?" crooned Reagan. "Trying to clean up your mess? You and Maggie think you can put a pretty little bow on this whole thing, but you can't. You can't ever fix this. You wanna come in here and scoop my guts back into my body? You wanna put a bandy on it and have Mommy kiss it all better?"

Ray's boney fists slammed into the wall. I jumped. Emma and Fern both cried out. Dust flew off of the boards, swirling through the storage room.

"Ray..."

I thought I'd seen Ray unhinged. I was wrong.

"YOU CAN'T FIX ME, OLLIE!"

SLAM! More dust. A board rattled.

"IT'S DONE! IT'S DONE FOREVER!"

SLAM! More dust and the board came loose on one end. A second board above it started to break free.

SLAM! The first board fell completely. The second was swinging by a single nail.

SLAM! SLAM! SLAM!

The Cutlass came to life, revving in time to Reagan's pounding. The second board fell.

SLAM! SLAM! SLAM! REV! REV! REV!

The pounding increased to a rapid staccato and the Cutlass was screaming now. Boards continued to rattle loose and I could see through the wall in several places. Through the dust, Ray was staring at me, not grinning, not bloodthirsty, but almost...sad. That was an emotion I had never considered him capable of.

"Ray?" I asked, uncertainly.

Hands grabbed me from behind and pulled me back. I had been walking toward my brother without even realizing it, drawn in like a moth, moving in a near dream-state. Fern threw me down onto the cold dirt and slammed the door shut, dropping the bolt in place.

I got to my feet and Fern and I hurried back across the yard, pulling Emma up off her knees as we passed. The Cutlass was still revving and Ray was still pounding, but without any real conviction. It was a tired dinner theater production, the same play every night, year after year. No one really believes in the story anymore and no one really wants to be there, but it's a job.

The three of us took refuge on the porch. Fern collapsed to the floor in a heap, whimpering to himself. Emma stood shivering next to me at the porch railing, tears shining on her cheeks, her bottom lip quivering. We stared at the corn crib until the revving and pounding died down completely.

"You were right, Oliver," Emma said sniffily. "We shouldn't have gotten him involved. That was too close."

"Are you okay?" I asked, not sure if I should put my arm around her or what. Physical touch has always made me uncomfortable, but I know it helps some people feel safe.

"You kinda fell apart back there," said Fern. "I've never seen you like that."

Emma didn't look at either of us. She just tugged at the sleeves of her cardigan, stretching them over her hands. "My dad...Before he..." She took a deep, steadying breath. "I don't like when people yell. I don't...I'm not going to talk about it. I'm fine, though." She wasn't fine, but she needed us to act like she was, so we did. Sometimes that's all people need, is a chance to act like things are fine.

"What a disaster," moaned Fern. He was still sprawled out on the floor of the porch.

"We got what we wanted, though," I said. "We know what they want from us."

"WHAT?!" blurted Fern. "We know nothing, Oliver! Well, we know that your brother wants Emma and I for...snacks...or playthings...or God only knows what. That was a complete waste of a heart attack!"

"Didn't you hear him?" I asked, not taking my eyes off the corn crib. "He said that Maggie thinks we can 'put a pretty little bow' on all of this."

"What does that mean?" asked Emma.

"It means that we're not done," I said. "Ray killed Maggie, but she's still here. I killed Ray, but he's still here. We both need to finish what we started."

"How?" asked Emma. "What's left to do?"

"I don't know," I said. "I've only ever killed one person before, and apparently I didn't do a very good job. But at least we know what to look for."

"This is so unfair," whined Fern as he sat upright. "Can we go back in time to when the gay Vietnamese kid was the weird one? Why do you white people have to take everything away from us minorities?"

"I'm so sorry, Fernando," said Emma, squatting down and hugging him. "We'll get rid of these ghosts and then you can go right back to being the weird one in the group."

Sniffling, Fern said, "I'd really like that."

-TWENTY-FIVE-
a rather abrasive summation
-(December, 1993)-

Now that the *Secretly Kings* project was out of our hands, we could focus all of our energies on finding a solution to my ghost problem. That was the plan, anyway. Dr. Jeffries had other ideas.

Apparently, some of the more precocious lads who had found copies of *Secretly Kings* had really embraced the punk rock ideals of anarchy and chaos. Several of them had taken it upon themselves to decorate the towns of Leopold and Gladden with graffiti, much of which included lyrics from songs I had put on the mixtape. As long as the graffiti was not on school property, Dr. Jeffries felt no obligation to involve himself, but that didn't last long.

On Monday, December 6, 1993, the buses pulled into the lot at the back of Leopold Jr./Sr. HIgh School. In five-foot tall letters, someone had painted a rather abrasive summation of what they thought of Dr. Jeffries. I will not reprint said message here, suffice it to say that it explored a level of obscenity that even Fern found excessive.

Three rows of perfectly spaced letters, reaching from the roofline all the way down to the sidewalk. I still don't know how they did it. Scaffolding? Repelling equipment? Had they rented a scissor lift? They had one weekend to complete the job, but it took several weeks to clean it up and, even then, the letters were still faintly visible if you knew what you were looking for. It became something of a school legend.

Dr. Jeffries was not amused, but he was sure that I'd had something to do with it.

"Mr. Barrow, have a seat," he said. His tone was blunt. "I have every reason to expel you. You can't deny that you had something to do with the graffiti on the gym."

I didn't even try to maintain a somber attitude. "I honestly had to ask Fern what some of those words meant, Dr. Jeffries. Whoever did it has a much more interesting vocabulary than I do."

He whipped his glasses off and dropped them on his desk. "The police are searching your house as we speak."

This caught me very much by surprise. "The police..." I said. The look on Dr. Jeffries's face was smug, to say the least.

"Yes, Mr. Barrow, the police," he folded his arms across his chest and leaned back in his chair. "Would you like to tell me what happened or would you like to tell the police?"

"Dr. Jeffries," I said, trying not to smile too widely, "I had nothing to do with the vandalism. The police aren't going to find anything in that house to connect me with it."

"This is not a game, Mr. Barrow," said Dr. Jeffries sternly. "You are in very serious trouble!"

"I didn't do anything," I said, openly laughing now. "You and the police are wasting your time."

"But I'll wager you know more about it than you're admitting," he said.

"You wanna know what I think?" I asked, growing very serious. "I think you've wasted your time demanding the respect of your students. You treat us like we're the most irritating part of your job instead of the best part of it. And, believe it or not, you're the biggest part of the problem that you're facing right now. You want the students of Leopold to be altruistic and charitable, but no one is showing us how. You tell us how you want us to act, and then condemn us for following the contrary example you set. These vandals, whoever they are, know what the problem is, and it's not them.

"You want us to learn to be part of a community, Dr. Jeffries, but you turn us against each other. You separate us into groups and tell us that the group that fits in is good while the group who gets bad grades or can't play sports is bad, and then you wonder why we're so combative. In your mind, if a person doesn't fit into the common standard, they are deviant and, therefore, guilty.

"Of course we're combative! We're combative because you're telling lies about us and everyone believes you. You treat us like criminals, so no one else gives us a chance. We're frustrated and anxious and afraid and the people who are supposed to help us are pushing us down further.

"You've got a bunch of hurt and frightened kids on your hands, and they're tired of being left alone to figure things out for themselves. You need to start caring about them or you're going to lose them, and when they go, they're going to take you down with them."

I left Dr. Jeffries's office without waiting for a reply.

By nature, I'm a very non-confrontational person, but there's something about people in authority who use their positions to abuse, belittle, or betray the trust of others that really sets me off. I'm at my most eloquent when someone is trying to defend or uphold injustice. Maybe I should have become a lawyer.

When I got off the bus that afternoon, I stood at the end of my driveway for a moment. It was starting to snow, just a little, and I pulled my musty, green army coat closer around me. I could feel the air thicken as I walked up the long driveway. It might have been my imagination, knowing that the police had been here, searching the house, but there was something strange about the place. Stranger than usual, I mean.

The police had not been gentle entering the house. The front door was quite literally hanging by a single hinge and the frame was in splinters. Every drawer had been pulled out and emptied onto the floor. The contents of every cabinet had been strewn about. It looked more like a robbery than a police search.

My first real suspicions that the search might not have been officially sanctioned by the police were triggered when I noticed that about a third of Dad's beer was gone from the fridge. I now suspect that the "police" who had trashed my house were local business owners and school board members whose property had been vandalized, like a last-minute posse in a Saturday-afternoon western.

I walked from room to room, utterly speechless, furious with the damage they had done. I can't imagine what they thought they would find, but they left nothing undisturbed. Even Maggie's and Reagan's rooms had been searched.

I took time to put my room back together, putting my mattress back in place, putting my sheets in the washing machine as they were covered in muddy boot prints. My bookshelf had been unceremoniously tipped over and all of my tapes had been dumped on the floor, scattered throughout the room as the individuals searching my home took no notice of them. Several had been stepped on, crushed underfoot. It took me a couple of hours to put my room back in order.

Once my room was settled, I checked Maggie's and Reagan's bedrooms. I wasn't worried about violating their personal space anymore. That had already been done. The mirror above Maggie's vanity had been knocked to the floor and lay in a glistening pile. Her dresser had been emptied and her mattress overturned. Then I checked Reagan's room. The Black Sabbath poster had been torn down and ripped in half. All of his clothes had been pulled out of the closet and piled up on the floor. The mattress was leaning crookedly against one wall. Someone had clearly gotten carried away.

I leaned against Reagan's door frame feeling helpless. This was all so unjust. I hadn't done anything wrong, but at Dr. Jeffries's accusation, a bunch of strangers came into my house and did their best to destroy everything. I was pretty sure that I would not be able to get over this offense for a long time.

I was right. I'm still working on it.

When I got home from school the next day, I swept up the broken mirror in Maggie's room and collected the fallen pictures. I found some wood glue and fixed a drawer that had broken during the search. I did everything I could to return her room to its former state. I made especially sure to put the rocking chair back in the carpet grooves.

I spent Wednesday afternoon cleaning Reagan's room. I washed his sheets and all of his clothes. I did my best to tape his poster back together and return it to its proper place. I vacuumed and dusted and even scrubbed his walls. It made quite a difference.

It was well past midnight by the time I was done. I had taken Reagan's bedsheets out of the dryer and was just putting them back on his bed when I heard an engine rev outside. The Cutlass.

My heart sped up. I had completely forgotten about the corn crib. Had they gone in there? I ran to my room and looked out the window.

The sodium arc light next to the corn crib cast the yard in an eerie, dim glow, but I could see clearly enough. The red doors had been pushed to either side. The chain had been cut and lay forgotten on the ground. Inside the darkness of the corn crib, I could just make out the rear end of the Cutlass, its brake lights flickering feebly.

"This isn't good." Maggie was standing in my doorway.

I turned to look at her. She looked frightened, but I wasn't buying it. "What do you want from me, Maggie?" I asked. "Stop playing games and tell me. I know you want me to...to finish all of this, whatever that means. I'm not smart enough to figure it out on my own, so you can either tell me, or..."

She actually smiled at me. It wasn't a malicious smile, but it also wasn't a nice smile. There was mischief behind it. She wasn't done playing with me yet. "Or what?" she asked.

"Or I'll leave," I said. "There's nothing here for me anymore, Maggie. Nothing I can't find someplace else. So you can either tell me what you want or you can wait for someone else to come along who's willing to solve your riddles."

"Daddy will come," she said with a shrug.

I laughed. "Dad's afraid to come home to his one living child and he won't even acknowledge the noises that come from the corn crib. How much attention do you think he'll spare for the silent ghost of the little girl upstairs?"

Her smile fell and she looked like she might yell. Instead, she disappeared down the hall and I heard her door slam.

Let her chew on that for a while, I thought, turning back to the window. Reagan was down there somewhere. He could come and go as he pleased, he had always been able to. He proved that when he wrote me his little note. What held him back? Surely not the chain. That was just a lie Dad told to himself so he could keep pretending things were normal.

I went back to Reagan's room and finished making his bed, looking around for anything I had missed. I had moved his nightstand when I vacuumed and I just now realized that it was crooked. I nudged it with my knee to move it straight, but nearly tipped it over in the process. As it tilted forward, the drawer slid out and I caught it just before it crashed to the floor.

I was struggling to fit it back in place when I noticed what lay at the bottom of the drawer. Beneath a layer of bottle caps and cigarette lighters and receipts and movie ticket stubs was a photograph of the three of us, Reagan, Maggie, and me. I must have been about two or three years old. Reagan was holding me in his lap with Maggie sitting next to him. He was reading to us. I was looking up at him with such awe and love. I don't ever remember feeling that way about him.

Reagan had kept this photo in his nightstand all these years. It was a memory of a time when Maggie and I had loved him and had looked up to him. He was our protector and our big brother. Once upon a time...

-TWENTY-SIX-
the Gladden antique store
-(December, 1993)-

"Simmy says you can come stay with us," said Emma in journalism the next day. "I told her about what the police did to your house. She's really mad at Dr. Jeffries." I hadn't told her my theory that the police hadn't actually been involved at all.

"It's not that bad," I lied. "I was able to fix the front door." I had fitted it back in place and nailed it shut. Dad would probably have a fit when he came home, though.

"It's an open invitation," she said.

"Thanks," I replied. "Tell her I really appreciate it."

We were approaching the end of our first semester and Miss Levine had handed back our very first assignment, the paragraph in which we had described ourselves.

"I want you to revisit this assignment," she said, walking slowly around the room as she spoke. "Some of you may want to simply edit your submissions while others may feel the need to do a complete rewrite. I'm not going to tell you what your submission needs. That's up to you. You will be handing in both the original and the revised, so keep that in mind. I will be doing a side-by-side comparison, so if you can't make it better, leave it alone." As she walked past the back row where Emma and I were sitting, she placed a cassette on my desk.

"What's this?" I asked, picking it up. At first I thought it was a copy of *Secretly Kings*, but it was a nondescript blank tape.

"You dropped it," said Miss Levine.

"No, I didn't," I said, looking up at her. "This isn't mine." She smiled and tapped a small pin on her sweater. It said, "Gabba-Gabba, Hey!" Miss Levine was a Ramones fan?!

"It's definitely yours, Oliver," she said, walking on.

I flipped the case open and pulled out the playlist. It was all Joy Division, Stiff Little Fingers, They Might Be Giants, The Damned, and some guy named Daniel Johnston. I watched Miss Levine as she wandered around the room, talking to the other students in the class. At one point she caught me staring at her and she started to laugh. My confusion must have shown on my face. I put the cassette in my pocket and got to work on my assignment.

I read over my paragraph from the beginning of the year.

"I've never been the type of person comfortable with making decisions. Whenever I do, things go wrong. I find myself far more comfortable in the passenger seat. I'm a follower, some might say a coward. I'm okay with that."

My plan was to change a word or two, maybe rewrite the last line. I wanted to make it look like I'd given it some thought without having to actually do so, which, in retrospect, would probably have been more work than actually making an effort.

But my anger with Dr. Jeffries was still fresh and, at that moment, the original paragraph didn't feel like me. I felt eloquent and righteous.

I clicked my pen a few times and went for a full rewrite. By the time the lunch bell rang, I had my first draft.

"I already have your Christmas present, Emma," said Fern as we sat down at our regular lunch table, "but I'm having trouble figuring out what to get you, Oliver."

"What are you talking about?" I asked. "You're not supposed to...Do NOT get me a Christmas present! Either of you!"

"Oh, I've had yours since the beginning of November," said Emma.

"WHAT?!" This was awful. I hadn't even considered this possibility. Was this the kind of nonsense that went with having friends? I wanted none of it.

I'm not sure why gift-giving fills me with such anxiety. If it's a middle-of-the-week, no-reason-at-all, saw-it-and-thought-of-you gift...Sure. I can do that.

But Christmas? Birthdays? Mother's Day? Those gifts need to be intentional and thoughtful and heartfelt. If you're not careful you can ruin someone's holiday. That's too much pressure.

"Calm down, Oliver," Emma said. "You don't have to get us anything."

"Yes, he does," said Fern, building a french fry log cabin.

"Just write a nice note or something," she said, ignoring Fern. "We know you care. We are your only friends, after all."

"Cash is fine if you don't have time to go shopping," said Fern.

I stared at my tray, unable to eat. I had completely lost my appetite.

When we went back to Journalism after lunch, I tried to put Christmas out of my head and focus on editing my paragraph, but it was difficult with my mind filled with Yuletide anxiety. I ended up turning in the unedited first draft that I wrote before lunch.

And I think, maybe, that it was good. Miss Levine gave me an A-, for what it's worth.

This is what I wrote:

"I used to avoid being the one to make decisions. Whenever I did, things went wrong, but I learned that, regardless of the consequences, I couldn't stay in the passenger seat. I liked being a follower, but the people driving took me to all the wrong places. I may not like being the one behind the wheel, but I've found that I'm far more careful with my life than others have been. And I get to decide who I'll be."

I spent the rest of the day worried about Christmas and didn't pay attention in any of my classes, which was unfortunate because finals were coming up and I needed to review. Kids might do better in school if they felt as strongly about their grades as they do about other, non-academic matters, but to be honest, I don't know that grades should be that important. I think worrying about your friends' Christmas gifts is far more admirable than worrying about your grades. People who focus on caring for others rather than on their own accomplishments are better for the world, in my opinion.

What did they want for Christmas? These were my only two friends in the world, and I had no idea what to get them. Mom and I hadn't really done Christmas. We celebrated with a junk food feast and whatever Christmas movies we found on TV. There was always a stocking for me with a couple of cassettes and novels, but I had never gotten her anything.

I called Emma that night. "Just tell me what I should get you guys for Christmas," I pleaded miserably. "Keep in mind, I don't have much money."

"Oh, lord, Oliver," she said. I could imagine her smiling patiently. "You don't have to get us anything. Like I said, we know you love us."

"Pretend I'm interviewing you for an article," I said, switching to a corny interviewer voice. "What are some of your favorite stores in and around Gladden?"

She sighed heavily before saying, "The antique store is really cool. They have a lot of random, old stuff. Unique things that you can't find anywhere else."

"Awesome," I said, writing it down. "And what about Fern? Any suggestions?"

"He'd probably say something like, 'Bring me the heads of my enemies,'" she said.

"Great idea," I replied, laughing. "Mrs. Pitt's head in a box. Perfect. Thanks, Emma."

"No problem, Oliver."

The antique store was amazing. I couldn't believe I'd never been inside. It was the kind of place only out-of-towners visited. The locals already owned plenty of antiques.

I walked through room after room filled with dusty furniture and tarnished fixtures. Crooked shelves sagged under the weight of ancient books that looked ready to crumble at a single touch. Old cribs and bassinets were filled with odds and ends. Headboards were stacked along the walls. There was a whole wall of old license plates.

I eventually found myself on the second floor in a space only slightly larger than my own bedroom. A yellowing, handwritten sign was tacked above the door. It read, "Every object in this room is part of the history of Gladden. Some were unearthed in the fields while others were found in attics or basements. Each item has a story, some of which remain secret." It gave me chills.

The walls were covered in shelves reaching up to the ceiling. There was no rhyme or reason to the collection. It was poorly curated, poorly cataloged, and utterly fascinating. Most of the objects had little tags with sparse information, like, "This shoe was found in 1986 in the northernmost pasture of the Joseph Grabill farm on Springfield Center Road," or "These glass insulators were discarded in a ditch when the first electric lines were installed across Gladden, ca. 1935."

There were dolls and toy trucks and leather aprons and hammers and rusted metal signs and lunchpails and boxes of nails and photographs and hubcaps and a spent shell casing that, according to the accompanying tag, may or may not have come from John Dillinger or one of his gang. It was an all-inclusive, chaotic whirlwind. I spent an hour in that room alone and didn't see a quarter of what was displayed. I promised myself I'd come back.

Wandering deeper into the antique shop, I discovered a small collection of beautiful keepsake boxes, most were empty, but one was filled with watercolors of wildflowers on small cards. They were lovely, innocent observations, done purely for the artist's own gratification. The box was small, but sturdy, and full of unexpected beauty. It reminded me of Emma. I paid the old man behind the counter eight dollars and carried my prize home like a crusader returning with the Holy Grail. I found several old rolls of Christmas paper in the basement and made quite a meal of wrapping Emma's gift.

I had hoped to find something for Fern at the antique store, but that wasn't really his kind of thing. All during school the next day, I wracked my brain, trying to generate a spark that would lead to the perfect gift, but nothing was forthcoming.

"Any luck on the gift search?" Emma asked at the beginning of fourth period.

"Yeah," I said. "I got your gift last night and I really hope you like it."

"I'm sure it will be amazing," she said. "What about Fern?"

"I'm about to take your advice," I said. "Should we sneak away to the library and see if we can catch Mrs. Pitt by surprise?"

"He'd probably appreciate it," she said, "but he's not worth prison."

In fifth period biology Mr. Reynolds showed us a movie about deep sea life, which was perfect. The lights were out so no one noticed that I was writing in my notebook instead of paying attention. Several kids were sleeping while others passed tightly folded messages back and forth. Compared to them, it just looked like I was taking notes.

Thirty minutes into class, I had made tremendous headway on my list. I had come up with nearly thirty ideas, almost one idea a minute, and eliminated every single one. The page was just one big collection of furiously crossed out suggestions. At the top I wrote in bold letters, "THE HEADS OF HIS ENEMIES!!!"

I sat up and stretched, glancing around the room. I was mildly surprised to see, two rows to my right, Julie Birdly. She, like many other students, was asleep, her head resting on her arms across the top of her desk. I watched her twin braids, trailing down her back, rise and fall slowly as she breathed. It was the deep, satisfied sleep of the self-righteous.

On a whim, I tore the list out of my notebook and got up from my desk, wadding the paper up into a ball. I made my way to the trash can, choosing a path that took me right past Julie's desk. I "accidentally" nudged her elbow as I passed, but she didn't respond. She was out cold.

I threw my paper into the trash can and, as I passed Mr. Reynold's desk, I casually grabbed the scissors protruding from his desktop organizer. Normally, Julie Birdly's best friend, Stacy Huck, sat directly behind Julie, but as soon as the lights were out, Stacy snuck across the room to sit near her boyfriend, Joshy Fritz, leaving her desk conveniently vacant.

Scissors in hand, I quietly slipped into Stacy's seat. Julie's breathing was very deep. I was a little envious. I hadn't slept that well in months. One of the drawbacks of living in a haunted house.

On the screen, an octopus was emitting a cloud of ink to escape from a predator. It was easily the most interesting moment in the video and everyone who wasn't asleep had their eyes locked on the action. By the time I returned to my own seat, the octopus had escaped while Julie Birdly slumbered on.

-TWENTY-SEVEN-
the dream
-(December, 1993)-

The last week of school before Christmas was rough. We had our semester finals which put everyone on edge, students and teachers alike. Emma already knew everything and Fern didn't care about his grades, so he wasn't worried, and normally I would have counted myself amongst that blissfully ignorant number, but I had never experienced finals week. I was blindsided by the intense demands and the heightened tension coming from all sides. It was like climbing into the backseat of a car for a nice ride to the grocery store and realizing, only after it was too late, that you had actually climbed into a tumble dryer.

In the end, I did alright. I wasn't an honor student, but I passed all of my classes. Algebra was a close call, but a D+ is still a pass in my book, and with room to spare.

"When should we exchange gifts?" asked Fern at lunch on Friday.

"Simmy and I want to have you both over for dinner during break," Emma said.

"Okay," I said eagerly. "My week is pretty wide open. Pick a time and I'll be there."

"What do you and your dad have planned?" Emma asked.

I shrugged. "Nothing," I said. "I don't know if he'll be home for Christmas."

"Oliver!" she gasped. "You have to come to my house on Christmas Day! You can't be alone on Christmas!"

"He won't be," said Fern. "He's got...other family."

"Yes, thank you, Fern," I said. "I want to be home in case he shows up. He hasn't had anyone home for Christmas for six years. I don't want him coming home to an empty house if I can help it. I appreciate the offer, though."

"Speaking of...other family," said Emma, "anything new with Maggie and Ray?"

"Not really," I said. "Once the police cut the chain off the corn crib, I thought Ray would become a much bigger problem, but he seems content to stay where he is. Other than when he wrote me that little note, I don't think he's left the corn crib."

"And Maggie?" asked Emma.

"I think I made her angry," I said. "I threatened to leave if she didn't level with me. I haven't heard from her since."

"Have you had any more ideas about what she wants?" asked Fern.

"Well, yes and no," I said. "I found a picture in Ray's nightstand and..." I didn't know how to explain it to them. The picture made me sad because it was a glimpse of a life that was on a trajectory that I never knew. We were on course for happiness, but something happened...or didn't happen...and things changed.

"...I think we were meant for something different," I said. "I think Ray wanted that other life. But if that's what he's hanging around for, it's too late."

Emma and Fern didn't say anything, but stared at me. I felt my face grow warm.

"This is all so strange," said Emma. "I don't really know how to process any of it."

"You?!" cried Fern, slamming his fork down on the table. "I'm an atheist! This means I have to find a whole new theology! My whole religion is ruined for me! You Christians talk about the Holy Spirit all the time and then when an unholy spirit shows up you freak out like you didn't think it was real! I don't believe in souls, but here they are! Refusing to leave! Talk about having trouble processing...Damn, Emma. Thanks for being insensitive..."

We couldn't help but laugh. Even in the midst of existential distress, Fern was funny.

I had a feeling that Emma understood, though, about families not turning out how they were meant to. She never talked about her past, but kids don't end up in foster care because everything went well. The only thing she ever said about her life before Miss Simms was in the way of a prophetic warning.

"There may be a time when I have to...leave," she said. "I can't tell you...I can't tell you where and I won't know when, but if it happens, just know that I'm okay."

Then she laughed at herself and said that she was probably being silly and we carried on like nothing had happened because what other option did we have? How do you address a statement like that except to pretend it's impossible? And it seemed impossible. When you're a kid, all the bad things seem impossible, even while they're happening...

The semester ended and everyone went home feeling so much lighter with finals behind us and Christmas on the horizon. I dug around in the basement near where I had found the wrapping paper and found a mildewed cardboard box with an ugly and battered aluminum Christmas tree. I rearranged the living room and put the tree up near the fireplace. I found our old stockings, too, but I was overcome with a sudden attack of painful nostalgia and, once I had a good cry and was able to pull myself together, I put them back where I'd found them. I was eventually able to locate some old ornaments and decorations that held no painful memories for me and set about making the place seem more festive.

I was wrapping some matted and frayed garland around the stairwell railing when I felt someone watching me. I looked up and saw Maggie standing at the top of the stairs. "He's not coming home, you know," she said. "He never comes home for Christmas."

"I'm not doing this for him," I said. "I'm doing this for us. We're still a family. We still matter."

"Not to him," she said. "Even before, he didn't like me. He didn't like you, either. And now that you're the only one left, he hates you even more."

I smiled up at her. "You ready to tell me what it is you need me to do for you?"

She glared at me, annoyed by my rational calm. "Your hair looks stupid." She stomped down the hallway to her room and slammed the door.

Outside, the Cutlass revved twice in agreement, and was silent.

I slept well that night, like Julie Birdly in fifth period biology. The house was decorated for Christmas, I had a long break from school, and I had plans to meet with my friends the next week. I felt relaxed for the first time in ages. I hadn't slept so well since before Mom had died.

I had a dream...

In my dream, I sat up in bed and stared at Mom's thrift store painting of the London street. The people were moving around, like an oil-based television show. I watched them wandering around, occasionally stopping to chat with one another. They knew each other. They were neighbors. After a few moments of watching, I noticed that one of them, a woman, seemed to be watching me back. It was hard to make out details, but it looked like she was wearing a yellow t-shirt and blue jeans. Everyone else in the painting was dressed in Victorian-era garb, but this person seemed dressed for a rock concert. She started walking up the street toward me and that's when I noticed that she was wearing green tennis shoes.

She walked right up to the frame and stopped. This close, her features were much clearer, but the image still moved and smeared as if the paint was fresh.

"Hi, Mom," I said.

"Hey, kiddo," she said. We stared at each other for a long time.

"I miss you, Mom," I said. "I wish you were here."

"I am here, Ollie. Just in a different way."

Neither of us spoke for a while. Finally I asked, "Mom? Why did you...Why did you poison us? Why did you think we needed to die?"

It took her a long time to answer. "I guess I did it for the same reason I took you away in the first place." She ran a hand through her oil paint hair. "I was afraid I would lose you. I almost took you away after Maggie died. I knew your brother was responsible and it was just a matter of time before he did the same thing to you, but I stayed. I don't know why. Every day, I expected to lose another child. It never occurred to me that it would be Reagan.

"After they saw what you did, they would have put you away in a hospital or in some home for juvenile delinquents," she said, shaking her head and looking down at her hands. "I would have lost all of my children, and what's a mother without her children?"

I watched her for a long time, soaking in her presence. I thought about trying to climb into the painting myself.

"I don't know what to do, Mom," I said, my voice cracking. "Maggie says she needs me, but she won't say why, and Ray...Ray's still so angry. And Dad won't come home. He just stays away. He's gotta be lonely, Mom." I was crying.

"Oliver," she said, "none of this should be your responsibility. Maggie and Reagan need to learn to fix their own problems and your father...Well, your father isn't going to find what he's looking for out there on the road, but he won't come home until he's searched every last mile, and there are so many miles. Your brother and sister are a lot like him in that way."

"I know it's not my responsibility, but sometimes..." I said, but Mom cut me off.

"That's not what I said, Oliver." Her voice was cold. "I said that it shouldn't be your responsibility. It *shouldn't* be, sweetie. But it is."

"What do I do?" I asked. I was weeping now. "How do I help them?" I had moved to the end of the bed and was sitting up on my knees. If someone had walked in right then, it would have looked like I was praying.

"Do you remember when you were little," Mom said, "and you and Maggie would play boardgames and whenever it looked like you were about to win, she would change the rules?"

I laughed, wiping away snot and tears. "And the next time we played, I'd be playing by the new rules and she would change them back again."

"Maggie refuses to lose." She said it with a hard, sharp finality.

"But she did lose," I said. "Ray..."

"She's not playing by those rules anymore, Ollie. The way she sees it, she's still in the game. She still has a chance to win."

"I can't fix it," I pleaded, shaking my head. "I don't understand..."

"You're right, Ollie," she said softly, as she backed away from the frame, "you can't fix this. It's not like that. This isn't about fixing, but about finishing. I know you can do it. I love you, Ollie. I have to go now. I'm so proud of you." She turned away and walked back up the street.

"MOM! DON'T GO!" I jumped off the bed and grabbed the frame of the painting, but as I did, music exploded in the air around me. The whole house shook with it. My teeth rattled and I fell to the floor, pressing my hands over my ears.

The song was unmistakable. "River" by Joni Mitchell. Mom's favorite for as long as I could remember.

I woke up with a shout, my face soaked with tears, my body soaked with sweat. I looked at the picture frame and wasn't surprised to see that it was slightly crooked. The soft voice of Joni Mitchell floated up from downstairs.

I found Dad in the living room, sitting in his ugly green chair, a beer in one hand, wiping tears from his eyes with the other.

"Merry Christmas, Dad," I said softly from the doorway.

"Oh! Hell!" he said, jumping up and turning off the music, hurriedly wiping his eyes with his sleeve. "I didn't mean to wake you, boy. Sorry." He sniffed and a look of alarmed confusion overwhelmed his face as he focused on me. "The hell...? What'd you do to your hair?"

My hand flew to my mohawk. Had it really been that long since we'd spoken face to face? "Oh, this...Well, I needed a haircut."

"You did that yourself?" he asked.

"Dad, are you okay?"

"Probably not," he said, with a dopey guffaw. He took the record off the turntable. "I don't know why, but I've had that song stuck in my head for two days. It was Delores's favorite, you know."

"I know," I said. "She used to sing it all the time. She said it was the only Christmas song she liked."

"I'm sorry I haven't been home," he said. I felt like he meant it.

"Don't apologize," I said, gently taking the record out of his hand. "You've got your life to live. I wasn't part of it for a long time and...things changed. I understand how it is. There's a lot of road out there."

"Yeah, but, uh..." He never finished the thought. Instead, he shrugged and went to the kitchen for another beer.

"How long are you home for, Dad?" I asked as I slid Joni back into her sleeve. It had been one of Mom's most prized possessions. She'd gone to a Joni Mitchell concert and gotten it autographed. Dad had kept it safe all these years. I carefully returned it to the shelf.

"Not long," he said with his head in the fridge. "This time of year pays real good. Most drivers have families, so they need the time off. Busiest time of year, too. And I don't need to run a reefer as long as I stay up north, 'cause it's so damn cold outside, so I save on fuel. I'd be an idiot to pass it up."

Yeah, I thought, *most drivers have families.*

"Hey, Dad, I don't know if you've seen your bedroom yet..." I explained about the people Dr. Jeffries had sent to search the house. Dad seemed unconcerned. He just looked foggily at the front door, saying that he'd fix it when he came home next month.

"They also cut the chain off the corn crib," I told him.

I could literally see him sober up right before my eyes. His bleary eyes cleared and the dopey, lazy look on his face hardened.

"Oh," he said, running his hand over his mouth. "Oh, hell..." He walked past me and looked out the back window to the corn crib. The sodium arc light was casting its unhelpful yellow glow over the yard. It was easy to see that the red corn crib doors were open, but nothing was visible inside.

"It's been pretty quiet since they cut the chain," I said. "You know...nothing weirder than usual, I mean."

Dad nodded and put his half-full beer can on the counter. "I gotta get to bed," he said shakily. "See you in the morning, boy." He patted me on the shoulder as he passed on his way to his bedroom.

By the time I woke up, he was gone.

-TWENTY-EIGHT-
a voice, a chime, a chant sublime
of peace on earth, good-will to men
-(December 22, 1993)-

I packed the Christmas gifts for my friends into my Australian rucksack, turned up the collar of the freshly-laundered military-issue field jacket that I had stolen from Dad, and headed out into the cold. I probably looked like Travis Bickle running errands for Santa Claus.

Emma greeted me at the door when I arrived. "I'm sorry you had to walk," she said. "Simmy's already deep in the eggnog."

"I hear that!" called Miss Simms, laughing heartily from the kitchen.

Fern was in the dining room, decorating a gingerbread man to look like a Ninja Turtle. "Amen, girlfriend!" he shouted, hurrying into the kitchen to join Miss Simms. I heard a slap followed by a pained cry from Fern.

"Stay away from that eggnog, boy!" yelled Miss Simms. "I'm not gonna tell you again!"

Emma took my coat and I put the gifts under the tree.

"I've never been to a Christmas party," I said. "Not really sure what to do."

"It's just us and Simmy," said Emma, leading me into the dining room where dozens of sugar cookies of various shapes were waiting to be decorated. I could see that Fern had made three Ninja Turtles so far. One more to go.

"Are you gonna do Splinter?" I asked.

"I was thinking about doing Bebop and Rocksteady," he said, nursing his slapped hand, "but once I finish Raph, I think I'll switch to Care Bears."

We sat around the dining room table for about an hour decorating cookies and laughing. Fern's were all pop-culture characters, Emma's were beautiful abstract designs, and mine were...awful. Visual art, no matter how I try, has never been my thing. I'm doomed to be an appreciator.

"Don't you worry about the ugly ones, baby," said Miss Simms, patting me on the shoulder. "We'll eat those first. Nobody needs to know." She took a mutant angel and bit off its head.

We cleared away the cookies and set the table for dinner. There was turkey and ham, green bean casserole, sweet potatoes with melted marshmallows on top, dressing, mashed potatoes, deviled eggs, dinner rolls...I have never, ever, in my entire life, experienced such a feast. It is the meal to which I have compared every celebratory meal since, and none has come close.

I began eating with such earnestness that everything around me faded away. At some point I became aware that the conversation had stopped. When I looked up from my plate, everyone was staring at me.

"What?" I said through a mouthful of ham and mashed potatoes.

"This should be a sport," said Fern in awe. "I would pay to watch this."

"Enjoying dinner?" asked Miss Simms with a smirk.

"Oh, God, yes," I said, diving back into the meal.

I went back for seconds of everything, and then thirds. Had Emma not warned me that there was pie, I would have kept eating until I burst.

When we had finally finished eating and cleared the table and washed the dishes, Miss Simms excused herself and started to leave.

"Wait! Miss Simms!" I said, stopping her. "You can't go yet. I have a gift for you!"

"Ugh," mumbled Fern. "Kiss-ass..."

I pulled her gift from beneath the tree. Judging by the size and shape, it was pretty obvious what it was.

"Oh!" she said in a confused but polite voice once she had pulled the paper off. "Joni Mitchell..."

I pointed to the front of the record cover. "See here," I said. "It's autographed. My mother had her sign it at a concert, like, twenty years ago or something. This was Mom's very favorite possession."

Miss Simms's mouth dropped open. "Oh, honey, I can't take this! It's too special!"

"That's why I want you to have it, Miss Simms," I said. "You're not just Emma's foster mom. You've kinda been a mom to all of us."

"Yeah," said Fern, nodding. "That's from all of us."

Tears spilled down Miss Simms's cheeks and she grabbed me in a rib-cracking hug. "This is just about the sweetest gift I've ever received, Oliver Barrow," she said, wiping her eyes with her sleeve. "And it's not just the eggnog making me say that."

She gave hugs all around and then excused herself again, clutching Mom's record to her chest as she went.

"I'll go first," said Emma, handing Fern and me identical packages. I peeled back the paper on my gift, trying to save the paper. The Barrows were always paper-savers, if we could help it. Fern's family was not, judging by the way he had his gift open in three seconds flat.

"Oh, my word," he said, holding up a t-shirt. "I adore this! It's absolutely perfect!" On the front of the shirt was a cartoon drawing of a stormtrooper wearing a full-length ball gown over his armor. He was standing in front of a mirror and the speech bubble above his head said, "Set blasters for 'stunning'!"

I opened my gift and found a black t-shirt with the classic Ramones presidential seal. "Emma!" I gasped. "Where did you find this?"

Emma made a locking gesture over her lips.

"And this is the original line-up!" I said, running my fingertips over Dee-Dee's name. I could have cried.

"Okay!" said Emma, breaking the spell. "I need a gift! Someone love me!"

"On it!" shouted Fern, pulling two large gift bags out from beneath the tree. They were each roughly the same size, but Emma's was relatively light and squishy while mine was heavy and clunky.

We peered into the bags and gasped loudly at the same time. Emma's bag was packed with skeins of yarn and knitting needles of various sizes. Mine was full of paperback books, and I mean full. There must have been two dozen books in there.

"Fernando Hanson!" Emma screamed, plunging her hands into the bag. "These are gorgeous! Ohhh...so soft..." She smashed her whole face down into the bag.

"Just watch out for the needles," said Fern. "'Merry Christmas! You're blind!'"

"Fern?" I asked, pulling out stacks of books. Mercedes Lackey, Eric Frank Russell, Larry Niven, Walter Tevis..."Where did you get all these?"

"There's this used bookstore in town," he said, smiling. "Hyde Bros. Opened last year. It's awesome."

"No, Fern," I said. "You're awesome. Thank you. I love it."

Emma still had her face buried in the yarn. "Thank you, Fern!" she mumbled through the yarn. "I love you so much!"

"Alright, my turn," I said, pulling the gifts out from under the tree. "You first, Emma."

She unwrapped her gift. "Oh, Oliver!" she said when she saw the keepsake box. "It's beautiful!" Then she opened the box and saw the drawings and watercolors. She gasped and pulled them out carefully, looking over each one. I explained how I had found them at the antique store.

"Are you...Are you crying?!" Fern asked.

"It's such a sweet gift," she said as she wiped her eyes. "Someone thought these flowers were beautiful enough to paint and here they are, all these years later. I'm so glad...so glad they didn't get thrown out or forgotten."

"Okay, Fern," I said, nervously. "Now you."

Fern took his gift and hefted it, noting how light it was. "Did you give me an empty box?" he asked, untying the ribbon that held it closed. He flipped the lid open and his jaw dropped.

Emma leaned forward to get a better look. "Oliver...?" she whispered. "What is that?"

"It's not exactly the head of one of his enemies," I said, "but it's as close as I could get."

"Who...?" said Fern, looking up at me, slightly disgusted. "What is this?"

"That braid," I said, "was cut, just as you see it, from the head of Julie Birdly while she slept through a video in my fifth period biology class."

Fern jumped to his feet. "OLIVER! OH! MY! GOD!" He cradled his gift as though he were holding a bar of solid gold. "This is...This is the most beautiful thing I've ever seen..."

"I wondered why she cut her hair," said Emma, thoughtfully. "I wish I could have seen her face when she noticed one of her braids was missing."

"Well, her new haircut looks absolutely hideous," said Fern, gleefully. "Oliver, you are an absolute legend."

"You could have been expelled for that," Emma said, looking at me with horrified wonder.

"I probably could have been arrested," I said. "Who knows? Maybe Jeffries would have had me shot."

"Well, thank you for risking your life on my behalf," said Fern. We all hugged.

"Emma," I said, from inside our weird little huddle. "Do you remember how you introduced yourself to me on the first day of school?"

"Ummm..." I could tell she was thinking hard. "I think I said something about being the most important person in your life, right?"

"It's still true," I said, squeezing harder. "It's true for both of you. I love you guys."

There were a few tears and then Fern said something insensitive and hilarious and we set about cleaning up the wrapping paper before spending the rest of the evening eating cookies and watching *Home Alone*. It was one of the most memorable Christmases I've ever experienced.

-TWENTY-NINE-

merry Christmas, I don't want to fight tonight

-(late December 22, early December 23, 1993)-

As I walked home that night, filled with love, Christmas cheer, and far too much food, I couldn't ignore the nagging sensation that something was wrong. This had been a perfect evening, but for some reason I felt a sense of guilt creeping up on me.

Here I was, having a nice holiday, laughing with my friends, completely ignoring Reagan and Maggie. According to Charles Dickens, Christmas is an important time for ghosts.

"This isn't about fixing, but about finishing." I heard Mom's words in the frigid December air. Like, actually heard them. I stopped dead in the middle of the ball diamond at the Gladden Communist Party (so the sign still proclaimed) and looked around. I was completely alone.

"Not about fixing," I whispered, my breath puffing into the night. "Well, that's good, 'cause I have no idea how to do that."

What about finishing? What did that even mean?

I hoisted my backpack, stuffed my hands in my pockets and hurried home, my mind swirling with too many questions and not enough answers.

As soon as I got home, I took a hot shower to banish the chill, but I still felt brittle. I just couldn't seem to get warm. A mohawk, I reflected, was not the smartest hairstyle for a northern Indiana winter. It provides little to no warmth while preventing you from wearing a hat. After my shower, I found a pair of scissors and a disposable razor and shaved my entire head, only to realize that I didn't have a hat.

The basement was full of random boxes of clothes and toys and old magazines. I could spend a week going through boxes looking for a hat, or I could ask someone who might actually know where to look.

"Hey, Maggie?" I said, knocking on her door.

The rocking chair stopped, but she didn't reply.

"Do you know where all of the wool hats are?" I asked.

The door flew open and banged against the wall. Maggie was sitting in her rocking chair, glaring at me.

"Wool hats?" she said, disdainfully. "What wool hats?"

"We used to have a whole box of hats and scarves and mittens," I said. "Do you know where they are?"

"Oh, those. Of course I know," she said, "but you were rude to me, so I'm not telling." The door slammed in my face.

"Fine," I said. "I'm sure Ray knows. I'll just go ask him."

The door banged open again, but this time Maggie was standing right there, looking up at me.

"Apologize," she demanded.

"For what?"

"For being rude the other night."

"How was I rude?" I asked incredulously. "I was very polite. You were the one who said that Dad hated me and that my hair looked stupid."

She looked up at my freshly shorn head. "It looks even worse now."

"See? Rude!" I said.

"Are you going to apologize?" she asked, crossing her arms.

I took a deep, steadying breath. "I'm sorry if you inferred any insult from my comments," I said, inclining my head toward her.

She squinted at me, not sure if she was being teased. "There might be some hats in the top of the coat closet downstairs," she said.

"Thank you, so much," I said, turning to go. I called over my shoulder as I went. "Christmas is in a few days. We should celebrate, you, me, and Ray."

She didn't say anything, as she watched me walk away, but I could feel the suspicion radiating from her like a heat lamp.

I found the hats, but they all smelled musty and had obviously not been washed or even aired out in years. I chose a few and hand-washed them in the kitchen sink, laying them out on the counter to dry. I chose one of the books Fern had given me and curled up on the couch. After a few minutes, I heard a noise at the doorway. Looking up, I saw Maggie standing there.

"We can't celebrate Christmas with you, Ollie," she said. "We can't do anything with you. That's not how it works. We aren't a family anymore."

"You're all the family I've got, Maggie," I said, setting my book aside. "Dad certainly doesn't think of me as family. He thought I was gone forever and he made peace with that. Me coming back didn't improve his life any. It just..."

"Ruined it," she said.

I thought about this and, as harsh as it sounded, it was true. "Yeah," I said. "I came back and ruined his life. So it's you and Ray or nobody."

"Then it'll have to be nobody, Ollie," she said. "We're not here so you can play house."

"Then why are you here?" I asked. "Why don't you come right out and tell me what it is that's keeping you here? No more games, Maggie. Let's put it all out there."

She shook her head. "I don't know you anymore," she said sadly. "You're not the same Ollie I used to know. We used to play games and tell stories, but now you don't want to play with me. You're mean."

"Knock it off, Maggie!" I stood up from the couch. I was getting angry. "Don't pull that crap with me! All you do is drop hints and ask riddles. I don't play games? EVERYTHING is a game with you!"

"Do you remember the day you died? You were playing games even then. You were playing jacks in the attic, right above Ray's room. You knew he was in pain and trying to rest, but you decided to make it worse for him. You banged on the floor until he couldn't stand it anymore. You always want to play games, Maggie, even when everyone else is tired of it!"

If I had ever doubted that Maggie and Reagan were blood siblings, the look she was giving me at that moment erased it all. She felt nothing but hate and loathing for me for bringing up that most sensitive moment: the end of her life. But I didn't care about that because something clicked in my brain, something that Mom had said.

"*Maggie refuses to lose,*" she told me. "*She's not playing by those rules anymore.*" Reagan had killed Maggie, but she wouldn't give up. She refused to lose. Maybe that was it. Maybe all she wanted was to beat Reagan.

This isn't about fixing, but about finishing. I needed to finish what I started so she could win.

Maggie's door slammed shut upstairs, but I barely noticed. I was too pleased with myself for having figured out...something. I didn't pat myself on the back, though, because I wasn't there yet. I was close, though. So close...

"I hate the thought of you in that house, all alone," Emma said over the phone the next day.

"I'm not alone," I said.

"That's the problem," she replied. "You should come stay with me and Simmy."

"That solves your problem," I said, "but it doesn't solve my problem. You get to feel better since I'm not living in a haunted house, but eventually I have to come back here."

"I know," said Emma, "but we're no closer to figuring this out than we were before. If you could just take a break..."

I hadn't told her about Mom coming to me in a dream or about any of my interactions with Maggie. I felt like I was close to having an answer, but if I was wrong, I didn't want to make a fool of myself by bragging about it beforehand.

"Things have been pretty quiet here lately," I said. "I've just been reading."

"The stuff Fern got you?" she asked. "Anything good?"

"There's some Bradbury I've never read before," I said. "*Dandelion Wine* and *Something Wicked This Way Comes*. I'm reading an old sci-fi novel called *Wasp* right now, but when I'm done, I'll try the Bradbury stuff." She seemed satisfied that I was well and, before hanging up, we made plans to get together for New Year's Eve.

The receiver was still swaying in the cradle when a voice behind me asked, "That your girlfriend?"

I looked slowly over my shoulder. Reagan was standing in the living room. I was in the kitchen. About twelve feet and a kitchen table separated us. "No, Emma's not my girlfriend."

"What's the matter? You gay?" he sneered. "Or is she?"

"No," I said. "Neither of us is gay." I decided to leave Fern out of it.

"Then what's the problem?" he asked, stepping forward. He staggered as though moving against a current.

"Did you really come in here to ask about my love life?"

"You never visit anymore," he said, his voice dropping down to a growl. "I was getting lonely."

For some reason, this act worked better in the corn crib with the swirling dust and the flickering flashlights. It lacked impact when set against our old plaid couch and macrame wall art.

"Really? Lonely?" I said. "You know you're welcome here any time, Ray. This is your house, too."

He sneered and chuckled at me some more, but rather than finding it startling or upsetting, I found it rather sad and pathetic.

"Maggie and I have been discussing Christmas plans," I said.

"Leave me out of this," Maggie said from upstairs. From where I stood, I could just see her feet on the top step.

"I decorated," I said, gesturing at the garland. "I even found an old artificial tree in the basement. It's incredible all the stuff I've come across down there. I should really clean it out. It's probably a fire hazard."

"And we all know how much you love to play with fire, don't we Ollie?" Reagan said, sounding not ominous, but like a boy trying to hold back tears. "I see you still have your scars, too."

I touched the side of my head, feeling the raised flesh there. "What should I have done, Ray?" I asked. "Should I have let you keep beating me? What was your plan with all of that gasoline?"

He had no response. Instead, he backed away toward the end of the living room, turning and walking into the shadows. A few moments later, the Cutlass gave a few feeble revs and fell silent once more.

"You shouldn't provoke him," said Maggie, still standing on the top step. "It's rude."

"It's not the worst thing I've done to him," I said. "He'll get over it."

-THIRTY-
the driving lesson
-(Christmas Eve, 1993)-

Friday, the 24th arrived, and I woke feeling hopeful and enthusiastic, two emotions with which I'd had little experience. I was much more familiar with fatalism. "Let's see what kind of nonsense the world throws at me today..."

I never made plans, because there were too many people intent on getting in my way and those people usually turned out to be smarter and more motivated than me. My plans typically failed, so I got used to stepping into the current of life and letting it carry me wherever it wanted. I figured it out as I went. On Christmas Eve, however, I inexplicably woke up with a plan, and it had a profound effect on my mood. Or maybe I was just really feeling the holiday vibes.

I lay in bed for a while staring at my ceiling and thought, *Is this how other people wake up? Is this how Emma feels all the time? She decides what to do and then...she does it? That doesn't seem safe.*

I finally climbed out of bed and pulled on my new Ramones t-shirt. That information is not relevant to the story, but it's a happy memory, so I wanted to share it.

I looked out my window at the corn crib. The doors were still open and I could see the back end of the Cutlass poking out of the shadows. "Morning, Ray," I whispered. The brake lights flashed at me, which I accepted as a cordial reply.

I walked down the hall and tapped on Maggie's door. "Good morning, Maggie."

"Good morning, Ollie," she replied gloomily.

I went down to the kitchen and made breakfast, feeling oddly optimistic. Like I said, I had a plan. I didn't know if it was a good plan or if I would even walk away from it alive, but it felt nice to have something to do.

After breakfast, I put on my shoes and coat and selected one of the wool hats I had cleaned and pulled it down over my bald head. I grabbed the envelope full of grocery money and stuffed it into an inside pocket of my coat before zipping it up.

It hadn't occurred to me that most of the stores in Gladden would be closed on Christmas Eve. The hardware was dark, as was the antique store, the General Store, the Pharmacy, the Gladden Napa, Crosscut Junction and Dairy Treat, the bank, the picture-framing place, the little tea-shop, and the new-age shop that sold crystals and incense. I walked through town, seeing shop after shop with darkened windows and CLOSED signs in the windows. One shop had a USE OTHER DOOR sign in the window that made me laugh out loud when I saw it.

When I reached the west edge of town I was relieved to discover that not all of the businesses in town were closed. Jim's Sunoco gas station and Eichel's grocery store were open, as was the Cedar Creek Carry Out, because people don't stop drinking just because it's the holidays. In fact, I'm pretty sure that's when some people start drinking.

I went to Eichel's first and stocked up on groceries. Nothing fancy, just my usual essentials. I was always pretty frugal because I never knew when another envelope of grocery money would show up on the kitchen table.

Next, I stopped at Jim's Sunoco and bought a galvanized five-gallon gas can and filled it up, which was a huge mistake. Five gallons of gasoline weighs about thirty pounds. I had to carry the gas can and my groceries all the way back across town with the gas can banging against the side of my leg the whole time. By the time I made it home, my knee was bruised, bleeding, and swollen. I had switched the gas can back and forth from my right side to my left, but I soon realized that I would be better off with one busted up knee than with two.

I left the gas can on the porch and went inside. I put away the groceries and filled up a plastic baggie with ice cubes to hold against my knee. My little excursion had taken about an hour and a half and I was exhausted. I fell asleep on the couch with the bag of ice on my knee and *How the Grinch Stole Christmas* playing on TV.

When I woke up, *It's a Wonderful Life* was on and the baggie was dripping all over the floor. I hobbled into the kitchen, depositing the bag in the sink before lurching upstairs to change into a pair of dry jeans.

I had woken up with a plan, and so far it had not gone as I had hoped. *Let the smart people plan things, Oliver*, I thought to myself. *You just listen to your tapes and read your books. You'll be much happier that way.*

I grabbed my current reading material off of my nightstand and was headed toward the stairs, fully intent on taking my own advice, when Maggie called from down the hall, "What did you do to your leg?"

"I got bit by a horse," I said, shrugging. "The Amish are out of control these days."

She didn't look amused. "I saw you with the gas can," she said. "Are you going to try to burn him again?"

"I don't think that would work," I said. "I tried it while he was alive and...no luck. Probably be a waste of time to try it again now."

"What are you doing, Ollie?" Maggie asked. There was real concern in her voice.

"I'm going to give Ray something he's been wanting for a long time," I said. "Kinda like a Christmas present."

"What about me?" she asked and I was reminded that, in spite of the whole "manipulative ghost"-thing, she was still just a little girl.

"If this works," I said, "we'll all get something we want."

It was mid-afternoon, but I had slept through lunch, so I ate an early dinner and iced my knee again. *A Christmas Story* was on, so I watched that for a while. I decided that I really love Christmas movies. They're all terrific. In Christmas movies, so few people have any real problems, it's great. We can just watch and laugh and ignore everything that wants to hurt us for a couple of hours.

By the time the movie was over, it was getting dark, which was not part of my plan. I thought about bailing and trying again the next day, but something told me that, once I started finding reasons to put it off, I would keep finding reasons and it would never get done.

I put on my ugly wool hat and my battered green coat and forced myself to go outside. The gas can was waiting for me on the front porch where I had left it and I carried it around to the back. There in the corn crib sat the Cutlass, catching the last dying light of the day. It was as ugly as ever, but my brother had put everything he had into it. As I stood looking, the hazard lights began to blink on and off, illuminating, faintly, the interior of the corn crib. In the amber glow, I could just make out the dark silhouette of someone sitting in the driver's seat.

I sighed, thinking of all the books sitting in my room that I would never get to read if this went wrong, but knowing that I'd never be at peace if I didn't at least try. I limped across the yard and into the corn crib.

I looked along the rear quarter panel on the driver's side, then on the passenger side, but I didn't find what I was looking for. My knee was aching and I was really ready to hang it up.

"It's behind the license plate," Reagan said from inside the car. "It's on a spring-hinge. Just fold it down."

I went to the rear bumper and pulled the license plate toward me and, just like he'd said, it folded down revealing the fuel cap. I opened it up and inserted the gas can nozzle, emptying the entire can into what I knew was an empty tank. When I had walked away from the car all those years ago, I had left it running. Dad didn't come home for days, which meant this gas-guzzler had been running that entire time, unless Mom had shut it off. I doubt she had, though. I didn't understand how Reagan had been revving the engine on an empty tank, but I also didn't understand how he had made that smoke detector go off when there was no battery in it. I didn't understand a lot of what was going on. I just did what came naturally and rolled with it.

I tossed the empty gas can aside and walked up to the driver's side door, pulling it open. "Scoot over, Ray," I said. "I'm driving."

He looked up at me and there was no anger, disdain, hatred, or criticism in his gaze. There was just a boyish hope. I was reminded that he, like Maggie, was just a child. We all were. The adults who we relied on had abandoned us. I had been lucky enough to find plenty of others to fill the void, but Maggie and Reagan were stuck with me. As if it wasn't bad enough that they had died gruesome and painful deaths, they now had me looking after them, their ridiculous baby brother.

"Seriously, man," I said when Reagan didn't move. "Move over or I'll sit on your lap." He slid across the bench seat to the passenger side and I sat down in the driver's seat.

"Do you know what you're doing?" he asked.

"Kind of," I said, "but you should know that the last time I drove a car, I killed a guy." The key was still in the ignition. I was worried that the battery would be dead, but, by some miracle, the engine turned over and, with a little tap on the accelerator, the car twisted under me. It wanted to drive.

"I never got around to replacing the brakes," he said.

"Does that matter?" I asked with a slight, nearly-hysterical chuckle.

"Probably not," he said. "Put it in reverse and barely touch the gas." Following his instructions, I managed to get the car out of the corn crib and down the driveway without hitting either the house or the Vega.

"Now what?" I asked. We were sitting at the end of the driveway and, in the faint glow of the dashboard lights, Reagan looked almost alive. His eyes were alight and he was on the verge of smiling.

"Are you really sure about this, Ollie?" he asked.

"No, Ray," I said, actually laughing. "I'm terrified! But I'm not backing out now. What do I do?"

"Give it just a tiny bit of gas and turn the wheel hard," he said. "Keep to the middle of the road unless you see a car coming. Then slow down and get over to the right, but don't put us in a ditch."

"What if there's an Amish buggy without lights and I don't see it until it's too late?" This was a very real possibility.

Reagan shrugged. "I dunno," he said, grinning.

"Oookay," I said, tapping the gas and turning left onto Armstrong Road. I drove away from Gladden, thinking that I could do less damage farther from town. I immediately regretted that choice because it was all farmland for miles and miles. There were no streetlights, no gas stations, nothing. Just roads, some paved, some dirt, some gravel, and it was so very dark.

"The dimmer switch is on the floor," he said. "You gotta really step on it."

I pressed down the floor-mounted dimmer switch with my toe and it gave a hard click. Suddenly, the world in front of us was illuminated by our high beams. "Thanks," I said. "That helps a lot."

"Turn left on Roth and open her up a bit," said Reagan, rolling his window down. I did as he asked and he stuck his head out the window. "Faster, Ollie! Just a little bit faster!" I pressed on the accelerator.

I saw ghostly white farmhouses zip past us in the night, the only indicators of the world around us. Everything was quiet and lonely. The Cutlass charged through the countryside, the 350 Rocket under the hood roaring in approval as we chewed up the road.

In the dark with the wind whipping in through Reagan's open window, it felt like we were flying. The car soaked up every bump, rolling like the shoulders of a running panther. For a few moments, I felt indestructible.

A railroad crossing sprang out of the darkness and we went over it at around fifty miles an hour. I nearly lost control on the other side as the car bounced and lurched on over-taxed shocks. Reagan started howling like a dog, his head still out the window.

"More!" he cried. "Give it more!"

I pressed my foot down and the engine responded. The speedometer read sixty-five, then seventy.

"MORE!" Reagan screamed. It was Christmas Eve, but there was no peace on this part of the earth. I was shattering it with my brother's ghost screaming by my side.

Soon I saw headlights crossing our path up ahead. A hint of red reflected our headlights back at us. We were approaching a stop sign. I dimmed the headlights again and gradually slowed us down, coming to a stop with State Road 1 stretching off in either direction.

"This is the worst driving lesson I could possibly imagine," I said.

"Turn left," said Reagan.

"Ray, this is a highway," I said. "I'm not sure I'm quite ready for that."

"It's just a state highway. You'll be fine," he said, slapping the dashboard. "Turn left. This'll take us into Leopold."

"Oh, great," I said, sarcastically. "Leopold, where the people are."

"GO, OLLIE!" he screamed and I turned onto Highway 1, pressing my foot down and launching us into the night.

It was very irresponsible of me, I now realize. At the time I didn't think it was a big deal. After all, Reagan was already dead, so I was only putting myself in danger. That was what I thought. I didn't consider the damage a 1.75-ton machine traveling at high-speed could do if it encountered, for example, anything else. The 1969 Oldsmobile Cutlass Supreme was a massive thing. Nothing else on the road in 1993 was a match for it. So...don't do what I did, kids. I was dumb. Don't be dumb.

Leopold was very sleepy that night, a cozy hamlet amidst miles of cornfields. Any other night, there would have been a fair amount of traffic, but it was Christmas Eve and everyone was at home, drinking probably, so when I inadvertently blasted through the four-way stop going seventy-five miles an hour, there was no one around to see me, thank God.

In spite of Reagan's objections, I slowed us down to something reasonably close to the speed limit and stayed on State Road 1. It was wide and well-lit and I was fairly certain I could find my way back home, though I nearly lost control going around the Cedarville curve.

"Ray," I said once he had pulled his head back inside the car and rolled up the window. "I need to apologize."

He didn't say anything.

"I know I was never a very good brother," I said. "I didn't treat you very well..."

"You lit me on fire, Ollie," he said coldly. "And then you murdered me with my own car."

"Yeahhh," I said. "You do bring up some excellent points, and, like I said, I want to apologize."

"You go ahead and apologize," he said, and I couldn't help but notice that the old cynicism was back in his voice. "But you don't even know what you're apologizing for. Not really. You think it's the fire and the murder, but there's so much more..."

"I know, Ray. I know."

"Oh, you know?!" he shouted. "Well, then, why don't you tell me? Go ahead and tell me all the things you're sorry for, Ollie."

"I'm sorry that Dad never told you how much he loved you!" I blurted out, which elicited a pained gasp from my brother. "I'm sorry that he was so caught up in himself that he couldn't tell his favorite child how important he was!"

"I wasn't..." he murmured.

"You weren't what? His favorite?" I laughed, matching his cynical tone. "He went to all of your little league games. He took you camping. He taught you how to drive. He taught you how to shave. Do you know who taught me how to shave? Danny Glover in *Lethal Weapon 2*. It was on TV one night and I watched it and there's a scene where he teaches his son to shave. That's how I learned."

"They made a second *Lethal Weapon* movie?"

"And I know that Mom took me away and Dad couldn't teach me any of those things," I said, very aware that I was starting to sound hysterical, but not caring. "He couldn't teach me then, but here I am, Ray. I came back. It's Christmas Eve and where is he? Do you know? 'Cause I sure don't. He's not here, that's all I know." I took several deep breaths to calm myself down, but I had to stop when I started to feel light-headed.

This little confession time was not part of my original plan, by the way. I just want to make that clear. We were just supposed to take the car out for a nice drive.

"I'm sorry that Mom didn't love you like she should have," I said. "Even before...before Maggie died. She always put Maggie first. No matter what happened, Mom always took Maggie's side. And then Maggie died and some part of Mom died, too. I noticed how she could never quite look at you. She knew, Ray. She knew what you did."

"That wasn't...I didn't mean to do it," he said. His voice sounded so small.

"I know, Ray. And I want to apologize for never letting you talk about it. It must have eaten you up. You were mean and you hated us, but I know you never meant to kill Maggie."

"Ollie," he said, "I didn't ever hate you. Never. I hated myself whenever I hurt you. I just wanted you to love me and to look up to me. But I never hated you."

"I wanted to love you, Ray," I said. "I wish you had been a better brother because I could have really used that in my life. You only taught me how to be cruel and how to fight. Whatever made you hate yourself made me hate you, too. I didn't want to, though. I really did want to love you.

"I'm sorry I didn't love you and I'm sorry for the fire and I'm sorry for the murder and I'm sorry I called you an asshole and I'm sorry for all of the things you'll never experience because of me. So many great things, Ray. Like *Beetlejuice*. And Alice in Chains! My God, Ray! You would have *loved* Alice in Chains!"

The roar of the engine had been steadily rising, my voice rising with it. I looked down at the speedometer and saw that it had climbed past ninety. Startled, I took my foot off the gas and let the car coast down to a reasonable fifty miles per hour. We pulled up to a four-way stop and there was no one around, so I turned the car around in the intersection and headed back toward home.

"Ollie," Reagan said. "I'm sorry."

"It's okay, Ray," I said. "You don't need to apologize. Maybe you should say something to Maggie, but you and me...We're good."

After a few moments of silence, he said, "Thank you. I've wanted this for a long time. I didn't think it would ever happen."

"You did a great job getting it running again, Ray," I said. "It really is a terrific old car."

"I'm not talking about the ride, Ollie," he said, motioning back and forth between us. "I'm talking about this. Us. Thank you."

And then he was gone. I felt a sudden emptiness where so much fear and hatred had been. There was a void, a welcome one, and it made me feel like crying.

I drove through Leopold and, at the four-way stop that I had ignored on our first pass, I turned right toward Gladden. I was about a mile away from home when the engine began to sputter and the car died on me. Five gallons didn't last long in a Cutlass Supreme.

I steered the car off to the side of the road, careful not to let it slide into the ditch. I had no idea what to do with it, so I left it where it was. I pulled my hat snug around my ears, stuffed my hands in my pockets, and started walking. I barely noticed my throbbing knee.

When I got home, I went straight upstairs and knocked on Maggie's door. "Hey, Maggie?" I said. "Can we talk?" The door swung open and she was standing at her window looking down at the corn crib.

"He's gone, isn't he?" she asked.

"I think so," I said. "I don't know where he's gone, but he's not here anymore. He found whatever it was he was looking for. I guess that makes you the winner."

"No it doesn't," she said, turning to look at me. "You're still here."

"I am," I said, "but this was always just between you and Ray. I was never playing."

"You were the prize," she said.

"I don't believe that for a second," I said. "You were in it for you, Maggie. And you beat him. He's gone. Congratulations." I turned to go.

"Merry Christmas, Ollie," she said.

I stopped, but didn't turn back. "Merry Christmas, Maggie." I heard the door click shut behind me.

I took a very hot shower and made some hot cocoa and settled down on the couch for a few hours with a book and an ice pack for my knee.

I went to bed well after midnight and slept most of the morning. I woke to a ringing phone.

"Merry Christmas, Oliver!" It was Emma and Miss Simms. We chatted a bit, wishing each other well, and then I called Fern and we did the same. I didn't mention the previous night's drive.

After I hung up with Fern, I wandered upstairs to my bedroom and crawled under the covers. I tried to go back to sleep, but something was...different. The house felt strange. I sat up again and looked around. Nothing was out of place. I shuffled down the hall to Maggie's room and knocked. There was no answer, so I opened the door and looked in. The air was cold. It felt more than empty. It felt abandoned. Maggie's rocking chair looked lifeless and forgotten.

I went back to my room and looked outside, half expecting to see the Cutlass parked in the corn crib, but it wasn't there. The house was truly empty. I was alone. Reagan and Maggie were gone.

I was overcome by a wave of loneliness and I cried for my dead siblings and for my dead mother and for my absent, lonely, frightened father who was far more afraid of his living child than he had ever been of his dead ones. I got dressed and was just about to leave my bedroom when something caught my eye. Mom's thrift store painting.

I looked at it closely, searching through the crowd. There in the back was a splash of bright yellow, a t-shirt perhaps, and beside it, a hint of turquoise and a spot of magenta.

I smiled, glad at the thought that Mom and Maggie were together somewhere. I took the painting down, though, because I didn't want them watching me anymore. I'd had far too much of that.

-THIRTY-ONE-
some things last a long time
-(1994 and on)-

I always thought I'd move away from Gladden as soon as I could. I was convinced that it was full of awful, self-serving, judgmental monsters, and while it does have its fair share, it has far more absolute gems. People who care quietly and constantly. These people are farmers. They plant seeds for...some day in the future, for some as-of-yet unknown need. They're patient and persistent and gradual. Everything they do takes time, but it lasts. How could I leave a place with such amazing people?

One such person was the manager of the antique store, a wonderfully interesting man named Mr. Moses. "I remember you," he said to me as I stood at the front counter in February of 1994. "You came in here last December and bought an old wooden box."

"Yeah," I said. "That was me."

"You had more hair then," he said with a friendly smirk. "Not much, but some."

I ran my hand across my scalp, which I had been shaving regularly. "The mohawk was causing problems," I said. "More trouble than it was worth."

"I wouldn't say that," Mr. Moses said. "Sometimes it's good to remind folks that their opinion doesn't rule the world. Now, tell me about this painting..."

Not sure what else to do with it, I had brought Mom's oil painting to him. "Well..." I said, not sure where to start, "my mother bought this for three dollars at a thrift store in Traverse City, Michigan."

"You're Rex and Delores's youngest boy, Oliver," he said, filling in a blank I hadn't realized was present. "That where she took you? Michigan?"

"Yes, sir," I said, surprised by his candor. He didn't dance around the uncomfortable truth. There wasn't any judgment, just statement. "She wasn't well for a long time, but I didn't notice. I don't suppose I had anything to compare it to."

"No one likes to think that their loved ones are slipping," Mr. Moses said. "And that's a lot to put on a kid. Should never have been in such a position. Go on..."

I went on. I told him about the movers packing everything up and bringing it to our house in Gladden and about hanging the painting up in my room.

"I had a dream that Mom was in the painting." I tried hard not to look at the painting as I said this, tried hard not to direct his attention to the very obviously out-of-place characters standing in the background.

"A dream..." he said. The look he gave me suggested he understood more than I wanted to say. "And you want to sell me the painting because the dream was so unsettling, is that right?"

"Not exactly," I said. If I sold the painting to Mr. Moses, he'd sell it to someone else and they'd hang it up in their house, unsuspecting hosts to Mom and Maggie. That didn't seem right. "I was hoping to donate it to the little museum upstairs."

"The museum..." Mr. Moses looked confused. "OH! The Gallery! Yeah, that's just a junk closet where we keep random oddities."

"I thought it was fascinating," I said. "Kind of a mess, but really interesting to look at."

"It certainly is a mess," said Mr. Moses, "but that's Gladden, isn't it? We've got farmers and woodworkers and modest Amish folk and the doctors and lawyers who live over in Brighton Heights and we've got corn-fed highschool football stars and mohawk-wearing punks. This whole town is one giant junk closet. The Gallery upstairs is just a miniature version of Gladden."

"Now," he said, fixing me with a squint, "why does that picture, which has nothing to do with Gladden as far as I can tell, belong with the other junk upstairs?"

I held the painting up and looked at it. Mom and Maggie stood far in the distance, looking in a shop window. They hadn't moved in weeks.

I tried to see what Mom had seen when she first bought it. Three dollars didn't seem like much, but that was far more than we could afford to spend on a painting at the time, especially a painting that Mom had immediately tucked into the back of her closet to be forgotten. What was it that she had seen?

I had forgotten about the painting when Mom hid it away, but that didn't mean she had. Had she been sneaking glances at the painting every time she opened her closet? Was it some kind of reminder? Was there something familiar here that she admired and longed for?

Mom and Maggie were there, but so were many other people. Neighbors and friends and family, not mine, but someone's. They held hands and laughed with each other. They were happy, not because of their situation, but because of their companions. It was a community of people helping and loving each other, something that Mom had always wanted, but never had.

"You keep calling the pieces in the Gallery 'junk,'" I said, looking up from the painting. "All of the glass insulators and old leather shoes, but it's not junk, Mr. Moses. That stuff is strange and interesting and noteworthy and, for various reasons, remarkable. Those odd pieces upstairs remind us that not everything makes sense, and that's okay, because everything can still have a place. Everything can belong. The farmers and the woodworkers and the Amish and the rich people all have a place here in Gladden. The athletes and the punks all live together. None of us are junk. We might not make sense, but we belong. Mom saw this painting and saw the people in it and I guess she imagined that, in spite of their differences, they loved each other. Maybe they loved each other because of their differences.

"I think this painting has everything to do with Gladden," I said. "It might not be the same buildings or the same people, but we have everything that makes a town great.

"For whatever reason, this painting reminded my Mom of her home. We might be a little dirty and a little drab and you might have to dig pretty deep to find the interesting stuff, but we're every bit as good as this London street."

Mr. Moses looked at me for several moments without speaking until, finally, he said, "Would you like a job?"

That's how it fell to me to organize the Gladden Gallery. I cleaned and arranged and curated everything. I updated all of the documentation on every item. I tracked down missing dates and contacted the original donors whenever possible. In a back room I found a large map of Gladden and the surrounding areas and, with Mr. Moses's permission, I hung it up and marked where each item came from. I did such a satisfactory job that the Gallery was moved to a larger room and, gradually, the collection grew.

It was not the kind of place tourists visited. The Gallery was of interest only to locals, and, on our busiest days, we counted half a dozen visitors. When not tending the Gallery, I cleaned the rest of the store.

I loved it. Mr. Moses would often tell me stories of his life, most of it spent in Gladden, but plenty of it spent overseas. He had been in the military, stationed in Japan, and I will not share any of his stories because they are not my stories to share. Also, most of them involve him operating a brothel and are, therefore, shockingly inappropriate.

I was something of an oddity in town, the last surviving descendant of a once-great Gladden family. Burned, kidnapped...Such a story. From time to time I regrew my mohawk, but people didn't seem to mind so much. I had Mr. Moses's approval and that carried a lot of weight.

As the Gallery grew and people visited more and more, whispers began to circulate. The painting, they said, changed ever so slightly from time to time. Sometimes there were different people in it and sometimes those new people resembled folks from town who had passed. I was tight-lipped about the painting, but I didn't dissuade any rumors.

While I stayed close to Gladden, Emma and Fern did not.

As I said, I never heard Emma's whole story, why she lived with Miss Simms and not her biological parents. She'd made it clear on several occasions, however, that she was happier with Miss Simms.

One day, near the end of our junior year, the unthinkable, the impossible, the worst thing happened. I found a note in my locker. It was from Emma. It said only that something had happened and that she and Miss Simms had to leave for a while, but she would get in touch with me when she could. Fern got a similar note in his locker.

Emma Seaway never returned to Gladden.

Fern and I made it through our senior year without Emma, but it was a close call. There were one-hundred and ten students in our graduating class and I was ranked eighty-sixth. A pass, and with room to spare.

While I kept my job at the antique store, Fern went to college and is now a moderately successful graphic artist. He and his husband designed and built an entire town for their cats in the basement of their house (they call it "Kittiesburg") and, as a result, they are very popular on social media. It's just as ridiculous as it sounds.

We do our best to stay in touch, but it's just a courtesy. Fern's entire life is public and I don't have a life at all, so neither of us ever have anything new to share. We never talk about Emma. It's clear that, if everything was okay, she would have contacted us long ago. If things went bad...we'd rather not know.

Dad died a few years ago. He was sitting on the front porch smoking a cigarette when he had a heart attack. They said he'd been dead three days before anyone found him.

Maybe I should have been checking on him more regularly, but he and I never really had a great relationship. We didn't hate each other, exactly, we just didn't think about each other. We spent so much time apart that we learned not to need each other. I think that was what he wanted most, for no one to need him. Family was an obligation he just couldn't handle. It should be noted that, after he died, I never saw any sign of him in Mom's thrift store painting. No matter what I think about him or how he chose to live his life, he didn't leave behind any unfinished business.

Reagan also never appeared in the painting, but I have reason to suspect that he's not entirely gone. After I left the Cutlass abandoned on the side of the road, I expected a call from the police once they'd run the plates and figured out who it belonged to, but no call ever came. The car, like its previous owner, simply vanished.

There are nights, however, when you can hear the roar of a 350-cubic inch, 5.7 liter, V8 engine chewing up the roads all around Gladden. He means no harm, but if you hear him coming, get out of his way, 'cause he's not stopping.

-EPILOGUE-
everything with love, whenever possible
-(August, 2023)-

The manager of the Gladden Antique Store was a middle-aged man with a bushy, gray beard. He was bald up top and going soft in the middle. Visitors typically found him to be friendly and knowledgeable, regardless of the topic of conversation. Books and music and movies, town history, driving directions, operating hours for various local businesses...Mr. Barrow knew much and was generous with his knowledge.

He also drove a bus for the local school district. He did this primarily for the insurance, but he found that driving a school bus came with unexpected perks.

Mr. Barrow had an unsettling upbringing full of tragedy and loss. He never had the chance for a normal life, but the kids on his bus generously gave him glimpses into their own lives, allowing him to experience, however briefly, their successes and failures and hopes and grievances and the victories that turned out to be losses and the heartbreaks that became incalculable strengths.

One grim youth frequently offered his pessimistic predictions concerning test results. Three exuberant siblings often shared with him the highs and lows, always with the most dramatic flair, that come with being in show choir. Another student announced that she'd made the junior olympic air rifle team. One young individual shared quietly that their parents didn't understand or accept their lifestyle. Another passenger cried while mourning the loss of a pet. Mr. Barrow's bus was always a safe place, for the passengers as well as the driver.

He watched them grow and he saw them become. He shared in their happy and sad moments. He attended band concerts and plays, went to fine arts nights and football games. He loved them and they loved him back. In a world with so very little peace and acceptance, Mr. Barrow gave freely of both, to whomever needed them.

Mr. Barrow listened as they learned their ABCs and then, mere moments later, listened as they talked about college visits and scholarship applications. They came and went, year after year, and his heart broke every time.

Each year he told himself, "I'm done with this." He thought, "I can't take it anymore. I can't say 'goodbye' again."

But he did say "goodbye", over and over. It was one of the few things he was good at. He'd had a lot of practice.

He needed those kids. He wouldn't have known what to do without them. They were the closest thing he had to a family. They brought him Christmas cards and he sang to them on their birthdays, loudly, obnoxiously, perhaps, but always with love.

He tried to do everything with love, whenever possible.

And while he was content, he was still very sad.

****

The Gladden Antique Store would have been a pretty dreary place had it not been for the constant antics of the Birdly twins. Mr. Barrow had hired them two summers ago as a favor to their father, Lewis Birdly, the youth pastor at Gladden Missionary. Mr. Barrow and Lewis were old acquaintances.

"Tucker!"

"Yeah, Mr. Barrow?" The young man who poked his head around the corner sported a tidy, blue mohawk. His earlobes were festooned with dangling ornaments. His t-shirt advertised a band called "Blaster the Rocket Man," a Christian punk band that Mr. Barrow had grown to like quite a lot.

"Mrs. Delagrange called this morning," Mr. Barrow said. "She found more boxes."

"Depression glass?" asked Tucker.

"That's what she says," said Mr. Barrow. "You and Darby mind picking it up for me? Feel free to take the truck. And grab lunch on your way back."

"Can I drive?" asked Tucker, eagerly.

"Well, I'm not sure I'm ready for Darby to climb behind the wheel at the moment," said Mr. Barrow. "He's still too heartsick from his breakup to be trusted. He's liable to drive you both right into the reservoir." Tucker grinned and disappeared around the corner.

"AND USE THE FURNITURE DOLLY THIS TIME!" yelled Mr. Barrow.

The Birdlys were good boys, a little spirited, but well-meaning. He hired them to move heavy stuff and clean things and run errands, but mostly he just liked their company. They had graduated from high school the year before and took classes at a community college in Fort Wayne. They made sure Mr. Barrow stayed up to date on matters of music and modern culture. Marvel movies were a frequent topic of conversation.

Mr. Barrow heard the back door slam as they left to go collect Mrs. Baxter's probably chipped and, therefore, worthless depression glass. He settled himself on a stool behind the counter and turned his attention to his battered paperback.

The antique shop door opened, causing the bell above it to dance and jingle.

"Morning, Oliver," said Allen, the postman, as he tossed the day's incoming mail onto the countertop and retrieved the outgoing from a small, wire basket.

"Morning, Allen," said Oliver. "How are things?"

"Things are hot," said Allen, offering a long-suffering smile and a shrug as he ducked back out into the August heat.

Oliver set his paperback aside and scooped up the stack of mail. Several bills, some political fliers (straight into the recycling with those), and a small, beige envelope addressed to "Oliver Barrow, % The Gladden Antique Store."

Oliver bypassed the other envelopes in favor of the beige one, turning it over in his hand to look for a return address. There was none. Using a tarnished brass letter opener, he opened the envelope, revealing two items. One was a watercolor that he recognized from thirty years prior. It was a wildflower and had once been accompanied by several other similar paintings housed in an ornate box that he had purchased in the very shop he now managed.

The other item was a photograph. A small woman his age was sitting on a beach. On her left sat a handsome man with a broad grin and, on her right, a short, black woman with an even broader grin. Behind them stood a young boy and girl, eleven or twelve years-old, perhaps. The boy looked exactly like his father and the girl looked exactly like her mother. On the back of the photograph was the following handwritten note:

Dear Oliver,

I am sorry it's taken so long to get in touch. It wasn't safe to do so until recently. As you can see from this picture, changed names and locations have not kept me from experiencing life, though it has made things somewhat more complicated. Again, I am sorry.

Though I can't tell you everything (nor do I want to), I will acknowledge that I owe you a very long and detailed explanation, which I prefer to give you face-to-face, hopefully over dinner. You can meet my husband and our kids, and Simmy is dying to see you. During all of our years of coming and going, sometimes hastily, she has never let go of that Joni Mitchell record you gave her.

I miss you, Oliver, and I can't wait to see you soon.

Love,

Emma

Oliver read the letter three times before flipping it over and studying the photo. She hadn't changed much, not thirty years worth, anyway. Her hair was still long and frizzy, but with a little gray. Her sunglasses mimicked the purple frames she had worn all those years ago. Oliver had never seen his friend without her cardigan, but in the picture, there on the beach, her arms were bare and he could see scars running up and down, from wrist to elbow. The sight broke his heart and he wondered how many secrets she had kept from him and Fern.

Emma had included a contact number with the note and Oliver pulled his phone out of his pocket and dialed, but rather than complete the call, he hesitated. What would he say? They had been friends, briefly, thirty years ago. True, there had been very few friends since, but how awkward would that conversation be?

Emma would have all sorts of interesting stories about the different places she and Miss Simms had been and all of the people they'd met. She had gotten married and had kids. They had full lives and had experienced so many things together. And what would he, Oliver, have to contribute to that conversation?

"I drive a school bus and, between routes, I manage an antique store where the big draw is a haunted painting."

Maybe not, Oliver told himself as he put his phone down on the counter. *Maybe memories are best.*

He tucked the photograph and the watercolor back inside the envelope and set it aside, scooping up the bills. He had the old letter opener in his hand and was just about to open the first bill when the little bell over the door tinkled, though the door had not opened. Oliver looked at the bell as it danced gently on its spring. He shrugged mentally and returned his attention to the bills, but the bell rang again, this time more insistently.

Dropping the bills (but not the letter opener), Oliver marched around the counter and up to the door (on which was displayed, for no discernable reason, a wrinkled and worn sign reading, "USE OTHER DOOR,"), pulling it open and sticking his head out into the oppressive heat. He looked left and right, but there was no one loitering along the wooden sidewalk or anywhere nearby. Tucker and Darby had left in the truck several minutes ago.

Returning to the cool dark of the antique store, he looked up at the bell. There was no chance of it malfunctioning. It was not electric. It was simply an old bell on a spring. When the door opened, it hit the bell, causing it to ring. It was old-fashioned, which people liked. The only way it could ring was if something made physical contact, but there was nothing and no one nearby, except for Oliver, who became embarrassingly aware that he was gripping the letter opener with a white-knuckled ferocity.

He returned to the counter and stared at the bell for a moment before picking up one of the envelopes. Again, the bell rang, but Oliver did not drop the envelope. Instead, he intentionally moved the blade of the letter opener under the flap, and, with a stubborn flourish, slit it open. The bell jangled furiously, the spring jumping up and down like mad.

"WHAT?!" shouted Oliver, jumping up from his stool. "WHAT DO YOU WANT?!" He felt like Ebeneezer Scrooge.

Outside, an engine roared, the type of big-block engine that most people these days find offensive. Something the color of very old mustard flashed by the window. The bell above the door continued to ring and, in the next room, all of the rocking chairs began creaking back and forth. After several tense seconds, the roar of the car diminished as it raced down the road, the rocking chairs in the next room ceased their creaking, and the bell above the door fell silent. When Oliver looked down at the envelope in his hand, he found, not a bill, but the small, beige envelope.

After several steadying breaths, Oliver picked up his phone and pressed the green "call" button.

Milton Keynes UK
Ingram Content Group UK Ltd.
UKHW010117011223
433552UK00004B/269